The Secret Passage

The Secret Passage

Fergus Hume

MINT EDITIONS

The Secret Passage was first published in 1905.

This edition published by Mint Editions 2021.

ISBN 9781513278384 | E-ISBN 9781513278841

Published by Mint Editions®

 MINT
EDITIONS
minteditionbooks.com

Publishing Director: Jennifer Newens
Design & Production: Rachel Lopez Metzger
Project Manager: Micaela Clark
Typesetting: Westchester Publishing Services

Contents

I

THE COTTAGE

W hat Is your name?"

"Susan Grant, Miss Loach."

"Call me ma'am. I am Miss Loach only to my equals. Your age?"

"Twenty-five, ma'am."

"Do you know your work as parlor-maid thoroughly?"

"Yes, ma'am. I was two years in one place and six months in another, ma'am. Here are my characters from both places, ma'am."

As the girl spoke she laid two papers before the sharp old lady who questioned her. But Miss Loach did not look at them immediately. She examined the applicant with such close attention that a faint color tinted the girl's cheeks and she dropped her eyes. But, in her turn, by stealthy glances, Susan Grant tactfully managed to acquaint herself with the looks of her possible mistress. The thoughts of each woman ran as follows,—

Miss Loach to herself. "Humph! Plain-looking, sallow skin, rather fine eyes and a slack mouth. Not badly dressed for a servant, and displays some taste. She might turn my old dresses at a pinch. Sad expression, as though she had something on her mind. Honest-looking, but I think a trifle inquisitive, seeing how she examined the room and is stealing glances at me. Talks sufficiently, but in a low voice. Fairly intelligent, but not too much so. Might be secretive. Humph!"

The thoughts of Susan Grant. "Handsome old lady, probably nearly sixty. Funny dress for ten o'clock in the morning. She must be rich, to wear purple silk and old lace and lovely rings at this hour. A hard mouth, thin nose, very white hair and very black eyebrows. Got a temper I should say, and is likely to prove an exacting mistress. But I want a quiet home, and the salary is good. I'll try it, if she'll take me."

Had either mistress or maid known of each other's thoughts, a conclusion to do business might not have been arrived at. As it was, Miss Loach, after a few more questions, appeared satisfied. All the time she kept a pair of very black eyes piercingly fixed on the girl's face, as though she would read her very soul. But Susan had nothing to conceal, so far as Miss Loach could gather, so in the end she resolved to engage her.

"I think you'll do," she said nodding, and poking up the fire, with a shiver, although the month was June. "The situation is a quiet one. I hope you have no followers."

"No, ma'am," said Susan and flushed crimson.

"Ha!" thought Miss Loach, "she has been in love—jilted probably. All the better, as she won't bring any young men about my quiet house."

"Will you not read my characters, ma'am?"

Miss Loach pushed the two papers towards the applicant. "I judge for myself," said she calmly. "Most characters I read are full of lies. Your looks are enough for me. Where were you last?"

"With a Spanish lady, ma'am!"

"A Spanish lady!" Miss Loach dropped the poker she was holding, with a clatter, and frowned so deeply that her black eyebrows met over her high nose. "And her name?"

"Senora Gredos, ma'am!"

The eyes of the old maid glittered, and she made a clutch at her breast as though the reply had taken away her breath. "Why did you leave?" she asked, regaining her composure.

Susan looked uncomfortable. "I thought the house was too gay, ma'am."

"What do you mean by that? Can any house be too gay for a girl of your years?"

"I have been well brought up, ma'am," said Susan quietly; "and my religious principles are dear to me. Although she is an invalid, ma'am, Senora Gredos was very gay. Many people came to her house and played cards, even on Sunday," added Susan under her breath. But low as she spoke, Miss Loach heard.

"I have whist parties here frequently," she said drily; "nearly every evening four friends of mine call to play. Have you any objection to enter my service on that account?"

"Oh, no, ma'am. I don't mind a game of cards. I play 'Patience' myself when alone. I mean gambling—there was a lot of money lost and won at Senora Gredos' house!"

"Yet she is an invalid I think you said?"

"Yes, ma'am. She was a dancer, I believe, and fell in some way, so as to break her leg or hurt her back. She has been lying on a couch for two years unable to move. Yet she has herself wheeled into the drawing-room and watches the gentlemen play cards. She plays herself sometimes!"

Miss Loach again directed one of her piercing looks at the pale face of the girl. "You are too inquisitive and too talkative," she said suddenly, "therefore you won't suit me. Good-day."

Susan was quite taken aback. "Oh, ma'am, I hope I've said nothing wrong. I only answered your questions."

"You evidently take note of everything you see, and talk about it."

"No, ma'am," said the girl earnestly. "I really hold my tongue."

"When it suits you," retorted Miss Loach. "Hold it now and let me think!"

While Miss Loach, staring frowningly into the fire, debated inwardly as to the advisability of engaging the girl, Susan looked timidly round the room. Curiously enough, it was placed in the basement of the cottage, and was therefore below the level of the garden. Two fairly large windows looked on to the area, which had been roofed with glass and turned into a conservatory. Here appeared scarlet geraniums and other bright-hued flowers, interspersed with ferns and delicate grasses. Owing to the position of the room and the presence of the glass roof, only a subdued light filtered into the place, but, as the day was brilliant with sunshine, the apartment was fairly well illuminated. Still, on a cloudy day, Susan could imagine how dull it would be. In winter time the room must be perfectly dark.

It was luxuriously furnished, in red and gold. The carpet and curtains were of bright scarlet, threaded with gold. The furniture, strangely enough, was of white polished wood upholstered in crimson satin fringed with gold. There were many pictures in large gilded frames and many mirrors similarly encircled with gilded wood. The grate, fender and fire-irons were of polished brass, and round the walls were numerous electric lamps with yellow shades. The whole room represented a bizarre appearance, flamboyant and rather tropical in looks. Apparently Miss Loach was fond of vivid colors. There was no piano, nor were there books or papers, and the only evidence as to how Miss Loach passed her time revealed itself in a work-basket and a pack of cards. Yet, at her age, Susan thought that needlework would be rather trying, even though she wore no glasses and her eyes seemed bright and keen. She was an odd old lady and appeared to be rich. "I'll engage you," said Miss Loach abruptly; "get your box and be here before five o'clock this afternoon. I am expecting some friends at eight o'clock. You must be ready to admit them. Now go!"

"But, ma'am, I—"

"In this house," interrupted Miss Loach imperiously, "no one speaks to me, unless spoken to by me. You understand!"

"Yes, ma'am," replied Susan timidly, and obeyed the finger which pointed to the door. Miss Loach listened to the girl's footsteps on the stairs, and sat down when she heard the front door close. But she was up again almost in a moment and pacing the room. Apparently the conversation with Susan Grant afforded her food for reflection. And not very palatable food either, judging from her expression.

The newly-engaged servant returned that same afternoon to the suburban station, which tapped the district of Rexton. A trunk, a bandbox and a bag formed her humble belongings, and she arranged with a porter that these should be wheeled in a barrow to Rose Cottage, as Miss Loach's abode was primly called. Having come to terms, Susan left the station and set out to walk to the place. Apart from the fact that she saved a cab fare, she wished to obtain some idea of her surroundings, and therefore did not hurry herself.

It was a bright June day with a warm green earth basking under a blue and cloudless sky. But even the sunshine could not render Rexton beautiful. It stretched out on all sides from the station new and raw. The roads were finished, with asphalt footpaths and stone curbing, the lamp-posts had apparently only been lately erected, and lines of white fences divided the roads from gardens yet in their infancy. Fronting these were damp-looking red brick villas, belonging to small clerks and petty tradesmen. Down one street was a row of shops filled with the necessaries of civilization; and round the corner, an aggressively new church of yellow brick with a tin roof and a wooden steeple stood in the middle of an untilled space. At the end of one street a glimpse could be caught of the waste country beyond, not yet claimed by the ferry-builder. A railway embankment bulked against the horizon, and closed the view in an unsightly manner. Rexton was as ugly as it was new.

Losing her way, Susan came to the ragged fringe of country environing the new suburb, and paused there, to take in her surroundings. Across the fields to the left she saw an unfinished mansion, large and stately, rising amidst a forest of pines. This was girdled by a high brick wall which looked older than the suburb itself. Remembering that she had seen this house behind the cottage of Miss Loach, the girl used it as a landmark, and turning down a side street managed to find the top of a crooked lane at the bottom of which Rose Cottage was situated. This lane showed by its very crookedness that it belonged to the

ancient civilization of the district. Here were no paths, no lamps, no aggressively new fences and raw brick houses. Susan, stepping down the slight incline, passed into quite an old world, smacking of the Georgian times, leisurely and quaint. On either side of the lane, old-fashioned cottages, with whitewash walls and thatched roofs, stood amidst gardens filled with unclipped greenery and homely flowers. Quickset hedges, ragged and untrimmed, divided these from the roadway, and to add to the rural look one garden possessed straw bee-hives. Here and there rose ancient elm-trees and grass grew in the roadway. It was a blind lane and terminated in a hedge, which bordered a field of corn. To the left was a narrow path running between hedges past the cottages and into the country.

Miss Loach's house was a mixture of old and new. Formerly it had been an unpretentious cottage like the others, but she had added a new wing of red brick built in the most approved style of the jerry-builder, and looking like the villas in the more modern parts of Rexton. The crabbed age and the uncultured youth of the old and new portions, planted together cheek by jowl, appeared like ill-coupled clogs and quite out of harmony. The thatched and tiled roofs did not seem meet neighbors, and the whitewash walls of the old-world cottage looked dingy beside the glaring redness of the new villa. The front door in the new part was reached by a flight of dazzling white steps. From this, a veranda ran across the front of the cottage, its rustic posts supporting rose-trees and ivy. On the cottage side appeared an old garden, but the new wing was surrounded by lawns and decorated with carpet bedding. A gravel walk divided the old from the new, and intersected the garden. At the back, Susan noted again the high brick wall surrounding the half-completed mansion. Above this rose tall trees, and the wall itself was overgrown with ivy. It apparently was old and concealed an unfinished palace of the sleeping beauty, so ragged and wild appeared the growth which peeped over the guardian wall.

With a quickness of perception unusual in her class, Susan took all this in, then rang the bell. There was no back door, so far as she could see, and she thought it best to enter as she had done in the morning. But the large fat woman who opened the door gave her to understand that she had taken a liberty.

"Of course this morning and before engaging, you were a lady," said the cook, hustling the girl into the hall, "but now being the housemaid, Miss Loach won't be pleased at your touching the front bell."

"I did not see any other entrance," protested Susan.

"Ah," said the cook, leading the way down a few steps into the thatched cottage, which, it appeared was the servants' quarters, "you looked down the area as is natural-like. But there ain't none, it being a conservitery!"

"Why does Miss Loach live in the basement?" asked Susan, on being shown into a comfortable room which answered the purpose of a servants' hall.

The cook resented this question. "Ah!" said she with a snort, "and why does a miller wear a white 'at, Miss Grant, that being your name I take it. Don't you ask no questions but if you must know, Miss Loach have weak eyes and don't like glare. She lives like a rabbit in a burrow, and though the rooms on the ground floor are sich as the King might in'abit, she don't come up often save to eat. She lives in the basement room where you saw her, Miss Grant, and she sleeps in the room orf. When she eats, the dining-room above is at her service. An' I don't see why she shouldn't," snorted the cook.

"I don't mean any—"

"No offence being given none is taken," interrupted cook, who seemed fond of hearing her own wheezy voice. "Emily Pill's my name, and I ain't ashamed of it, me having been cook to Miss Loach for years an' years and years. But if you had wished to behave like a servant, as you are," added she with emphasis, "why didn't you run round by the veranda and so get to the back where the kitchen is. But you're one of the new class of servants, Miss Grant, 'aughty and upsetting."

"I know my place," said Susan, taking off her hat.

"And I know mine," said Emily Pill, "me being cook and consequently the mistress of this servants' 'all. An' I'm an old-fashioned servant myself, plain in my 'abits and dress." This with a disparaging look at the rather smart costume of the newly-arrived housemaid. "I don't 'old with cockes feathers and fal-de-dals on 'umble folk myself, not but what I could afford 'em if I liked, being of saving 'abits and a receiver of good wages. But I'm a friendly pusson and not 'ard on a good-lookin' gal, not that you are what I call 'andsome."

Susan seated beside the table, looked weary and forlorn, and the good-natured heart of the cook was touched, especially when Susan requested her to refrain from the stiff name of Miss Grant.

"You an' me will be good friends, I've no doubt," said Emily, "an' you can call me Mrs. Pill, that being the name of my late 'usband, who died of gin in excess. The other servants is housemaid and page, though

to be sure he's more of a man-of-all-work, being forty if he's a day, and likewise coachman, when he drives out Miss Loach in her donkey carriage. Thomas is his name, my love." The cook was rapidly becoming more and more friendly, "and the housemaid is called Geraldine, for which 'eaven forgives her parents, she bein' spotty and un'ealthy and by no means a Bow-Bell's 'eroine, which 'er name makes you think of. But there's a dear, I'm talking brilliant, when you're dying for a cup of tea, and need to get your box unpacked, by which I mean that I sees the porter with the barrer."

The newly-arrived parlor-maid was pleased by this friendly if ungrammatical reception, and thought she would like the cook in spite of her somewhat tiresome tongue. For the next hour she was unpacking her box and arranging a pleasant little room at the back. She shared this with the spotty Geraldine, who seemed to be a good-natured girl. Apparently Miss Loach looked after her servants and made them comfortable. Thomas proved to be amiable if somewhat stupid, and welcomed Susan to tea affably but with sheepish looks. As the servants seemed pleasant, the house comfortable, and as the salary was excellent, Susan concluded that she had—as the saying is—fallen on her feet.

The quartette had tea in the servants' hall, and there was plenty of well-cooked if plain victuals. Miss Loach dined at half-past six and Susan assumed her dress and cap. She laid the table in a handsome dining-room, equally as garish in color as the apartment below. The table appointments were elegant, and Mrs. Pill served a nice little meal to which Miss Loach did full justice. She wore the same purple dress, but with the addition of more jewellery. Her sharp eyes followed Susan about the room as she waited, and at the end of the dinner she made her first observation. "You know your work I see," she said. "I hope you will be happy here!"

"I think I will, ma'am," said Susan, with a faint sigh.

"You have had trouble?" asked Miss Loach quickly.

"Yes, ma'am!"

"You must tell me about it to-morrow," said the old lady rising. "I like to gain the confidence of my servants. Now bring my coffee to the room below. At eight, three people will arrive—a lady and two gentlemen. You will show them into the sitting-room and put out the card-table. Then you can go to the kitchen and wait till I ring. Be sure you don't come till I do ring," and Miss Loach emphasized this last order with a flash of her brilliant eyes.

Susan took the coffee to the sitting-room in the basement and then cleared the table. Shortly before eight o'clock there was a ring at the front door. She opened it to a tall lady, with gray hair, who leaned on an ebony cane. With her were two men, one a rather rough foolish-looking fellow, and the other tall, dark, and well-dressed in an evening suit. A carriage was just driving away from the gate. As the tall lady entered, a breath of strong perfume saluted Susan's nostrils. The girl started and peered into the visitor's face. When she returned to the kitchen her own was as white as chalk.

II

THE CRIME

The kitchen was rather spacious, and as neat and clean as the busy hands of Mrs. Pill could make it. An excellent range polished to excess occupied one end of the room; a dresser with blue and white china adorned the other. On the outside wall copper pots and pans, glittering redly in the firelight, were ranged in a shining row. Opposite this wall, a door led into the interior of the house, and in it was the outer entrance. A large deal table stood in the center of the room, and at this with their chairs drawn up, Geraldine and the cook worked. The former was trimming a picture-hat of the cheapest and most flamboyant style, and the latter darned a coarse white stocking intended for her own use. By the fire sat Thomas, fair-haired and stupid in looks, who read tit-bits from the Daily Mail for the delectation of Mrs. Pill and Geraldine.

"Gracious 'eavens, Susan," cried the cook, when Susan returned, after admitting the visitors, "whatever's come to you?"

"I've had a turn," said Susan faintly, sitting by the fire and rubbing her white cheeks.

At once Mrs. Pill was alive with curiosity. She questioned the new parlor-maid closely, but was unable to extract information. Susan simply said that she had a weak heart, and set down her wan appearance to the heat. "An' on that accounts you sits by the fire," said Mrs. Pill scathingly. "You're one of the secret ones you are. Well, it ain't no business of mine, thank 'eaven, me being above board in everythink. I 'spose the usual lot arrived, Susan?"

"Two gentlemen and a lady," replied Susan, glad to see that the cooks thoughts were turning in another direction.

"Gentlemen!" snorted Mrs. Pill, "that Clancy one ain't. Why the missus should hobnob with sich as he, I don't know nohow."

"Ah, but the other's a real masher," chimed in Geraldine, looking up from her millinery; "such black eyes, that go through you like a gimlet, and such a lovely moustache. He dresses elegant too."

"Being Miss Loach's lawyer, he have a right to dress well," said Mrs. Pill, rubbing her nose with the stocking, "and Mr. Clancy, I thinks, is someone Mr. Jarvey Hale's helpin', he being good and kind."

Here Geraldine gave unexpected information.

"He's a client of Mr. Hale's," she said indistinctly, with her mouth full of pins, "and has come in for a lot of money. Mr. Hale's introducing him into good society, to make a gent of him."

"Silk purses can't be made out of sows' ears," growled the cook, "an' who told you all this Geraldine?"

"Miss Loach herself, at different times."

Susan thought it was strange that a lady should gossip to this extent with her housemaid, but she did not take much interest in the conversation, being occupied with her own sad thoughts. But the next remark of Geraldine made her start. "Mr. Clancy's father was a carpenter," said the girl.

"My father was a carpenter," remarked Susan, sadly.

"Ah," cried Mrs. Pill with alacrity, "now you're speaking sense. Ain't he alive?"

"No. He was poisoned!"

The three servants, having the love of horrors peculiar to the lower classes, looked up with interest. "Lor!" said Thomas, speaking for the first time and in a thick voice, "who poisoned him?"

"No one knows. He died five years ago, and left mother with me and four little brothers to bring up. They're all doing well now, though, and I help mother, as they do. They didn't want me to go out to service, you know," added Susan, warming on finding sympathetic listeners. "I could have stopped at home with mother in Stepney, but I did not want to be idle, and took a situation with a widow lady at Hampstead. I stopped there a year. Then she died and I went as parlor-maid to a Senora Gredos. I was only there six months," and she sighed.

"Why did you leave?" asked Geraldine.

Susan grew red. "I wished for a change," she said curtly.

But the housemaid did not believe her. She was a sharp girl and her feelings were not refined. "It's just like these men—"

"I said nothing about men," interrupted Susan, sharply.

"Well, then, a man. You've been in love, Susan, and—"

"No. I am not in love," and Susan colored more than ever.

"Why, it's as plain as cook that you are, now," tittered Geraldine.

"Hold your noise and leave the gal be," said Mrs. Pill, offended by the allusion to her looks, "if she's in love she ain't married, and no more she ought to be; if she'd had a husband like mine, who drank every day in the week and lived on my earnings. He's dead now, an' I gave 'im a 'andsome tombstone with the text: 'Go thou and do likewise' on it, being a short remark, lead letterin' being expensive. Ah well, as I allays say, 'Flesh is grass with us all.'"

While the cook maundered on Thomas sat with his dull eyes fixed on the flushed face of Susan. "What about the poisoning?" he demanded.

"It was this way," said Susan. "Father was working at some house in these parts—"

"What! Down here?"

"Yes, at Rexton, which was then just rising into notice as a place for gentlefolks. He had just finished with a house when he came home one day with his wages. He was taken ill and died. The doctor said he had taken poison, and he died of it. Arsenic it was," explained Susan to her horrified audience.

"But why did he poison himself?" asked Geraldine.

"I don't know: no one knew. He was gettin' good wages, and said he would make us all rich."

"Ah," chimed in Thomas suddenly, "in what way, Susan?"

"He had a scheme to make our fortunes. What it was, I don't know. But he said he would soon be worth plenty of money. Mother thought someone must have poisoned him, but she could not find out. As we had a lot of trouble then, it was thought father had killed himself to escape it, but I know better. If he had lived, we should have been rich. He was on an extra job down here," she ended.

"What was the extra job?" asked Thomas curiously.

Susan shook her head. "Mother never found out. She went to the house he worked on, which is near the station. They said father always went away for three hours every afternoon by an arrangement with the foreman. Where he went, no one knew. He came straight from this extra job home and died of poison. Mother thought," added Susan, looking round cautiously, "that someone must have had a wish to get rid of father, he knowing too much."

"Too much of what, my gal?" asked Mrs. Pill, with open mouth.

"Ah! That's what I'd like to find out," said Susan garrulously, "but nothing was ever known, and father was buried as a suicide. Then mother, having me and my four brothers, married again, and I took the name of her new husband."

"Then your name ain't really Grant?" asked Geraldine.

"No! It's Maxwell, father being Scotch and a clever workman. Susan Maxwell is my name, but after the suicide—if it was one—mother felt the disgrace so, that she made us all call ourselves Grant. So Susan Grant I am, and my brothers of the old family are Grant also."

"What do you mean by the old family?"

"Mother has three children by her second husband, and that's the new family," explained Susan, "but we are all Grants, though me and my four brothers are really Maxwells. But there," she said, looking round quietly and rather pleased at the interest with which she was regarded, "I've told you a lot. Tell me something!"

Mrs. Pill was unwilling to leave the fascinating subject of suicide, but her desire to talk got the better of her, and she launched into a long account of her married life. It seemed she had buried the late Mr. Pill ten years before, and since that time had been with Miss Loach as cook. She had saved money and could leave service at once, if she so chose. "But I should never be happy out of my kitchen, my love," said Mrs. Pill, biting a piece of darning-cotton, "so here I stay till missus goes under."

"And she won't do that for a long time," said Thomas. "Missus is strong. A good, kind, healthy lady."

Geraldine followed with an account of herself, which related chiefly to her good looks and many lovers, and the tyranny of mistresses. "I will say, however, that after being here a year, I have nothing to complain of."

"I should think not," grunted Thomas. "I've been twenty years with Miss Loach, and a good 'un she is. I entered her service when I was fifteen, and she could have married an earl—Lord Caranby wanted to marry her—but she wouldn't."

"Lor," said Mrs. Pill, "and ain't that his lordship's nephew who comes here at times?"

"Mr. Mallow? Yes! That's him. He's fond of the old lady."

"And fond of her niece, too," giggled Geraldine; "not but what Miss Saxon is rather sweet."

"Rather sweet," growled the cook, "why, she's a lovely gal, sich as you'll never be, in spite of your fine name. An' her brother, Mr. Basil, is near as 'andsome as she."

"He ain't got the go about him Miss Juliet have," said Thomas.

"A lot you know," was the cook's retort. "Why Mr. Basil quarrelled with missus a week ago and gave her proper, and missus ain't no easy person to fight with, as I knows. Mr. Basil left the house and ain't been near since."

"He's a fool, then," said Thomas. "Missus won't leave him a penny."

"She'll leave it to Miss Juliet Saxon, which is just the same. I never did see brother and sister so fond of one another as those two. I believe she'd put the 'air of 'er head—and lovely 'air it is, too—under his blessed feet to show him she loves him."

"She'd do the same by Mr. Mallow," said Geraldine, tittering.

Here Susan interrupted. "Who is the old lady who comes here?"

"Oh, she's Mrs. Herne," said the cook. "A cross, 'aughty old thing, who fights always. She's been coming here with Mr. Jarvey Hale and Mr. Clancy for the last three years. They play whist every evening and go away regular about ten. Missus let's 'em out themselves or else rings for me. Why, there's the bell now," and Mrs. Pill rose.

"No! I go," said Susan, rising also. "Miss Loach told me to come when she rang."

Mrs. Pill nodded and resumed her seat and her darning. "Lor bless you, my love, I ain't jealous," she said. "My legs ain't as young as they was. 'Urry, my dear, missus is a bad 'un to be kept waitin'."

Thus urged, Susan hastened to the front part of the house and down the stairs. The door of the sitting-room was open. She knocked and entered, to find Mr. Clancy, who looked rougher and more foolish than ever, standing by the table. Miss Loach, with a pack of cards on her lap, was talking, and Susan heard the concluding sentence as she entered the room.

"You're a fool, Clancy," said Miss Loach, emphatically. "You know Mrs. Herne doesn't like to be contradicted. You've sent her away in a fine rage, and she's taken Hale with her. Quite spoilt our game of—ah, here's Susan. Off with you, Clancy. I wish to be alone."

The man would have spoken, but Miss Loach silenced him with a sharp gesture and pointed to the door. In silence he went upstairs with Susan, and in silence left the house. It was a fine night, and Susan stopped for a moment at the door to drink in the fresh air. She heard the heavy footsteps of a policeman draw near and he passed the house, to disappear into the path on the opposite side of the road. When Susan returned to the kitchen she found supper ready. Soon the servants were seated at the table and talking brightly.

"Who does that house at the back belong to?" asked Susan.

"To Lord Caranby," said Thomas, although not directly addressed. "It's unfinished."

"Yes and shut up. Lord Caranby was in love with a lady and built that house for her. Before it was ready the lady died and Lord Caranby left the house as it was and built a high wall round it. He then went travelling and has been travelling ever since. He never married either, and his nephew, Mr. Cuthbert Mallow, is heir to the title."

"I thought you said Lord Caranby loved Miss Loach?"

"No, I didn't. I said she could have married him had she played her cards properly. But she didn't, and Lord Caranby went away. The lady who died was a friend of missus, and they were always together. I think missus and she were jealous of Lord Caranby, both loving him. But Miss Saul—that was the other lady—died, and Lord Caranby left the house as it stands, to go away."

"He won't allow anyone to set a foot in the house or grounds," said Mrs. Pill, "there ain't no gate in the wall—"

"No gate," echoed Susan astonished.

"Not a single 'ole as you could get a cat through. Round and round the place that fifteen-feet wall is built, and the park, as they calls it, is running as wild as a cow. Not a soul has set foot in that place for the last fifteen years. But I expect when Mr. Mallow comes in for the title he'll pull it down and build 'ouses. I'm sure he ought to: it's a shame seeing land wasted like that."

"Where is Lord Caranby now?"

"He lives in London and never comes near this place," said Thomas.

"Is Miss Loach friendly with him now?" "No, she ain't. He treated her badly. She'd have been a better Lady Caranby than Miss Saul"— here Thomas started and raised a finger. "Eh! wasn't that the front door closing?"

All listened, but no sound could be heard. "Perhaps missus has gone to walk in the garding," said cook, "she do that at times."

"Did you show 'ern out?" asked Thomas, looking at Susan.

"Only Mr. Clancy," she answered, "the others had gone before. I heard what Miss Loach was saying. Mr. Clancy had quarrelled with Mrs. Herne and she had gone away with Mr. Hale. Then Miss Loach gave it to him hot and sent him away. She's all alone."

"I must have been mistaken about the door then," said he.

"Not at all," chimed in Mrs. Pill. "Missus is walking as she do do in the garding, singing and adornin' self with flowers."

After this poetic flight of fancy on the part of the cook, the supper ended. Thomas smoked a pipe and the housemaid cleared away. Mrs. Pill occupied her time in putting her few straggling locks in curl-papers.

While Susan was assisting Geraldine, the bell rang. All started. "I thought missus had gone to bed," cried the cook, getting up hurriedly. "She'll be in a fine rage if she finds us up. Go to bed, Geraldine, and you, Thomas. Susan, answer the bell. She don't like us not to be gettin' our beauty sleep. Bless me it's eleving."

The clock had just struck as Susan left the kitchen, and the three servants were bustling about so as to get to bed before their sharp-eyed old mistress found them. Susan went down the stairs. The door of the sitting-room was closed. She knocked but no voice told her to enter. Wondering if the bell had been rung by mistake, Susan knocked again, and again received no answer. She had a mind to retreat rather than face the anger of Miss Loach. But remembering that the bell had rung, she opened the door, determined to explain. Miss Loach was seated in her usual chair, but leaning back with a ghastly face. The glare of the electric lamp fixed in the ceiling, shone full on her white countenance, and also on something else. The bosom of her purple gown was disarranged, and the lace which adorned it was stained with blood. Startled by her looks Susan hurried forward and gazed searchingly into the face. There was no sign of recognition in the wide, staring eyes. Susan, quivering with dread, touched Miss Loach's shoulder. Her touch upset the body and it rolled on the floor. The woman was dead. With a shriek Susan recoiled and fell on her knees. Her cry speedily brought the other servants.

"Look!" cried Susan pointing, "she is dead—murdered!"

Geraldine and Mrs. Pill shrieked with horror. Thomas preserved his stolid look of composure.

III

A Mysterious Death

To be the husband of a celebrated woman is not an unmixed blessing. Mr. Peter Octagon found it to be so, when he married Mrs. Saxon, the widow of an eminent Q.C. She was a fine Junoesque tragic woman, who modelled herself on the portraits of the late Mrs. Siddons. Peter, on the contrary, was a small, meek, light-haired, short-sighted man, who had never done anything in his unromantic life, save accumulate a fortune as a law-stationer. For many years he lived in single blessedness, but when he retired with an assured income of three thousand a year, he thought he would marry. He had no relatives, having been brought up in a Foundling Hospital, and consequently, found life rather lonely in his fine Kensington house. He really did not care about living in such a mansion, and had purchased the property as a speculation, intending to sell it at a profit. But having fallen in with Mrs. Saxon, then a hard-up widow, she not only induced him to marry her, but, when married, she insisted that the house should be retained, so that she could dispense hospitality to a literary circle.

Mrs. Octagon was very literary. She had published several novels under the nom-de-plume of "Rowena." She had produced a volume of poems; she had written a play which had been produced at a matinee; and finally her pamphlets on political questions stamped her, in the opinion of her immediate circle, as a William Pitt in petticoats. She looked upon herself as the George Eliot of the twentieth century, and dated events from the time of her first success. "That happened before I became famous," she would say. "No, it was after I took the public by storm." And her immediate circle, who appreciated her cakes and ale, would agree with everything she said. The Kensington house was called "The Shrine of the Muses!" and this title was stamped on her envelopes and writing-paper, to the bewilderment of illiterate postmen. It sounded like the name of a public-house to them.

Peter was quite lost in the blaze of his wife's literary glory. He was a plain, homely, small man, as meek as a rabbit, fond of his garden and fireside, and nervous in society. Had he not committed the fatal mistake of wedding Mrs. Saxon, he would have taken a cottage in the country and cultivated flowers. As it was, he dwelt in town and was ordered to escort Mrs. Octagon when she chose to "blaze," as she put it, in her friends' houses. Also there was a reception every Friday when literary London gathered round "Rowena," and lamented the decline of Art. These people had never done anything to speak of, none of them were famous in any wide sense, but they talked of art with a big "A," though what they meant was not clear even to themselves. So far as could be ascertained Art, with a big "A," was concerned with something which did not sell, save to a select circle. Mrs. Octagon's circle would have shuddered collectively and individually at the idea of writing anything interesting, likely to be enjoyed by the toilers of modern days. Whatever pictures, songs, books or plays were written by anyone who did not belong to "The Circle," these were considered "pretty, but not Tart!" Anything successful was pronounced "Vulgar!" To be artistic in Mrs. Octagon's sense, a work had to possess obscurity, it had to be printed on the finest paper with selected type, and it had to be sold at a prohibitive price. In this way "Rowena" had produced her works, and her name was not known beyond her small coterie. All the same, she intimated that her renown was world-wide and that her fame would be commensurate with the existence of the Anglo-Saxon race. Mrs. Lee Hunter in the Pickwick Papers, also labored under the same delusion.

With Peter lived Mrs. Saxon's children by the eminent Q.C. Basil, who was twenty-five, and Juliet age twenty-two. They were both handsome and clever, but Juliet was the more sensible of the two. She detested the sham enthusiasm of The Circle, and appreciated Peter more than her mother did. Basil had been spoilt by his mother, who considered him a genius, and had produced a book of weak verse. Juliet was fond of her brother, but she saw his faults and tried to correct them. She wished to make him more of a man and less of an artistic fraud, for the young man really did possess talents. But the hothouse atmosphere of "The Shrine of the Muses!" would have ruined anyone possessed of genius, unless he had a strong enough nature to withstand the sickly adulation and false judgments of those who came there. Basil was not strong. He was pleasant, idle, rather vain, and a little inclined to be dissipated. Mrs. Octagon did not know that Basil was fond of dissipation. She thought him a model young Oxford man, and hoped he would one day be Laureate of England.

Afternoon tea was just ended, and several of Mrs. Octagon's friends had departed. Basil and Mr. Octagon were out, but the latter entered with a paper in his hand shortly after the last visitor took her leave. Mrs. Octagon, in a ruby-colored velvet, looking majestic and self-satisfied, was enthroned—the word is not too strong—in an arm-chair, and Juliet was seated opposite to her turning over the leaves of a new novel produced by one of The Circle. It was beautifully printed and bound, and beautifully written in "precious" English, but its perusal did not seem to afford her any satisfaction. Her attention wandered, and every now and then she looked at the door as though expecting someone to enter. Mrs. Octagon disapproved of Juliet's pale cheeks and want of attention to her own fascinating conversation, so, when alone, she took the opportunity to correct her.

"My child," said Mrs. Octagon, who always spoke in a tragic manner, and in a kind of blank-verse way, "to me it seems your cheeks are somewhat pale."

"I had no sleep last night," said Juliet, throwing down the book.

"Your thoughts concerned themselves with Cuthbert's face, no doubt, my love," said her mother fondly.

"No, I was not thinking of him. I was worried about—about—my new dress," she finished, after vainly casting about for some more sensible reason.

"How foolish children are. You trouble about your dress when you should have been thinking of the man who loves you."

"Does Cuthbert love me?" asked Juliet, flushing.

"As Romeo loved your namesake, sweetest child. And a very good match it is too," added Mrs. Octagon, relapsing into prose. "He is Lord Caranby's heir, and will have a title and a fortune some day. But I would not force you to wed against your will, my dear."

"I love Cuthbert and Cuthbert loves me," said Juliet quickly, "we quite understand one another. I wonder why he did not come to-day."

"Ah," said her mother playfully, "I saw that your thoughts were otherwise. Your eyes wandered constantly to the door. He may come late. By the way, where is my dearest son?"

"Basil? He went out this morning. I believe he intended to call on Aunt Selina."

Mrs. Octagon lost a trifle of her suave manner, and became decidedly more human. "Then I wish he would not call there," she said sharply. "Selina Loach is my own sister, but I do not approve of her."

"She is a poor, lonely dear, mother."

"Poor, my child, she is not, as I have every reason to believe she is well endowed with this world's goods. Lonely she may be, but that is her own fault. Had she behaved as she should have done, Lady Caranby would have been her proud title. As to dear," Mrs. Octagon shrugged her fine shoulders, "she is not a woman to win or retain love. Look at the company she keeps. Mr. Hale, her lawyer, is not a nice man. I have espied something evil in his eye. That Clancy creature is said to be rich. He needs to be, if only to compensate for his rough way. They visit her constantly."

"You have forgotten Mrs. Herne," said Juliet, rising, and beginning to pace the room restlessly and watch out of the window.

"I have never met Mrs. Herne. And, indeed, you know, that for private reasons I have never visited Selina at that ridiculous house of hers. When were you there last, Juliet, my child?"

The girl started and appeared embarrassed. "Oh, a week ago," she said hurriedly, then added restlessly, "I wonder why Basil does not come back. He has been away all day."

"Do you know why he has called on your aunt, my dear?"

"No," said Juliet, in a hesitating manner, and turned again to look out of the window. Then she added, as though to escape further questioning, "I have seen Mrs. Herne only once, but she seemed to me a very nice, clever old woman."

"Clever," said Mrs. Octagon, raising her eyebrows, which were as strongly marked as those of her sister, "no. She does not belong to The Circle."

"A person can be clever without that," said Juliet impatiently.

"No. All the clever people in London come here, Juliet. If Mrs. Herne had been brilliant, she would have found her way to our Shrine."

Juliet shrugged her shoulders and curled her pretty lip. She did not appreciate her privileges in that house. In fact, a word distinctly resembling "Bother!" escaped from her mouth. However, she went on talking of Mrs. Herne, as though to keep her mother from questioning her further.

"There is a mystery about Mrs. Herne," she said, coming to the fire; "for I asked Aunt Selina who she was, and she could not tell me."

"That is so like Selina," rejoined Mrs. Octagon tartly, "receiving a person of whom she knows nothing."

"Oh, she does know a little. Mrs. Herne is the widow of a Spanish merchant, and she struck me as being foreign herself. Aunt Selina has known her for three years, and she has come almost every week to play whist at Rose Cottage. I believe she lives at Hampstead!"

"It seems to me, Juliet, that your aunt told you a great deal about this person. Why did you ask?"

Juliet stared into the fire. "There is something so strange about Mrs. Herne," she murmured. "In spite of her gray hair she looks quite young. She does not walk as an old woman. She confessed to being over fifty. To be sure, I saw her only once."

Mrs. Octagon grew rather cross. "I am over fifty, and I'm sure I don't look old, you undutiful child. When the soul is young, what matters the house of clay. But, as I was saying," she added hastily, not choosing to talk of her age, which was a tender point with her, "Selina Loach likes low company. I know nothing of Mrs. Herne, but what you say of her does not sound refined."

"Oh, she is quite a lady."

"And as to Mr. Clancy and Mr. Jarvey Hale," added Mrs. Octagon, taking no notice, "I mistrust them. That Hale man looked as though he would do a deed of darkness on the slightest provocation."

So tragic was her mother's manner, that Juliet turned even paler than she was. "Whatever do you mean?" she asked quickly.

"I mean murder, if I must use so vulgar and melodramatic a word."

"But I don't understand—"

"Bless me," cried Mrs. Octagon, becoming more prosaic than ever, "there is nothing to understand. But Selina lives in quite a lonely house, and has a lot of money. I never open the papers but what I expect to read of her death by violence."

"Oh," murmured Juliet, again crossing to the window, "you should not talk like that, mother!"

Mrs. Octagon laughed good-naturedly. "Nonsense, child. I am only telling you my thoughts. Selina is such a strange woman and keeps such strange company that she won't end in the usual way. You may be sure of that. But, after all, if she does die, you will come in for her money and then, can marry Cuthbert Mallow."

Juliet shuddered. "I hope Aunt Selina will live for many a long day, if that is what you think," she said sharply. "I want none of her money. Cuthbert has money of his own, and his uncle is rich also."

"I really hope Cuthbert has enough to justify him gambling."

"He does not gamble," said Juliet quickly.

"Yes he does," insisted Mrs. Octagon. "I have heard rumors; it is but right you should hear about—"

"I want to hear nothing. I thought you liked Cuthbert."

"I do, and he is a good match. But I should like to see you accept the Poet Arkwright, who will yet be the Shakespeare of England."

"England has quite enough glory with the Shakespeare she has," rejoined Juliet tartly, "and as to Mr. Arkwright, I wouldn't marry him if he had a million. A silly, ugly, weak—"

"Stop!" cried Mrs. Octagon, rising majestically from her throne. "Do not malign genius, lest the gods strike you dumb. Child—"

What Mrs. Octagon was about to say further must remain ever a mystery, for it was at this moment that her husband hurried into the room with an evening paper in his hand. "My dear," he said, his scanty hair almost standing on end with horror, "such dreadful news. Your aunt, Juliet, my dear—"

"Selina," said Mrs. Octagon quietly, "go on. There is nothing bad I don't expect to hear about Selina. What is it?"

"She is dead!"

"Dead!" cried Juliet, clasping her hands nervously. "No!"

"Not only dead, but murdered!" cried Mr. Octagon. His wife suddenly dropped into her throne and, being a large fleshly woman, her fall shook the room. Then she burst into tears. "I never liked Selina," she sniffed, "even though she was my own sister, but I am sorry—I am dreadfully—oh, dear me! Poor Selina!"

By this time all the dramatic posing of Mrs. Octagon had gone by the wall, and she showed herself in her true colors as a kind-hearted woman. Juliet hurried to her mother and took one of her hands. The elder woman started, even in the midst of her tears. "My child, your hand is as cold as ice," she said anxiously. "Are you ill."

"No," said the girl hurriedly and evidently trying to suppress her emotion, "but this dreadful news! Do you remember what you said?"

"Yes—but I never expected I would be a true prophetess," sobbed Mrs. Octagon. "Peter," with sudden tartness, "why don't you give me the details. Poor Selina dead, and here am I in ruby velvet!"

"There are not many details to give," said Peter, reading from the newspaper, "the police are keeping quiet about the matter."

"Who killed her?"

Juliet rose suddenly and turned on the electric light, so that her step-father could see to read more clearly. "Yes," she said in a firm voice, belied by the ghastly whiteness of her face, "who killed her?"

"It is not known," said Mr. Octagon. "Last night she entertained a few friends—to be precise, three, and she was found by her new parlor-maid dead in her chair, stabbed to the heart. The weapon has not been found, nor has any trace of the murderer been discovered."

"Entertained friends," muttered Mrs. Octagon weeping, "the usual lot. Mr. Hale, Mrs. Herne and Mr. Clancy—"

"Yes," said Peter, somewhat surprised, "how do you know?"

"My soul, whispered me," said Mrs. Octagon tragically, and becoming melodramatic again, now that the first shock was over. "One of those three killed her. Who struck the fatal blow?—the villain Hale I doubt not."

"No," cried Juliet, "it was not Mr. Hale. He would not harm a fly."

"Probably not," said her mother tartly, "a fly has no property—your Aunt Selina had. Oh, my dear," she added, darting away at a tangent, "to think that last night you and Basil should have been witnesses of a melodrama at the Marlow Theatre, at the very time this real tragedy was taking place in the rural country."

"It's a most dreadful affair," murmured Peter, laying aside the paper. "Had I not better go down to Rose Cottage and offer my services?"

"No," said Mrs. Octagon sharply, "don't mix yourself up in this dreadful affair. Few people know that Selina was my sister, and I don't want everyone to be condoling with me on this tragedy."

"But we must do something," said Juliet quickly.

"We will wait, my dear. But I don't want more publicity than is necessary."

"But I have told some of our friends that Aunt Selina is a relative."

"Then you should not have done so," replied her mother, annoyed. "However, people soon forget names, and the thing may not be noticed."

"My dear," said Octagon, seriously, "you should not be ashamed of your sister. She may not have your renown nor rank, still—"

"I know my own knowing," interrupted the lady rather violently, and crushing her meek husband with a look. "Selina and I are strangers, and have been for years. What are the circumstances of the case? I have not seen Selina for over fifteen years. I hear nothing about her. She suddenly writes to me, asking if my dear children may call and see her— that was a year ago. You insisted that they should go, Peter, because relatives should be friendly. I consented, as I heard from Mr. Hale that Selina was rich, and fancied she might leave her money to my children. Juliet has called several times—"

"More than that," interrupted Juliet in her turn, "both Basil and I have called nearly every month. We sometimes went and did not tell you, mother, as you seemed so annoyed that we should visit her."

"I consented only that you might retain her goodwill and get what money she might leave," said Mrs. Octagon obstinately. "There is nothing in common between Selina and me."

"There was nothing in common," put in Octagon softly.

"I know she is dead. You need not remind me of that unpleasant fact, sir. And her death is worthy of her strange, and I fear not altogether reputable life."

"Oh, mother, how can you? Aunt Selina was the most particular—"

"There—there," said her mother who was much agitated, "I know more than you do. And between ourselves, I believe I know who killed her. Yes! You may look. And this death, Juliet, ends your engagement with Cuthbert."

IV

DETAILS

What Mrs. Octagon meant by her last enigmatic remark it is impossible to say. After delivering it in her usual dramatic manner, she swept from the room, leaving Juliet and her step-father staring at one another. Peter was the first to break the silence.

"Your mother appears to be very positive," said he.

"About my giving up Cuthbert?" asked Juliet sharply.

"About the crime. She hinted that she guessed who killed the poor lady. I never knew Miss Loach myself," added Mr. Octagon, seating himself and ruffling his scanty locks, a habit with him when perplexed, "but you said you liked her."

"Yes, Aunt Selina was always very nice to me. She had strange ways, and, to tell you the truth, father," Juliet always addressed Peter thus, to his great delight, "she was not so refined as mother—"

"Few people are so refined as my wife, my dear."

"As to mother knowing who killed her," pursued Juliet, taking no notice of this interpolation, "it's nonsense. She said she believed Mr. Hale or Mr. Clancy—"

"Surely not," interposed Mr. Octagon anxiously, "both these gentlemen have participated in the delights of our literary Circle, and I should be loath to credit them with violence."

"I don't believe either has anything to do with the matter. Mother doesn't like them because they were such good friends to Aunt Selina. Can you guess why mother quarrelled with aunt, father?"

"No, my dear. Your mother has some grudge against her. What it is I do not know. She never told me. But for over fifteen years your mother spoke little of your aunt and never called to see her. I was quite astonished when she consented that you and Basil should call. Did your aunt ever speak of your mother?"

"Very little, and then she was cautious—what she said. But this is not the question," continued the girl, leaning her chin on her hand and staring into the fire; "why does mother say I must break my engagement with Cuthbert on account of this death?"

"Perhaps she will explain."

"No; she left the room to avoid an explanation. Cuthbert certainly saw Aunt Selina once or twice, but he did not care for her. But he can have nothing to do with the matter. Then again, mother, up till now, was always pleased that I should marry Cuthbert."

"Yes," said Octagon, twiddling his thumbs; "she has known Mr. Mallow ever since he was a child. Both your aunt and your mother were great friends of Lord Caranby's in their youth, over twenty years ago. I believe at one time Selina was engaged to him, but he was in love with a young lady called Miss Saul, who died unexpectedly."

"I know," said Juliet; "and then Lord Caranby abandoned the house he was building at Rexton, and it has been shut up all these years. Aunt Selina told me the story. When I asked mother for details, she refused to speak."

"Your mother is very firm when she likes."

"Very obstinate, you mean," said Juliet, undutifully. "However, I am not going to give up Cuthbert. I love him and he loves me. I intend to marry him whatever mother may say."

"But if your mother refuses her consent?"

"I am over age."

As she spoke her brother entered the room hurriedly. Basil Saxon was as fair and weak-looking as his sister was dark and strong in appearance. He was smartly dressed, and in a rather affected way. His hair was long, he wore a moustache and a short imperial, and talked in a languid way in a somewhat obscure manner. These were the traits Juliet disliked in Basil. She would rather have seen him a spruce well-groomed man about town like Cuthbert. But at the present moment Basil's face was flushed, and he spoke hurriedly, evidently laboring under great stress of emotion.

"Have you heard the news?" he said, dropping into a chair and casting a side look at the evening paper which Peter still held.

"If you mean about the death—"

"Yes; Aunt Selina has been murdered. I called to see her this morning, and found the house in the possession of the police. All day I have been down there with Mallow."

"With Cuthbert," said Juliet, starting and growing red. "What was he doing there?"

"He came down to Rexton to see about the unfinished house. Lord Caranby has returned to England, and he has thoughts of pulling it down. Mallow came to have a look at the place."

"But he can't get in. There is a wall round the grounds."

"He climbed over the wall," said Basil, quickly, "and after looking through the house he came out. Then he saw me, and I told him what had happened. He appeared dreadfully shocked."

Juliet shivered in spite of the heat of the day and the fire, near which she was seated. "It is strange he should have been there."

Her brother threw a keen glance at her. "I don't see that!" he exclaimed. "He gave his reason for being in the neighborhood. He came up with me, and is coming on here in a few moments. This is why he did not turn up this afternoon."

Juliet nodded and appeared satisfied with this explanation. But she kept her eyes on her brother when he entered into details about the crime. Her emotions during the recital betrayed themselves markedly.

"I saw the detective," said Basil, with quicker speech than usual. "He is a first-rate chap called Jennings, and when he heard I was Miss Loach's nephew he didn't mind speaking freely."

"What did you learn?" asked Mr. Octagon.

"Enough to make the mystery surrounding the death deeper than ever."

"What do you mean?" asked his sister, restlessly. "Can't the murderer be found?"

"Not a trace of him can be discovered."

"Why do you say 'him.' It might have been a woman."

"No," rejoined Basil positively, "no woman could have struck so hard a blow. Aunt Selina was stabbed to the heart. She must have been killed as she was rising from her chair, and death, so the doctor says, must have been instantaneous."

"Has the weapon been found?" asked Juliet in a low voice.

Basil turned quickly in his chair, and looked at her sharply. "No!" he said, "not a sign of any weapon can be found, nor can it be discovered how anyone got into the house. Though to be sure, she might have admitted her visitor."

"Explain! explain," cried Mr. Octagon, ruffling his hair.

"Well, to tell the story in detail," said his step-son, "the way it happened is this. Aunt Selina had Mr. Hale and Mr. Clancy and Mrs. Herne to their usual game of whist. Clancy, as it appears from the report of what the new parlor-maid overheard, quarrelled with Hale and Mrs. Herne. They left before ten o'clock. At all events, when she entered the room in answer to my aunt's summons, she found only Mr. Clancy, and aunt was scolding him for having provoked Mrs. Herne by contradicting her. Apparently Mrs. Herne had gone away under the wing of Hale. Then aunt sent Clancy away at ten o'clock. The parlor-maid returned to the kitchen and there had supper. She heard the bell ring at eleven, and found aunt dead in the sitting-room, stabbed to the heart."

"Heard the bell ring?" echoed Juliet. "But how could aunt ring if she had been killed?"

"She might have rung as she was dying," said Basil, after a pause. "It seems she was seated near the button of the bell and could have touched it without rising. She might have rung with a last effort, and then have died before the parlor-maid could get to the room."

"Or else," said Mr. Octagon, anxious to prove his perspicuity, "the assassin may have stabbed her and then have touched the bell."

"What!" cried his step-son derisively, "to summon a witness. I don't think the assassin would be such a fool. However, that's all that can be discovered. Aunt Selina is dead, and no one knows who killed her."

"Was the house locked up?" "The front door was closed, and the windows were bolted and barred. Besides, a policeman was walking down Crooked Lane a few minutes before eleven, and would have seen anyone leaving the house. He reported that all was quiet."

"Then the assassin might have rung the bell at eleven," said Peter.

"Certainly not, for he could never have escaped immediately afterwards, without the policeman seeing him."

"He might have got out by the back," suggested Juliet.

"My dear girl, what are you thinking of. That wall round Lord Caranby's mansion blocks any exit at the back. Anyone leaving the house must go up the lane or through that part at the bottom. The policeman was near there shortly before eleven and saw no one leaving the house."

"But, look here," said Mr. Octagon, who had been ruminating; "if, as the doctor says, death was instantaneous, how could your aunt have rung the bell?"

"Yes," added Juliet. "And even had death not taken place at once, it could not have been more than a few minutes before eleven when the blow was struck. Aunt might have had strength to crawl to the bell and touch it, but the assassin could not have escaped from the house, seeing—as you say—the policeman was on guard."

"Aunt died instantaneously," insisted Basil.

"Then she could not have sounded the bell," said Juliet triumphantly.

"The assassin did that," said Peter.

"And thus called a witness," cried Basil. "Ridiculous!"

"Then how do you explain the matter?"

"I can't explain. Neither can the detective Jennings. It's a mystery."

"Could any of the servants—" began Peter.

"No," interrupted Saxon. "The four servants were having supper in the kitchen. They are innocent. Well, we'll see what the inquest reveals. Something may be found before then likely to elucidate the mystery. But here comes Mallow. He questioned Jennings also, so you can question him if you like. Does mother know?"

"Yes. And she doesn't want the fact of her relationship to your aunt talked about."

Basil understood at once. "No wonder," he said, shrugging his shoulders. "It is not a pleasant affair for a woman of mother's celebrity to be mixed up with."

Meantime, Juliet having heard the ring at the front door, escaped from the room to see her lover. She met him divesting himself of his overcoat in the hall, and ran to him with outstretched hands. "But why have you got on an overcoat this warm day?" she asked.

"I have a cold. I caught one last night," said Cuthbert, kissing her.

"Where were you last night?" asked Juliet, drawing him into a side room. "I thought you were coming to the Marlow Theatre with Basil and me."

"Yes. But my uncle arrived unexpectedly in England and sent for me to his hotel in Guelph street—the Avon Hotel, you know. He will insist on a fire even in June, and the room was so hot that I caught cold when I came out. I had to go down to Rexton to-day on his business, and put on a coat so as to avoid catching further cold. But why this room, Juliet?"

"Father and Basil are in the drawing-room. They are talking of the murder, and I don't want to hear any more about it."

"There are pleasanter things to talk about," said Mallow. "I knew Basil would come crammed with news. Has he told you—"

"He told us everything he could gather from the detective. It seems that the crime is quite a mystery."

"Quite. Why your aunt should be killed, or how the assassin escaped, after killing her, cannot be discovered. Jennings is in high glee about it. He loves a puzzle of this sort."

"Do you know him?" asked Juliet anxiously.

"Oh, yes. Jennings is a gentleman. He was at Eton with me. But he ran through his money and took up the detective business. He is very clever, and if anyone will learn the truth, he will. Now, my theory—"

Juliet put her hand over his mouth. "Don't," she said. "I have had enough horrors for this afternoon. Let us talk of ourselves."

"I would rather do this," said Mallow, and kissed her.

Mallow was a handsome fellow, tall and slim, with a rather military carriage. His face was clean-shaven save for a small straw-colored moustache, which showed up almost white against the bronze of his face. He was more of an athlete than a student, and this was one reason why Juliet was fond of him. She had seen so much of literary circles that she always vowed she would marry a man who never opened a book. Cuthbert nearly fulfilled this requirement, as he read little, save novels and newspapers. He was well known in sporting circles, and having a good private income, owned race-horses. He was always irreproachably dressed, good-humored and cheerful. Consequently he was popular, and if not overburdened with brains, managed to make himself agreeable to the world, and to have what the Americans call "a good time." He had travelled much and was fond of big-game shooting. To complete his characterization, it is necessary to mention that he had served in the Boer War, and had gained a D.S.O. But that was in the days before he met Juliet or he might not have risked a life so precious to her.

Juliet was dark and rather little, not at all like her Junoesque mother. She was extremely pretty and dressed to perfection. Having more brains and a stronger will than Mallow, she guided him in every way, and had already succeeded in improving his morals. With so gentle and charming a mentor, Cuthbert was quite willing to be led into the paths of virtue. He adored Juliet and she loved him, so it appeared that the marriage would be quite ideal.

"Much as we love one another," said Cuthbert when the lovers were seated on the sofa. "I wonder you can talk of anything but this horrid murder."

"Because there is nothing to talk of," rejoined the girl impatiently; "according to Basil, the case is most mysterious, so it is useless for us to worry over it until something tangible is discovered. But I want to speak to you seriously—" here Juliet hesitated.

"Well, go on," said Cuthbert, taking her hand.

"Mother says—" began Juliet, then hesitated again. "Promise me you will keep to yourself what I am about to tell you."

"Certainly. I never was a fellow to chatter."

"Then mother says that this murder will put a stop to our marriage."

Mallow stared, then flushed up to his ears. "What on earth does she mean by that?" he asked aghast.

Juliet looked searchingly at him. "Do you know of any impediment?"

"I? Of course I don't. I am sorry for the death of your aunt, but I really don't see what it has to do with you and me."

Juliet drew a breath of relief. "Mother hints that she knows who committed the crime, and—"

"What! She knows. How does she know?"

"I can't say. She refuses to speak. She was not on good terms with Aunt Selina and they never saw one another for over fifteen years. But mother is much disturbed about the murder—"

"That is natural. A sister is a sister however much one may have quarrelled. But why should this death stop our marriage?"

"I know no more than you do. Here is mother. Ask her yourself."

It was indeed Mrs. Octagon who entered the room. She looked very pale, but otherwise was perfectly composed. In silence she gave her hand to Cuthbert, and kept her black eyes fixed steadily on his face. The young man flushed and turned away, whereat Mrs. Octagon sighed. Juliet broke an embarrassed silence.

"Mother," she said, "I have told Cuthbert what you said."

"Then you had no right to," said Mrs. Octagon sternly.

"Oh, I think she had," said Mallow, rather annoyed. "Seeing you hint that this crime will stop our marriage."

Mrs. Octagon did not answer. "Is your uncle in town?" she asked.

"Yes. He arrived from the continent a day or two ago."

"I thought so," she said, half to herself, and strove to repress her agitation. "Mr. Mallow, my daughter can't marry you."

"Why not? Give your reason."

"I have no reason to give."

"But you must. Is it on account of this murder?"

"It is. I told Juliet so. But I cannot explain."

The lovers looked at one another in a dazed fashion. The woman's objection seemed to be senseless. "Surely you don't think Cuthbert killed Aunt Selina?" said Juliet, laughing in a forced manner.

"No. I don't suspect him."

"Then whom do you suspect?" demanded Mallow.

"That I decline to say."

"Will you decline to say it to the police?"

Mrs. Octagon stepped back a pace. "Yes, I should," she faltered.

Cuthbert Mallow looked at her, wondering why she was so agitated, and Juliet stole her hand into his. Then he addressed her seriously.

"Mrs. Octagon," he said, "your remark about my uncle leads me to think you suspect him."

"No I don't. But you can't marry Juliet on account of this crime."

"Then you hear me," said Mallow, driven into a corner, "from this moment I devote myself to finding out who killed your unfortunate sister. When the assassin is discovered you may consent to our marriage."

But he spoke to empty air. Mrs. Octagon had left the room, almost before the first words left his mouth.

V

LORD CARANBY'S ROMANCE

C uthbert was considerably perplexed by the attitude of Juliet's mother. She had always been more than kind to him. On the announcement that he wished to marry her daughter, she had expressed herself well pleased, and during the engagement, which had lasted some six months, she had received him as Juliet's intended husband, with almost ostentatious delight. Now, for some inexplicable reason, she suddenly changed her mind and declined to explain. But rack his brains as he might, Cuthbert could not see how the death of a sister she had quarrelled with, and to whom she had been a stranger for so long, could affect the engagement.

However, there was no doubt in his mind that the refusal of Mrs. Octagon to approve of the marriage lay in the fact that her sister had met with a violent end. Therefore Mallow was determined to see Jennings, and help him to the best of his ability to discover the assassin. When the criminal was brought to justice, either Mrs. Octagon's opposition would be at an end, or the true reason for its existence would be revealed. Meantime, he was sure that she would keep Juliet out of his way, and that in future he would be refused admittance to the "Shrine of the Muses." This was annoying, but so long as Juliet remained true, Cuthbert thought he could bear the exclusion. His betrothed—as he still regarded the girl—could meet him in the Park, at the houses of mutual friends, and in a thousand and one places which a clever woman like her could think of. And although Cuthbert knew that Mrs. Octagon had frequently regretted the refusal of her daughter to marry Arkwright, and would probably try and induce her to do so now that matters stood thus, yet he was not afraid in his own heart. Juliet was as staunch as steel, and he was certain that Mr. Octagon would be on his side. Basil probably would agree with his mother, whose lead he slavishly followed. But Mallow had rather a contempt for Basil, and did not count his opposition as dangerous.

On leaving the "Shrine of the Muses," the young man's first intention was to seek out Jennings and see what progress he was making in the matter. But on reflection he thought he would call again on his uncle and question him regarding his knowledge of Mrs. Octagon. It seemed to Cuthbert that, from the woman's question as to whether Lord Caranby had returned from abroad, and her remark on hearing that he had, some suspicion was in her mind as to his being concerned in the crime. Yet, beyond the fact that the unfinished house stood behind the cottage where the crime had been committed and belonged to Lord Caranby who had known the dead woman in the past, Cuthbert could not see how Mrs. Octagon could constitute a latter-day connection between her dead sister and her old friend. But Lord Caranby might be induced to talk—no easy matter—and from what he said, the mystery of Mrs. Octagon's attitude might be elucidated. Only in the past—so far as the perplexed young man could conjecture—could be found the reason for her sudden change of front.

Cuthbert therefore sent a wire to his uncle, stating that he wished to see him after eight o'clock on special business, and then went home to dress.

While thus employed, he thought over means and ways to make Caranby open his mouth. The old lord was a silent, grave man, who never uttered an unnecessary word, and it was difficult to induce him to be confidential. But invariably he had approved of his nephew's engagement, although he had never seen Juliet, so it might be that he would speak out—if there was anything to say—in order to remove any impediment to the match. It depended upon what information he received as to how Mallow would act.

At half-past eight he drove to the Avon Hotel and was shown up at once to his uncle's sitting-room. That he should live in an hotel was another of Caranby's eccentricities. He had a house in town and three in the country, yet for years he had lived—as the saying is—on his portmanteau. Even the villa at Nice he owned was unoccupied by this strange nobleman, and was usually let to rich Americans. When in England he stopped at the Avon Hotel and when in the country remained at any inn of the neighborhood in which he might chance to find himself wandering. And wandering is an excellent word to apply to Lord Caranby's peregrinations. He was as restless as a gipsy and far more aimless. He never appeared to take an interest in anything: he was always moving here, there and everywhere, and had—so far as Cuthbert knew—no object in life. His reason for this Cainlike behavior, Caranby never condescended to explain.

When his nephew entered the room, looking smart and handsome in his accurate evening suit, Caranby, who was seated near the fire, stood up courteously to welcome him, leaning on his cane. He suffered from sciatica, and could not walk save with the assistance of his stick. And on this account also, he always insisted on the room being heated to an extraordinary degree. Like a salamander he basked in the heat, and would not allow either door or window to be opened, even in the midst of summer, when a large fire made the apartment almost unendurable. Cuthbert felt as though he were walking into a Turkish bath, and sat as far away from the fire as he could. After saluting him, his uncle sank back into his seat and looked at him inquiringly.

Lord Caranby was tall and thin—almost emaciated—with a lean, sallow, clean-shaven face, and a scanty crop of fair hair mixed with gray. His eyes were sunken but full of vitality, although usually they were grave and somewhat sad. His hands were deformed with gout, but for all that he wore several costly rings. He was perfectly dressed, and as quiet and composed as an artist's model. When he spoke it was in an unemotional way, as though he had exhausted all expression of his feelings early in life. Perhaps he had, for from what Cuthbert had heard from his uncle, the past of that nobleman was not without excitement. But Caranby's name was rarely mentioned in London. He remained so much abroad that he had quite dropped out of the circle to the entry of which his rank entitled him. His age was sixty-five.

"You are surprised at seeing me again to-night," said Cuthbert.

"I am never surprised at anything," replied his uncle dryly, "but we exhausted all we had to say to one another before eight o'clock last night, at which time you left. I therefore don't know why you have come this evening. Our conversation is bound to be dull, and—excuse me—I can't afford to be bored at my age."

"I cannot say that our conversation was particularly agreeable last night," rejoined Mallow, equally dryly, "we talked business and money matters, and about your will."

"And about your engagement also," said Caranby without a vestige of a smile. "That should interest a young man of your ardent temperament. I certainly thought the subject amused you."

"Would you be surprised to learn that my engagement has been broken off since our conversation," said Cuthbert, crossing his legs.

"No! Who can account for the whims of a woman. After all, perhaps you are to be congratulated on not marrying a weathercock."

"Juliet has nothing to do with the breaking of our engagement. Her mother objects."

"I understood for the last six months that her mother not only approved, but was delighted."

"That is the strange part, sir. On hearing of the death of her sister, Mrs. Octagon suddenly changed her mind, and told me that the marriage could not take place."

"Did she give any reason?"

"She declined to do so."

"The same woman," muttered Caranby, "always mysterious and unsatisfactory. You say her sister is dead?"

Cuthbert cast a look at the Globe, which lay on a small table near Caranby's elbow. "If you have read the papers, sir—" "Yes! I have read that Miss Loach has been murdered. You went down to Rexton to-day. I presume you heard something more than the details set forth by the press."

Cuthbert nodded. "It appears to be a mystery."

Caranby did not reply, but looked into the fire. "Poor Selina!" he said half to himself. "A sad end for such a charming woman."

"I should hardly apply that word to Miss Loach, sir. She did not appear to be a lady, and was by no means refined."

"She must have changed then. In her young days she and her sister were the handsomest women in London."

"I believe you were engaged to one of them," said Mallow politely.

"Yes," replied his uncle grimly. "But I escaped."

"Escaped?"

"A strange word is it not, but a suitable one."

Cuthbert did not know what to make of this speech. "Have I your permission to smoke?" he asked, taking out his case.

"Yes! Will you have some coffee?"

"Thank you. I had some before I came here. Will you—" he extended the case of cigarettes, which Caranby declined.

"Ring for Fletcher to get me my chibouque."

"It is in the corner. We will dispense with Fletcher with your permission." And Cuthbert brought the chibouque to his uncle's side. In another minute the old man was smoking as gravely as any Turk. This method of consuming tobacco was another eccentricity. For a few moments neither spoke. Then Caranby broke the silence.

"So you want me to help you to find out Mrs. Octagon's reason?"

"I do," said Mallow, rather surprised by Caranby's perspicuity.

"What makes you think I can explain?"

Cuthbert looked at his cigarette. "I asked you on the chance that you may be able to do so," he said gravely. "The fact is, to be frank, Mrs. Octagon appears to think you might have something to do with the crime."

Caranby did not seem surprised, but smoked imperturbably. "I don't quite understand."

The young man related how Mrs. Octagon had inquired if the Earl was back from the Continent, and her subsequent remark. "Of course I may be unduly suspicious," said he. "But it suggested—"

"Quite so," interrupted the old gentleman gravely. "You are quick at putting two and two together. Isabella Octagon hates me so much that she would gladly see me on the scaffold. I am not astonished that she suspects me."

"But what motive can she impute—"

Caranby laid aside the long coil he was holding and laughed quietly to himself. "Oh, she'll find a motive if it suits her. But what I cannot understand is, why she should accuse me now. She has had ample opportunity during the past twenty years, since the death of Miss Saul, for instance."

"She did not exactly accuse you."

"No, a woman like that would not. And then of course, her sister dying only last night affords her the opportunity of getting me into trouble. But I am afraid Mrs. Octagon will be disappointed of her revenge, long though she has waited."

"Revenge! remember, sir, she is the mother of Juliet."

"I sincerely hope Juliet does not take after her, then," said Lord Caranby, tartly. "To be perfectly plain with you, Cuthbert, I could never understand why Mrs. Octagon sanctioned your engagement with her daughter, considering you are my nephew."

"I don't understand," said Mallow, staring and uneasily.

Caranby did not answer immediately. He rose and walked painfully up and down the room leaning heavily on his cane. Mallow offered his arm but was impatiently waved aside. When the old man sat down again he turned a serious face to his nephew. "Do you love this girl?"

"With all my heart and soul."

"And she loves you?"

"Of course. We were made for one another."

"But Mrs. Octagon—"

"I don't like Mrs. Octagon—I never did," said Mallow, impetuously, "but I don't care two straws for her opposition. I shall marry Juliet in spite of this revenge she seems to be practising on you. Though why she should hope to vex you by meddling with my marriage, I cannot understand."

"I can put the matter in a nutshell," said Caranby, and quoted Congreve—

"Heaven has no rage like love to hatred turned
Nor Hell a fury like a woman scorned.'"

"Oh," said Mallow, dropping his cigarette, and a whole story was revealed to him in the quotation.

"A gentleman doesn't talk of these things," said Caranby abruptly, "and for years I have held my tongue. Still, as Mrs. Octagon does not hesitate to strike at me through you, and as your happiness is at stake, and the happiness of the girl you love, I shall tell you—so far as I can guess—why the woman behaves in this way."

"If you please, sir," and Cuthbert settled himself to listen.

"About twenty years ago," said Caranby, plunging headfirst into his subject, "Isabella and Selina Loach were well-known in society. They were the daughters of a country squire—Kent, I remember—and created a sensation with their beauty when they came to town. I fell in love with Selina, and Isabella—if you will pardon my vanity—fell in love with me. She hated her sister on my account. I would have married Selina, but her father, who was hard up, wished her to marry a wealthy American. Isabella, to part Selina from me, helped her father. What arguments they used I do not know, but Selina suddenly changed in her manner towards me. Out of pique—you may think this weak of me, Cuthbert, but I was a fool in those days—I became engaged to a girl who was a singer. Her name was Emilia Saul, and I believe she was of Jewish extraction. I liked her in a way, and she had a wonderful power over me. I proposed and was accepted."

"But if you had really loved Miss Loach—"

"I should have worn the willow. I told you I was foolish, and, moreover, Miss Saul fascinated me. Selina was cold, Emilia was charming, and I was weak. Therefore, I became engaged to Emilia, and Selina—as I heard, arranged to marry her wealthy American. I believe she was angry at my apparently forgetting her so soon. But she was in fault, not I."

Cuthbert looked at his smart shoes. "Had I loved Selina," said he slowly, "I should have remained true to her, and have married her in spite of the objection of her father—"

"And of her sister Isabella—Mrs. Octagon that is; don't forget that, Cuthbert. And I could scarcely run away with a girl who believed stories about me."

"What sort of stories?" asked Mallow, remembering certain rumors.

"The sort that one always does tell of an unmarried man," retorted Caranby. "Scandalous stories, which Isabella picked up and retailed to Selina. But I never pretended to be a saint, and had Selina really loved me she would have overlooked certain faults. I did love her, Cuthbert. I did all in my power to prove my love. For a time I was engaged to her, and when she expressed a wish that I should build her a house after her own design, I consented."

"The house at Rexton!" exclaimed the young man.

"Exactly. I got an architect to build it according to designs suggested by Selina. When our engagement was broken and I became—out of pique, remember—engaged to Miss Saul, I still went on building the house. Selina, I believe, was very angry. One week when I was out of London she went down with her sister to see the house, and there met Emilia."

"Ah! then there was trouble?"

"No; there was no time for a quarrel, if that is what you mean. When the three met, Emilia was walking across a plank on the unfinished second story. On seeing the Loach girls—this is Isabella's tale—Emilia lost her footing and fell thirty feet. She was killed almost instantaneously, and her face was much disfigured. This took place during the dinner hour when the workmen were absent. When they returned, the body was found and recognized by the clothes."

"Did not the girls remain?"

"No. They took fright at the accident and returned home. But here a fresh disaster awaited them. Mr. Loach was dead. He died suddenly of heart disease. Selina at once broke her engagement with the American, and—"

"And returned to you?"

"Strangely enough she did not. I never saw her again. After the death of the father the girls went to the Continent, and only came back after two years abroad. Then Isabella, after vainly trying to get me to marry her, became the wife of Saxon, then a rising barrister. Selina went to Rexton and shut herself up in the house she now has."

"The house she did have," corrected Cuthbert, "you forget she is dead."

"Yes. I tried to see her, but she refused to look on my face again, alleging that I had treated her badly by becoming engaged to Miss Saul. That poor soul was buried, and then I shut up the house and left it as it is now. I travelled, as you know, for years, and I am travelling still, for the matter of that," added Caranby with a sigh, "all Selina's fault. She was the only woman I ever loved."

"But was there not an inquest held on Emilia's body?"

"Oh yes, and Isabella gave evidence as to the accident. Selina was too ill to appear. But there was no need. The cause of the death was plain enough. Moreover, Emilia had no relatives who cared to make inquiries. She left very little money, so those she had, did not trouble themselves."

"It is a strange story," said Cuthbert, looking puzzled. "Had you an idea that Emilia may have been pushed off the plank by Selina?"

"Certainly not," rejoined Caranby indignantly. "She was a good and kind girl. She would not do such a thing."

"Humph!" said Mallow, remembering the eagle nose and thin lips of Miss Loach. "I'm not so sure of that."

"Isabella, who was passionate, might have done it," resumed Caranby, "often did I wish to speak to her on the subject, but I never did. And after all, the jury brought in a verdict of accidental death, so there was no use making trouble."

"Had Emilia no relatives who might have made inquiries?"

"I believe she had a brother who was a clerk in an office, but, as I said, she left no money, so he did not bother himself. I saw him after the death, and the sight of him made me glad I had not married his sister. He looked a thorough blackguard, sly and dangerous. But, as I said, Emilia came of low people. It was only her fine voice and great talents that brought her into the society where I met her. I have never heard of her brother since. I expect he is dead by this time. It is over twenty years ago. But you can now understand why Mrs. Octagon objects to the marriage. She has never forgiven me for not making her my wife."

Cuthbert nodded again. "But I can't understand why she should have consented at all, only to alter her mind when Selina died."

"I can't understand that myself. But I decline to mix myself up in the matter. You will have to learn the reason yourself."

"I intend to," said Mallow rising, "and the reason I am certain is connected with the violent death of her sister!" A speech to which Caranby replied by shaking his head. He did not agree with the idea.

"And you see, in spite of Mrs. Octagon's hint, I had no reason to kill Selina," said Caranby gravely. "I cannot understand why Isabella should accuse me—"

VI

A PERPLEXING CASE

The morning after his visit to Lord Caranby, Mallow was unexpectedly called to Devonshire on account of his mother's illness. Mrs. Mallow was a fretful hypochondriac, who always imagined herself worse than she really was. Cuthbert had often been summoned to her dying bed, only to find that she was alive and well. He expected that this summons would be another false alarm, but being a dutiful son, he tore himself away from town and took the mid-day express to Exeter. As he expected, Mrs. Mallow was by no means so bad as she hinted in her wire, and Cuthbert was vexed that she should have called him down, but she insisted that he should remain, and, unwilling to cause her pain, he did so. It was four days before he returned to London. But his visit to Exeter was not without results, for he asked his mother about Caranby's romance. Mrs. Mallow knew all about it, and highly disapproved of her brother-in-law.

"He's crazy," she said vigorously, when the subject was brought up one evening. "All his life he has been queer. Your father should have had the title, Cuthbert!"

"Well, I shall have it some day," said her son soothingly. "Caranby is not likely to marry."

"Yes, but I'll never be Lady Caranby," lamented Mrs. Mallow, who was intensely selfish and egotistical. "And I should have adorned the title. Such an old one as it is, too. But I'm glad that horrid Selina Loach never became his wife. Even that Saul girl would have been better."

"Don't speak evil of the dead, mother."

"I don't see why we should praise the bad dead," snapped Mrs. Mallow. "I never liked either Isabella nor Selina. They were both horrid girls and constantly quarrelling. They hardly ever spoke to one another, and how you can contemplate marrying the daughter of Isabella, I really don't know. Such a slight to me. But there, I've said all I had to say on the subject."

To do her justice, Mrs. Mallow certainly had, and never ceased nagging at Cuthbert to break the engagement. Had she known that Mrs. Octagon had forbidden the marriage she would have rejoiced, but to save making awkward explanations to a woman who would not hold her tongue, Cuthbert said nothing about the breach.

"Did you like Miss Saul, mother?" he asked.

"I only saw her on the concert platform," said Mrs. Mallow, opening her eyes, "gracious, Cuthbert, I never associated myself with those sort of people. Caranby was infatuated with her. To be sure, he got engaged to spite Selina, and she really did treat him badly, but I believe Miss Saul—such a horrid Hebrew name, isn't it—hypnotized him. He forgot her almost as soon as she died, in spite of his ridiculous idea of shutting up that house. And such valuable land as there is at Rexton too. Well, I hope this violent death of Selina will be a warning to Caranby. Not that I wish him any harm, in spite of your being next heir to the title, and we do need money."

While Mrs. Mallow rambled on in this diffusive manner, Cuthbert was thinking. When she ended, "Why should this death be a warning to Caranby?" he asked quickly.

"Good gracious, Cuthbert, don't get on my nerves. Why?—because I believe that Selina pushed Miss Saul off that plank and killed her. She was just the kind of violent girl who would do a thing like that. And Miss Saul's relatives have waited all these years to kill Selina, and now she's dead, they will kill Caranby because he did not marry the wretched girl."

Cuthbert stared. "Mother, what are you talking about? Caranby told me that Miss Saul had only one brother, and that probably he was dead."

"Ah," said Mrs. Mallow, "he didn't tell you that Miss Saul's father was arrested for coining or passing false money, I forget which. I believe the brother was involved also, but I can't be sure. But I only know the girl was dead then, and the Saul family did not move in the matter, as the police knew too much about them.

"Good gracious!" shuddered the lady, "to think if she had lived, Caranby would have married into that family and have cheated you of the title."

"Are you sure of what you say, mother?"

"Of course I am. Look up any old file of newspapers and you'll read all about the matter. It's old history now. But I really won't talk any more of these things, Cuthbert. If I do, there will be no sleep for me to-night. Oh dear me, such nerves as I have."

"Did you ever see Miss Saul, mother?"

"I told you I did on the platform. She was a fine, large, big girl, with a hook nose and big black eyes. Rather like Selina and Isabella, for I'm sure they have Jewish blood in their veins. Miss Saul—if that was her real name—might have passed as a relative of those horrid Loach girls."

"Mrs. Octagon and her sister who died are certainly much alike."

"Of course they are, and if Miss Saul had lived they would have been a kind of triplets. I hate that style of beauty myself," said Mrs. Mallow, who was slim and fair, "so coarse. Everyone called those Loach girls pretty, but I never did myself. I never liked them, and I won't call on Mrs. Octagon—such a vulgar name—if you marry fifty of her wretched daughters, Cuthbert."

"Don't say that, mother. Juliet is an angel!"

"Then she can't be her mother's daughter," said Mrs. Mallow obscurely, and finished the discussion in what she considered to be a triumphant manner. Nor would she renew it, though her son tried to learn more about the Loach and Saul families. However, he was satisfied with the knowledge he had acquired.

While returning next day to London, he had ample time to think over what he had been told. Miss Selina Loach had certainly shut herself up for many years in Rose Cottage, and it seemed as though she was afraid of being hurt in some way. Perhaps she even anticipated a violent death. And then Mrs. Octagon hinted that she knew who had killed her sister. It might not have been Caranby after all, whom she meant, but one of the Saul family, as Mrs. Mallow suggested.

"I wonder if it is as my mother thinks," mused Cuthbert, staring out of the window at the panorama of the landscape moving swiftly past. "Perhaps Selina did kill Miss Saul, and shut herself up to avoid being murdered by one of the relatives. Caranby said that Selina did not go to the inquest, but pretended she was ill. Then she and her sister went to the continent for two years, and finally, when they returned, Selina instead of taking her proper place in society as Isabella did, shut herself up as a recluse in Rose Cottage. The Saul family appear to have been a bad lot. I should like to look up that coining case. I wonder if I dare tell Jennings."

He was doubtful of the wisdom of doing this. If he told what he knew, and set Jennings on the track, it might be that a scandal would arise implicating Mrs. Octagon. Not that Cuthbert cared much for her, but she was Juliet's mother, and he wanted to avert any trouble likely to cause the girl pain. A dozen times on the journey Cuthbert altered his mind. First he thought he would tell Jennings, then he decided to hold his peace. This indecision was not like him, but the case was so perplexing, and such serious issues were involved, that the young man felt thoroughly worried.

Hitherto he had seen nothing new about the case in the papers, but on reaching Swindon he bought a few and looked through them. His search was rewarded by finding an article on the crime. The inquest had been held, and the jury had brought in a verdict of "Murder against some person or persons unknown!" But it was plainly stated that the police could not find a clue to the assassin. The article in question did not pretend to solve the mystery, but collocated the facts so as to put the case in a nutshell.

"The facts are these," said the journal, after a preliminary introduction. "A quiet maiden lady living at Rose Cottage, Rexton, received three friends to a card-party. Difference arising—and such things will arise amongst the best when cards are in question—two of the friends, Mrs. Herne, an old lady and life-long friend of the deceased, and Mr. Hale, a lawyer of repute and the legal adviser of Miss Loach, depart before ten o'clock. In her evidence Mrs. Herne stated that she and Mr. Hale left at half-past nine, and her assertion was corroborated by Mr. Hale himself. Mr. Clancy, the third friend, left at ten, being shown out by the maid Susan Grant, who then returned to the kitchen. She left Miss Loach seated in her usual chair near the fire, and with a pack of cards on her lap. Probably the deceased lady intended to play a game of 'Patience'!

"The four servants, three women and a man, had their supper. During the supper the man asserted that he heard the front door open, but as Miss Loach was in the habit of walking in the garden before retiring, it was thought that she had gone out to take her usual stroll. Whether the man heard the door open or shut he was not quite sure. However, thinking his mistress was walking in the garden as usual, the man paid no further attention to the incident. At eleven (precisely at eleven, for the kitchen clock struck), the sitting-room bell rang. Susan Grant entered the room, and found Miss Loach seated in her chair exactly as she had left her, even to the fact that the cards were in her lap. But she had been stabbed to the heart with some sharp instrument and was quite dead. The front door was closed and the windows barred.

"Now it is certain that Miss Loach met her death between the hours of ten and eleven. Susan Grant saw her alive at ten, seated in her usual chair with the cards on her lap, and at eleven, she there found her dead, still with the cards. It would seem as though immediately after the servants left the room someone had stabbed the deceased to the heart, before she had time to rise or even alter her position. But Susan Grant asserts that no one was in the room. There was only one door, out of which she departed. The bedroom of Miss Loach on the basement floor had a door which opened into the passage, as did the sitting-room door. No one could have entered until the servant departed. The passage was lighted with electricity, but she did not observe anyone about, nor did she hear a sound. She showed out Mr. Clancy and then returned to the kitchen. Certainly the assassin may have been concealed in the bedroom and have stolen into the sitting-room when Susan Grant was showing out Mr. Clancy. Perhaps then he killed the deceased suddenly, as we said before. He could have then come up the stairs and have escaped while the servants were at supper. It might have been the murderer who opened the door, and was overheard by Thomas.

"The policeman was on duty about ten, as he was seen by Susan Grant when she showed Mr. Clancy to the door. The policeman also asserted that he was again on the spot—i.e., in the roadway opposite the cottage—at eleven. At these times the assassin could not have escaped without being seen. There is no exit at the back, as a high wall running round an unfinished house belonging to the eccentric Lord Caranby blocks the way. Therefore the assassin must have ventured into the roadway. He could then have walked up the lane into the main streets of Rexton, or have taken a path opposite to the gate of Rose Cottage, which leads to the railway station. Probably, after executing the crime, he took this latter way. The path runs between quickset hedges, rather high, for a long distance, past houses, and ends within fifty yards of the railway station. The criminal could take the first train and get to town, there to lose himself in the wilderness of London.

"So far so good. But the strangest thing about this most mysterious affair is that the bell in the sitting-room rang two minutes before Susan Grant entered the room to find her mistress dead. This was some time after the closing of the door overheard by Thomas; therefore the assassin could not have escaped that way. Moreover, by this time the policeman was standing blocking the pathway to the station. Again, the alarm was given immediately by the other servants, who rushed to the sitting-room on hearing Susan's scream, and the policeman at once searched the house. No one was found.

"Now what are we to make of all this? The doctor declares that Miss Loach when discovered had been dead half an hour, which corresponds with the time the door was heard to open or shut by Thomas. So far, it would seem that the assassin had escaped then, having committed the crime and found the coast inside and outside the house clear for his flight. But who rang the bell? That is the question we ask. The deceased could not have done so, as, according to the doctor, the poor lady must have died immediately. Again, the assassin would not have been so foolish as to ring and thus draw attention to his crime, letting alone the question that he could not have escaped at that late hour. We can only offer this solution.

"The assassin must have been concealed in the bedroom, and after Susan ascended the stairs to let Mr. Clancy out, he must have stolen into the sitting-room and have killed the old lady before she could even rise. She might have touched the bell, and the button (the bell is an electric one) may have got fixed. Later on, the heat of the room, warping the wood round the ivory button, may have caused it to slip out, and thus the bell would have rung. Of course our readers may say that when pressed down the bell would have rung continuously, but an examination has revealed that the wires were out of order. It is not improbable that the sudden release of the button may have touched the wires and have set them ringing. The peal is described as being short and sharp. This theory is a weak one, we are aware, but the whole case is so mysterious that, weak as it is, we can offer no other solution.

"Mrs. Herne, the servants, and Messrs. Hale and Clancy were examined. All insist that Miss Loach was in her usual health and spirits, and had no idea of committing suicide, or of being in any danger of sudden death. The weapon cannot be discovered, nor the means—save as we suggest above—whereby the assassin can have made his escape. The whole affair is one of the most mysterious of late years, and will doubtless be relegated to the list of undiscovered crimes. The police have no clue, and apparently despair of finding one. But the discovery of the mystery lies in the bell. Who rang it? or did it ring of itself, as we suggest above."

Cuthbert laid down the paper with a shrug. The article did not commend itself to him, save as the means of making a precis of the case. The theory of the bell appeared excessively weak, and he could not understand a man being so foolish as to put it forward.

"If the button was pressed down by Miss Loach, the bell would have rung at once," argued Cuthbert; "and when it slipped up, even with the heat, the ringing would have stopped. But the bell rang at eleven, and the girl was in the room two minutes later. Someone must have rung it. But why did someone do this, and how did someone escape after ringing in so fool-hardy a manner?"

He could not find an answer to this question. The whole case was indeed most perplexing. There seemed absolutely no answer to the riddle. Even supposing Miss Loach had been murdered out of a long-delayed revenge by a member of the Saul family—and that theory appeared ridiculous to Mallow—the question was how did the assassin escape? Certainly, having regard to the cards still being on the lap of the deceased, and the closing of the door at a time when the policeman was not in the vicinity, the assassin may have escaped in that way. But how did he come to be hidden in the bedroom, and how did he kill the old lady before she had time to call out or even rise, seeing that he had the whole length of the room to cross before reaching her? And again, the escape of the assassin at this hour did not explain the ringing of the bell. Cuthbert was deeply interested, and wondered if the mystery would ever be solved. "I must see Jennings after all," he thought as the train steamed into Paddington.

And see Jennings he did, sooner than he expected. That same evening when he was dressing to go out, a card was brought. It was inscribed "Miles Jennings." Rather surprised that the detective should seek him out so promptly, Cuthbert entered his sitting-room. Jennings, who was standing with his back to the window, saluted him with a pleasant smile, and spoke to him as to an equal. Of course he had every right to do so since he had been at school with Mallow, but somehow the familiarity irritated Cuthbert.

"Well, Jennings, what is it?"

"I came to ask you a few questions, Mallow."

"About what?"

"About the murder at Rose Cottage."

"But, my dear fellow, I know nothing about it."

"You knew Miss Loach?"

"Yes. I saw her once or twice. But I did not like her."

"She is the aunt of the young lady you are engaged to marry?"

Mallow drew himself up stiffly. "As a matter of fact she is," he said with marked coldness. "But I don't see—"

"You will in a minute," said Jennings briskly. "Pardon me, but are you in love with another woman?"

Mallow grew red. "What the devil do you mean by coming here to ask me such a question?" he demanded.

"Gently, Mallow, I am your friend, and you may need one."

"What do you mean. Do you accuse me of—"

"I accuse you of nothing," said Jennings quickly, "but I ask you, why did you give this photograph, with an inscription, to the servant of the murdered woman."

"I recognize my photograph, but the servant—"

"Susan Grant. The picture was found in her possession. She refuses to speak," here the detective spoke lower, "in case you get into trouble with the police."

VII

The Detective

The two men looked at one another, Jennings searchingly, and Cuthbert with a look of mingled amazement and indignation. They were rather like in looks, both being tall, slim and fair-haired. But Mallow wore a mustache, whereas the detective, possibly for the sake of disguising himself on occasions, was clean-shaven. But although Jennings' profession was scarcely that of a gentleman, he looked well-bred, and was dressed with the same quiet taste and refinement as characterized Mallow. The public-school stamp was on both, and they might have been a couple of young men about town discussing sport rather than an officer of the law and a man who (it seemed from Jennings' hints) was suspected of complicity in a crime.

"Do you mean this for a jest?" said Cuthbert at length.

"I never jest on matters connected with my profession, Mallow. It is too serious a one."

"Naturally. It so often involves the issues of life and death."

"In this case I hope it does not," said Jennings, significantly.

Cuthbert, who was recovering his composure, sat down with a shrug. "I assure you, you have found a mare's nest this time. Whatever my follies may have been, I am not a criminal."

"I never thought you were," rejoined the other, also taking a seat, "but you may have become involved with people who are criminals."

"I dare say half of those one meets in society are worthy of jail, did one know what is done under the rose," returned Cuthbert; "by the way, how did you come so opportunely?"

"I knew you had gone out of town, as I came a few days ago to see you about this matter, and inquired. Your servant said you were in Devonshire—"

"I went to see my mother who was ill," said Mallow quickly.

"I guessed as much. You said something about your mother living in Exeter when we met last. Well, I had Paddington watch for your return, and my messenger—"

"Your spy, you mean," said Mallow angrily.

"Certainly, if you prefer the term. Well, your spy—I mean my spy, reported that you were back, so I came on here. Are you going out?"

"I was, but if you wish to arrest me—"

"Nonsense, man. I have only come to have a quiet chat with you. Believe me, I wish you well. I have not forgotten the old Eton days."

"I tell you what, Jennings, I won't stand this talk from any man. Are you here as a gentleman or as a detective?"

"As both, I hope," replied the other dryly, "but are we not wasting valuable time? If you wish to go out this evening, the sooner we get to business the better. Will you answer my questions?"

"I must know what they are first," said Cuthbert defiantly.

Jennings looked irritated. "If you won't treat me properly, I may as well leave the matter alone," he said coldly. "My position is quite unpleasant enough as it is. I came here to an old schoolfellow as a friend—"

"To try and implicate him in a crime. Thanks for nothing."

Jennings, whose patience appeared to be exhausted, rose. "Very well, then, Mallow. I shall go away and hand over the matter to someone else. I assure you the questions must be answered."

Cuthbert made a sign to the other to be seated, which Jennings seemed by no means inclined to obey. He stood stiffly by his chair as Mallow paced the room reflectively. "After all, I don't see why we should quarrel," said the latter at length.

"That's just what I've been driving at for the last ten minutes."

"Very good," said Mallow soothingly, "let us sit down and smoke. I have no particular engagement, and if you will have some coffee—"

"I will have both cigarette and coffee if you will help me to unravel this case," said Jennings, sitting down with a smoother brow.

"But I don't see what I can—"

"You'll see shortly. Will you be open with me?"

"That requires reflection."

"Reflect as long as you like. But if you decline, I will hand the case over to the next man on the Scotland Yard list. He may not deal with you so gently."

"I don't care how he deals with me," returned Mallow, haughtily; "having done no wrong, I am not afraid. And, what is more, Jennings, I was coming to see you as soon as I returned. You have only forestalled our interview."

"What did you wish to see me about?"

"This case," said Cuthbert, getting out a box of cigarettes and touching the bell. "The deuce!" said Jennings briskly, "then you do know something?"

Cuthbert handed him the box and gave an order for coffee. "Any liqueur?" he asked in friendly tones.

"No. I never drink when on—ah—er—pleasure," said the other, substituting another word since the servant was in the room. "Well," he asked when the door closed, "why did you wish to see me?"

"To ask if you remember a coining case that took place some twenty years ago?"

"No. That was before my time. What case is it?"

"Some people called Saul were mixed up in it."

"Humph! Never heard of them," said Jennings, lighting his cigarette, "but it is strange you should talk of coining. I and several other fellows are looking for a set of coiners now. There are a lot of false coins circulating, and they are marvellously made. If I can only lay my hands on the coiners and their factory, there will be a sensation."

"And your reputation will be enhanced."

"I hope so," replied the detective, reddening. "I want a rise in my salary, as I wish to marry. By the way, how is Miss Saxon?"

"Very well. You met her, did you not?"

"Yes! You took me to that queer house. What do they call it? the— 'Shrine of the Muses'—where all the sham art exists. Why do you look so grave, old boy?"

The two men, getting more confidential, were dropping into the language of school-days and speaking more familiarly. Mallow did not reply at once, as his servant had just brought in the coffee. But when each gentleman was supplied with a cup and they were again alone, he looked gravely at Miles. "I want to ask your advice," he said, "and if you are my friend—"

"I am, of course I am."

"Well, then, I am as interested in finding out who killed Miss Loach as you are."

"Why is that?" demanded Jennings, puzzled.

"Before I answer and make a clean breast of it, I should like you to promise that you will get no one I know into trouble."

Jennings hesitated. "That is a difficult matter. Of course, if I find the assassin, even if he or she is one of your friends, I must do my duty."

"Oh, I don't expect anything of that sort," said Mallow easily, "but why do you say 'he' or 'she'?"

"Well, the person who killed Miss Loach might be a woman."

"I don't see how you make that out," said Cuthbert reflectively. "I read the case coming up in the train to-day, and it seems to me from what The Planet says that the whole thing is a mystery."

"One which I mean to dive into and discover," replied Miles. "I do not care for an ordinary murder case, but this is one after my own heart. It is a criminal problem which I should like to work out."

"Do you see your way as yet?" asked Cuthbert.

"No," confessed Jennings, "I do not. I saw the report you speak of. The writer theorizes without having facts to go on. What he says about the bell is absurd. All the same, the bell did ring and the assassin could not have escaped at the time it sounded. Nor could the deceased have rung it. Therein lies the mystery, and I can't guess how the business was managed."

"Do you believe the assassin rang the bell?"

Miles shrugged his shoulders and sipped his coffee. "It is impossible to say. I will wait until I have more facts before me before I venture an opinion. It is only in detective novels that the heaven-born Vidocq can guess the truth on a few stray clues. But what were you going to tell me?"

"Will you keep what I say to yourself?"

"Yes," said Jennings, readily enough, "so long as it doesn't mean the escape of the person who is guilty."

"I don't ask you to betray the confidence placed in you by the authorities to that extent," said Mallow, "just wait a moment."

He leaned his chin on his hand and thought. If he wished to gain the hand of Juliet, it was necessary he should clear up the mystery of the death. Unaided, he could not do so, but with the assistance of his old schoolfellow—following his lead in fact—he might get at the truth. Then, when the name of the assassin of her sister was known, the reason of Mrs. Octagon's strange behavior might be learned, and, moreover, the discovery might remove her objection. On the other hand, Cuthbert could not help feeling uneasy, lest Mrs. Octagon had some secret connected with the death which made her refuse her consent to the match, and which, if he explained to Jennings what he knew, might become known in a quarter which she might not approve of. However, Mallow was certain that, in spite of Mrs. Octagon's hint, his uncle had nothing to do with the matter, and he had already warned her— although she refused to listen—that he intended to trace the assassin. Under these circumstances, and also because Jennings was his friend and more likely to aid him, than get anyone he knew and respected into trouble, the young man made up his mind to tell everything.

"The fact is, I am engaged to Juliet Saxon," he began, hesitatingly.

"I know that. She is the daughter of that absurd Mrs. Octagon, with the meek husband and the fine opinion of herself."

"Yes. But Juliet is the niece of Miss Loach."

"What!" Jennings sprang from his chair with a look of surprise; "do you mean to tell me that Mrs. Octagon is Miss Loach's sister."

"I do. They quarrelled many years ago, and have not been friendly for years. Mrs. Octagon would never go and see her sister, but she did not forbid her children being friendly. As you may guess, Mrs. Octagon is much distressed about the murder, but the strange thing is that she declares this death renders it impossible for me to marry her daughter."

Jennings looked searchingly at his friend. "That is strange. Does she give no reason?"

"No. But knowing my uncle knew her when she was a girl, I thought I would ask him what he thought. He told me that he had once been engaged to Miss Loach, and—"

"Well, go on," said Miles, seeing Cuthbert hesitating.

"There was another lady in the case."

"There usually is," said Jennings dryly. "Well?"

"The other lady's name was Saul—Emilia Saul."

"Oh," Miles sat down again. He had remained standing for a few moments. "Saul was the name you mentioned in connection with the coining case of twenty years ago."

Cuthbert nodded, and now, being fully convinced that he badly needed Jennings' aid, he told all that he had heard from Caranby, and detailed what his mother had said. Also, he touched on the speech of Mrs. Octagon, and repeated the warning he had given her. Miles listened quietly, but made no remark till his friend finished.

"You have told me all you know?" he asked.

"Yes. I want you to help me. Not that I think what I have learned has anything to do with the case."

"I'm not so sure of that," said Jennings musingly, his eyes on the carpet. "Mrs. Octagon bases her refusal to allow the marriage on the fact of the death. However, you have warned her, and she must take the consequence."

"But, my dear Jennings, you don't think she has anything to do with the matter. I assure you she is a good, kind woman—"

"With a violent temper, according to your mother," finished Jennings dryly. "However, don't alarm yourself. I don't think she is guilty."

"I should think not," cried Mallow, indignantly. "Juliet's mother!"

"But she may have something to do with the matter all the same. However, you have been plain with me, and I will do all I can to help you. The first thing is for us to follow up the clue of the portrait."

"Ah, yes! I had quite forgotten that," said Mallow, casting a look on the photograph which lay near at hand. "Just pass it, will you."

Miles did so. "You say you recognize it," he said.

"I recognize my own face. I had several portraits done like this. I think this one—" Mallow looked at the inscription which he read for the first time, and his face grew pale.

"What is it?" asked Miles eagerly.

"I don't know," faltered the other uneasily.

"You recognize the inscription?"

"Yes, I certainly wrote that."

"It is quite a tender inscription," said Miles, his eyes on the disturbed face of the other. "'With my dear love,' it reads."

Cuthbert laid down the portrait and nodded. "Yes! That is the inscription," he said in low tones, and his eyes sought the carpet.

"You wrote that to a servant."

"What servant?"

"The new parlor-maid engaged by Miss Loach on the day of her death—Susan Grant."

"I remember the name. I saw it in the papers."

"Do you know the girl well?" asked Jennings.

"I don't know her at all."

"Come now. A man doesn't give a portrait with such an inscription to any unknown girl, nor to one he is not in love with."

"Jennings," cried Mallow indignantly, "how can you think—" his voice died away and he clenched his hands.

"What am I to think then?" demanded the detective.

"What you like."

"That you love this Susan Grant?"

"I tell you I never set eyes on her," said Cuthbert violently.

"Then how does she come into possession of your portrait?" asked the other. Then seeing that Mallow refused to speak, he laid a persuasive hand on his shoulder. "You must speak out," he said quickly, "you have told me so much you must tell me all. Matters can't stand as they are.

No," here Jennings looked straight into Mallow's eyes, "you did not give that portrait to Susan Grant."

"I never said so."

"Don't be an ass, Mallow. You say you don't know the girl, therefore you can hardly have given her the photograph. Now the inscription shows that it was given to a woman you are in love with. You told me when you introduced me to Miss Saxon that she was the only woman you ever loved. Therefore you gave this portrait with its tender inscription to her."

"I—I can't say."

"You mean you won't trust me," said Jennings.

Cuthbert rose quickly and flung off his friend's arm. "I wish to Heaven I had never opened my mouth to you," he said.

"My dear fellow, you should show more confidence in me. I know quite well why you won't acknowledge that you gave this photograph to Miss Saxon. You think it will implicate her in the matter."

"Jennings!" cried Cuthbert, his face growing red and fierce.

"Wait a moment," resumed the other calmly and without flinching. "I can explain. You gave the photograph to Miss Saxon. She gave it to Miss Loach, and Susan Grant falling in love with your face, took possession of it. It was found in her trunk."

"Yes—yes, that's it!" cried Mallow, catching at a straw. "I did give the photograph to Juliet, and no doubt she gave it to her aunt. It would be easy for this girl to take it. Though why she should steal it," said Cuthbert perplexed, "I really can't say!"

"You don't know her?" asked Jennings.

"No. Really, I don't. The name is quite unknown to me. What is the girl like in appearance?" Jennings described Susan to the best of his ability, but Cuthbert shook his head. "No, I never saw her. You say she had this photograph in her trunk?" Then, on receiving an affirmative reply, "She may have found it lying about and have taken it, though why she should I can't say."

"So you said before," said Jennings dryly. "But strange as it may appear, Mallow, this girl is in love with you."

"How do you know that?"

"Well, you see," said Miles, slowly. "After the murder I searched the boxes of the servants in the house for the weapon."

"But there was no danger of them being accused?"

"No. Nor would I have searched their boxes had they not insisted. But they were all so afraid of being accused, that they wished to exonerate themselves as much as possible. The fact that the whole four were in the kitchen together at the time the crime was committed quite clears them. However, they insisted, so I looked into their boxes. I found this photograph in the box of the new housemaid. She refused to state how it came into her possession, and became so red, and wept so much, that I soon saw that she loved you."

"But I tell you it's ridiculous. I don't know the girl—and a servant, too. Pshaw!"

"Well, then, I must get her to see you, and possibly some explanation may be made. I took possession of the photograph—"

"Why? On what grounds should my photograph interest you, Jennings?"

"On the grounds that you are a friend of mine, and that I knew your face the moment I saw it. I naturally asked the girl how it came into her possession, as I know your tastes don't lie in the way of pretty parlor-maids, however attractive. It was her reply which made me take the portrait and come to ask you for an explanation."

"What reply did she make?" demanded Cuthbert, exasperated by the false position he was placed in.

"She said that she would explain nothing in case you should get into trouble with the police. Can you explain that?"

"No," said Mallow, perplexed. "I really cannot be responsible for the vagaries of a parlor-maid. I don't know the name Susan Grant, and from your description of her appearance, I never set eyes on her. I am quite sure your explanation is the correct one. Juliet gave it to her aunt, and for some ridiculous reason this girl stole it."

"But her remark about the police."

Mallow made a gesture of helplessness, and leaned his elbow on the mantelpiece. "I can't guess what she means. Well, what will you do now, Jennings?"

"First, I shall get the girl to come here and see you. Then I shall ask Miss Saxon why she gave the photograph to Miss Loach. You were not a favorite with the old lady, I gather."

"On the contrary, she liked me much more than I did her."

"You see. She liked you so much that she insisted on having your photograph. I must ask Miss Saxon when she gave it. Will you let me bring this girl to see you to-morrow?"

"Certainly. But it's all very unpleasant."

The detective rose to go. "Most matters connected with a crime are, my dear fellow," said he calmly. "I only hope there will not be any more unpleasantness."

"What do you mean?"

"I can't say what I mean—yet."

"You are mysterious, Jennings."

"I am perplexed. I don't seem to advance. However, I intend to follow up the clue of your photograph, though if the explanation I suggest is the true one, there's nothing more to be said. But the girl, Susan Grant, has not the look of a thief."

"That means, I gave her the photograph," said Cuthbert haughtily.

"Not necessarily," rejoined Jennings, putting on his overcoat. "But I will not theorize any more. Wait till I confront the girl with you in a few days. Then we may force her to speak."

Cuthbert shrugged his shoulders. "As you please. But I really am at a loss to think what she will say."

"So am I," said Jennings, as they walked to the door. "That is why I am anxious to see her and you together. And, after all, I may have found only a mare's nest."

"You certainly have so far as I am concerned. By the way, when is the body to be buried?"

"The day after to-morrow. Then the will has to be read. I hope the old lady will leave you some money, Mallow. She was reported to be rich. Oh, by the way, I'll look up that Saul coining case you speak of."

"Why?" asked Mallow, bluntly and uneasily.

"It may have some bearing on this matter. Only in the past will we find the truth. And Miss Selina Loach certainly knew Miss Saul."

As Jennings departed the postman came up the stairs with the late letters. Cuthbert found one from Juliet and opened it at once. It contained one line—

"Don't see the police about aunt's death—Juliet."

Cuthbert Mallow slept very badly that night.

VIII

The Course of True Love

The most obvious thing for Cuthbert to do was to seek Juliet and ask for an explanation of her mysterious note. He went to the "Shrine of the Muses" the very next day, but was informed that Miss Saxon and her mother had gone out of town and would not be back for a few days. He could not learn where they were, and was leaving the house somewhat disconsolately when he met Basil.

"You here, Mallow," said that young gentleman, stopping short, "have you been to see my mother?"

"I went to see Juliet," replied Cuthbert, not sorry that the meeting had taken place, "but I hear she is out of town."

"Well, not exactly. The fact is, she and my mother have gone down to Rose Cottage and intend to stop there until the funeral is over and the will is read."

"The will?" echoed Mallow.

"Yes. Aunt Selina is likely to leave a great deal of money. I expect it will all go to Juliet. She never liked me."

"Yet you were frequently at her house."

"I was," confessed Basil candidly. "I tried to make myself as civil as possible, so that she might remember me. Between ourselves, Mallow, I am deuced hard up. My mother hasn't much money, I have none of my own, and old Octagon is as stingy as he well can be."

This sounded well coming from an idler who never did a stroke of work, and who lived on the charity of his step-father. But Basil had peculiar views as to money. He considered himself a genius, and that Peter should be proud to support him until, as he phrased it, he had "stamped his name on the age"! But the stamping took a long time, and Basil troubled himself very little about the matter. He remarked that genius should not be forced, and loafed away the greater portion of his days. His mother kept him in pocket-money and clothes, Peter supplied board and lodging, and Basil got through life very pleasantly. He wished to be famous, to have his name in every mouth and his portrait in every paper; but the work that was necessary to obtain these desirable things he was unwilling to do. Cuthbert knew that the young fellow had been "born tired"! and although something of an idler himself, liked Basil none the more for his laziness. Had Mallow been poor he would certainly have earned his bread, but he had a good income and did not work. And, after all, he only pursued the way of life in which he had been brought up. But Basil was poor and had his career to make, therefore he certainly should have labored. However, for Juliet's sake, Cuthbert was as polite as possible.

"If I were you, Saxon, I should leave cards alone," said Mallow.

"Nonsense! I don't play high. Besides, I have seen you at Maraquito's also losing a lot."

"I can afford to lose," said Cuthbert dryly, "you can't."

"No, by Jove, you're right there. But don't preach, Mallow, you ain't such a saint yourself."

"Can I help you with a cheque?"

Basil had good breeding enough to color.

"No! I didn't explain myself for that," he said coldly, "and besides, if Juliet comes in for Aunt Selina's money, I'll get some. Juliet and I always share."

This meant that Juliet was to give the money and Basil to spend it. Mallow was disgusted with this candid selfishness. However, he did not wish to quarrel with Basil, as he knew Juliet was fond of him, and moreover, in the present state of affairs, he was anxious to have another friend besides Mr. Octagon in the house. "Perhaps Miss Loach may have left you some money after all," he remarked.

"By Jove, I hope so. I'll be in a hole if she has not. There's a bill—" here he stopped, as though conscious of having said too much. "But that will come into Juliet's possession," he murmured.

"What's that?" asked Cuthbert sharply.

"Nothing—nothing—only a tailor's bill. As to getting money by the will, don't you know I quarrelled with Aunt Selina a week before her death. Yes, she turned me out of the house." Here Basil's face assumed what may be described as an ugly look. "I should like to have got even with the old cat. She insulted me."

"Gently, old fellow," said Mallow, seeing that Basil was losing his temper, and having occasionally seen him in fits of uncontrollable passion, "we're in the public street."

Basil's brow cleared. "All right," he said, "don't bother, I'll be all right when Juliet gets the money. By the way, mother tells me you are not going to marry her."

"Your mother is mistaken," rejoined Mallow gravely. "Juliet and I are still engaged. I do not intend to give her up."

"I told mother you would not give in easily," said Basil, frowning, "but you can't marry Juliet."

"Why not?" asked Cuthbert sharply; "do you know the reason?"

Basil appeared about to say something, then suddenly closed his mouth and shook his head.

Cuthbert pressed him. "If you know the reason, tell me," he said, "and I'll help you out of your difficulties. You know I love Juliet, and your mother does not seem to have any excuse to forbid the marriage."

"I would help you if I could, but I can't. You had better ask Juliet herself. She may tell you the reason."

"How can I find her?"

"Go down to Rose Cottage and ask to see her," suggested Basil.

"Your mother will not admit me."

"That's true enough. Well, I'll tell you what, Mallow, I'll speak to Juliet and get her to make an appointment to see you."

"I could write and ask her for one myself."

"Oh, no, you couldn't. Mother will intercept all letters."

"Upon my word—" began Mallow angrily, then stopped. It was useless to show his wrath before this silly boy, who could do no good and might do a deal of harm. "Very well, then," he said more mildly, "ask Juliet to meet me on the other side of Rexton, under the wall which runs round the unfinished house."

Basil started. "Why that place?" he asked nervously.

"It is as good as any other."

"You can't get inside."

"That's true enough. But we can meet outside. I have been inside though, and I made a mess of myself climbing the wall."

"You were inside," began Basil, then suddenly appeared relieved. "I remember; you were there on the day after Aunt Selina was killed."

"I have been there before that," said Cuthbert, wondering why the young man avoided his eye in so nervous a manner.

"Not at—at night?" murmured Saxon, looking away.

"Once I was there at night. Why do you ask?"

"Oh, nothing—nothing. I was just thinking it's a wild place in which to find one's self at night. By the way," added Basil, as though anxious to change a disagreeable subject, "do you think Jarvey Hale a nice fellow?"

"No, I don't. I have met him at Maraquito's, and I don't like him. He's a bounder. Moreover, a respectable lawyer has no right to gamble to the extent he does. I wonder Miss Loach trusted him."

"Perhaps she didn't know of his gambling," said Basil, his eyes wandering everywhere but to the face of his companion; "but, should you think Hale would be hard on a fellow?"

"Yes, I should. Do you owe him money?"

"A few pounds. He won't give me time to pay. And I say, Mallow, I suppose all Aunt Selina's affairs will be left in Hale's hands?"

"I can't say. It depends upon the will. If everything is left to Juliet, unconditionally, she may take her affairs out of Hale's hands. I should certainly advise her to do so. He's too intimate with Maraquito and her gambling salon to be a decent lawyer."

"You do seem down on gambling," said Basil, "yet you gamble yourself a lot. But I expect Juliet will change her lawyer. I hope she will."

"Why?" asked Cuthbert sharply.

"Oh," replied Basil, confused, "because I agree with you. A gambler will not make a good lawyer—or a good husband either," he added in an abrupt tone. "Good-day. I'll tell Juliet," and he was off before Mallow could find words to answer his last remark.

Cuthbert, walking back to his rooms, wondered if it was on account of the gambling that Mrs. Octagon objected to the marriage. He really did not gamble much, but occasionally he dropped into Maraquito's house, and there lost or won a few pounds. Here he had often met Basil, and without doubt the young man had told his mother. But he could hardly do this without incriminating himself. All the same, Basil was a thorough liar, and a confirmed tattler. He might have blackened Mallow's character, and yet have told a story to exonerate himself. His friendship appeared feigned, and Cuthbert doubted if he would really tell Juliet of the appointment.

"That young man's in trouble," thought Mallow, "he is anxious about Hale, and I shouldn't wonder if that respectable person had lent him a large sum of money. Probably he counts on getting the money from Juliet, should she inherit the fortune of Miss Loach. Also he seems annoyed that I should have been in Caranby's unfinished house at night. I wonder what he would say if he knew my reason for going there. Humph! I must keep that quiet. The only person I dare tell is Juliet; but I can't speak to her about the matter just yet. And after all, there is no need to mention my visit. It does not concern her in the least.

I wonder," here Cuthbert stopped, struck with an idea. "By George! can it be that Basil was near Rose Cottage on the night the crime was committed? Juliet may know that, and so, fearful lest he should be accused of the murder, asked me to stop proceedings. Can Basil Saxon be guilty? No," Mallow shook his head and resumed his walk, "he has not pluck enough to kill a fly."

After this he dismissed the matter from his thoughts and waited expectant of a letter from Juliet. None came, and he was convinced that Basil had not delivered the message. This being the case, Cuthbert determined to act for himself, and one afternoon went down to Rexton. That same evening he had an appointment with Jennings, who was to bring Susan Grant to Mallow's rooms. But the young man quite expected to be back in time to keep the appointment, and meantime he spent an hour wandering round Rexton in the vicinity of Rose Cottage. But afraid lest Mrs. Octagon should see him and keep Juliet within doors, he abstained from passing in front of the house and waited on the path which led to the station.

While watching the cottage, a young woman came along the path. She was neatly dressed and looked like a servant. Cuthbert pressed himself against the quickset hedge to allow her to pass, as there was very little room. The girl started as she murmured her thanks, and grew crimson on seeing his face. Cuthbert, not thinking, gave a passing thought to her looks and wondered why she had blushed. But when he saw her enter the gate of Rose Cottage—she looked back twice—he recalled the description of Jennings.

"By George!" he thought, "that was Susan Grant. I wish I had spoken to her. I wonder why she blushed. She can't be in love with me, as I never saw her before. All the same, it is strange about the portrait."

It was now about four o'clock, and Cuthbert fancied that after all it would be best to boldly ring at the door and ask admission, in spite of Mrs. Octagon.

But while hesitating to risk all his chances of seeing Juliet on one throw of fortune's dice, the matter was decided for him by the appearance of Juliet herself. She came out of the gate and walked directly towards the path. It would seem as though she expected to find Cuthbert, for she walked straight up to him and caught his hand. There was no one about to see their meeting, but Juliet was not disposed to behave tenderly.

"Why are you here?" she asked. "Susan Grant told me you—"

"Susan Grant!" echoed Cuthbert, resolved not to know too much in the presence of Juliet. "I saw her name in the papers. How does she know me?"

"I can't say," said Juliet quickly; "come along this way." She hurried along the narrow path, talking all the time. "She came in just now and said you were waiting in the by-path. I came out at once. I don't want my mother to see you."

"Really!" cried Cuthbert, rather nettled. "I don't see that I have any reason to avoid Mrs. Octagon."

"She will not allow me to see you. If she knew I was meeting you she would be very angry. We are here only till to-morrow. Now that Aunt Selina is buried and the will read, we return to Kensington at once. Come this way. Let us get into the open. I don't wish my mother to follow and find me speaking to you."

They emerged into a waste piece of land, distant a stone-throw from the railway station, but secluded by reason of many trees and shrubs. These, belonging to the old Rexton estate, had not yet been rooted up by the builder, and there ran a path through the heart of the miniature wood leading to the station. When quite screened from observation by the friendly leafage, Juliet turned quickly. She was pale and ill in looks, and there were dark circles under her eyes which told of sleepless nights. But she was dressed with her usual care and behaved in a composed manner.

"I wish you had not come, Cuthbert," she said, again taking his hand, "at least not at present. Later on—"

"I wanted to see you at once," said Mallow, determinedly. "Did not Basil tell you so?"

Juliet shook her head. "He said he met you the other day, but gave me no message."

"Then he is not the friend I took him to be," said Mallow angrily.

"Don't be angry with Basil," said Juliet, gently. "The poor boy has quite enough trouble."

"Of his own making," finished Cuthbert, thoroughly annoyed. "See here, Juliet, this sort of thing can't go on. I have done nothing to warrant my being treated like this. Your mother is mad to behave as she is doing. I insist on an explanation."

Juliet did not pay attention to this hasty speech. "How do you know Basil has troubles?" she asked hurriedly.

"Because I know he's a dissipated young ass," returned Mallow roughly; "and I daresay you know it also."

"Do you allude to his playing cards?" she asked quickly.

"Yes. He has no right to tell you these things. But I know he is in debt to Hale—he hinted as much the other day. I would say nothing of this to you, but that I know he counts on your paying his debts. I tell you, Juliet, it is wrong for you to do so."

"How do you know I can?" she asked.

"I know nothing," said Cuthbert doggedly, "not even if you have inherited the money of Miss Loach."

"I have inherited it. She left everything to me, save legacies to Thomas her servant, and to Emily Pill, the cook. It is a large fortune. The will was read on the day of the funeral. I have now six thousand a year."

"So much as that? How did your aunt make such a lot of money?"

"Mr. Hale speculated a great deal on her account, and, he is very lucky. At least so he told me. But the money is well invested and there are no restrictions. I can easily pay the few debts Basil owes, poor boy. You are too hard on him."

"Perhaps I am. But he is so foolish, and he doesn't like me. I believe he puts you against me, Juliet."

The girl threw her arms round his neck. "Nothing in the world would ever put me against you, Cuthbert," she whispered vehemently. "I love you—I love you—with all my heart and soul, with every fibre of my being do I love you. I don't care what mother says, I love you."

"Well, then," said Cuthbert, between kisses, "since you are now rich and your own mistress—not that I care about the money—why not marry me at once?"

Juliet drew back, and her eyes dilated with fear. "I dare not—I dare not," she whispered. "You don't know what you ask."

"Yes I do. Juliet, what is all this mystery about? I could not understand the meaning of your letter."

"Did you do what I asked?" she panted.

"It was too late. I had told Jennings the detective all I knew."

"You were not afraid?"

"Afraid!" echoed Cuthbert, opening his eyes. "What do you mean?"

She looked into his eyes. "No," she said to herself, "he is not afraid."

Cuthbert lost his temper. "I don't understand all this," he declared, "if you would only speak out. But I can guess why you wish me to stop the proceedings—you fear for Basil!"

She stepped back a pace. "For Basil?"

"Yes. From what he hinted the other day I believe he was about this place on the night of the—"

"Where are your proofs?" she gasped, recoiling.

"I have none. I am only speaking on chance. But Basil is in monetary difficulties—he is in debt to Hale—he counted on you inheriting the money of Miss Loach to pay his debts. He—"

"Stop! stop!" cried Juliet, the blood rising to her face, "this is only supposition. You can prove nothing."

"Then why do you wish me to hold my tongue?"

"There is nothing for you to hold your tongue about," she answered evasively. "You know nothing."

Cuthbert caught her hands and looked into her troubled eyes. "Do you, Juliet—do you? Put an end to this mystery and speak out."

She broke from him and fled. "No," she cried, "for your sake I keep silent. For your own sake stop the action of the detective."

IX

ANOTHER MYSTERY

When Jennings arrived that evening according to appointment, he found Mallow in a state of desperation. Juliet's conduct perplexed the young man to such an extent that he felt as though on the point of losing his reason. He was quite delighted when he saw Jennings and thus had someone with a clear head in whom to confide.

"What's the matter?" asked Jennings, who at once saw that something was wrong from Cuthbert's anxious face.

"Nothing, save that I am being driven out of my senses. I am glad you have come, Jennings. Things are getting more mysterious every day. I am determined to get to the bottom of this murder case if only for my own peace of mind. I am with you heart and soul. I have the detective fever with a vengeance. You can count on my assistance in every way."

"All right, my dear chap," said the other soothingly, "sit down and let us have a quiet talk before this girl arrives."

"Susan Grant. I saw her to-day."

"Did you speak to her?"

"No. I only guessed that she was the girl you talked about from your description and from the fact that she entered Rose Cottage."

"Ah," said Jennings, taking a seat, "so you have been down there?"

"Yes. I'll tell you all about it. I don't know if I'm sane or insane, Jennings. When does this girl arrive?"

The detective glanced at his watch. "At half-past eight. She'll be here in half an hour. Go on. What's up?"

"Read this," said Cuthbert, and passed along the note from Juliet. "I received that immediately after you went the other night."

Jennings read the note with a thoughtful look, then laid it aside and stared at his friend. "It is strange that she should write in that way," said he. "I should have thought she would wish to learn who killed her aunt. What does she mean?"

"I can't tell you. I met her to-day," and Cuthbert gave details of his visit to Rexton and the interview with Juliet. "Now what does she mean," he added in his turn, "talking as though I had something to do with the matter?"

"Someone's been poisoning her mind. That brother of hers, perhaps."

"What do you know of him?" asked Cuthbert quickly.

"Nothing good. He's an hysterical idiot. Gambles a lot and falls into rages when he loses. At times I don't think he's responsible for his actions."

Mallow threw himself back in his chair biting his moustache. Every word Jennings spoke made him more confident that Basil had something to do with the crime. But why Juliet should hint at his own guilt Cuthbert could not imagine. Had he been calmer he might have hesitated to tell Jennings about Basil. But, exasperated by Juliet's half confidence, and anxious to learn the truth, he gave the detective a full account of his meeting with the young man. "What do you make of that?" he asked.

"Well," said Jennings doubtfully, "there's nothing much to go upon in what he said. He's in difficulties with Hale certainly—"

"And he seemed anxious about my having been in Caranby's grounds at night." "Were you there?"

"Yes. I did not intend to say anything about it, but I must tell you everything so that you can put things straight between me and Juliet. I can't understand her. But I am sure her mother and Basil are trying to influence her against me. I should not be surprised to learn that they accused me of this murder."

"But on what grounds?" asked Jennings quickly.

"We'll come to that presently. But I now see why neither Basil nor his mother want the marriage to take place. By the will of Miss Loach Juliet comes in for six thousand a year, which is completely at her own disposal. Mrs. Octagon and her pet boy want to have the handling of that. They know if Juliet becomes my wife I won't let them prey on her, so immediately Miss Loach died the mother withdrew her consent to the marriage, and now she is being backed up by Basil."

"But I thought Mrs. Octagon was well off?"

"No. Saxon, her late husband, left her very little, and Octagon, for all his meekness, knows how to keep his money. Both mother and son are extravagant, so they hope to make poor Juliet their banker. In some way they have implicated me in the crime, and Juliet thinks that I am in danger of the gallows. That is why she wrote that mysterious note, Jennings. To-day she asked me to stop proceedings for my own sake, which shows that she thinks me guilty. I could not get a further explanation from her, as she ran away. Hang it!" Cuthbert jumped up angrily, "if she'd only tell me the truth and speak straight out. I can't understand this silence on her part."

"I can," said Jennings promptly, "in some way Basil is mixed up in the matter, and his accusing you means his acknowledging that he was near Rose Cottage on the night of the crime. He funks making so damaging an admission."

"Ah, I daresay," said Cuthbert, "particularly as he quarrelled with his aunt a week before the death."

"Did he quarrel with her?"

"Of course. Didn't I tell you what he said to-day. He's in a fine rage with the dead woman. And you know what an uncontrollable temper he has. I've seen him rage at Maraquito's when he lost at baccarat. Silly ass! He can't play decently and lose his money like a gentleman. How Juliet ever came to have such a bounder for a brother I can't imagine. She's the soul of honor, and Basil—bah!"

"He quarrelled with his aunt," murmured Jennings, "and he has a violent temper, as we both knew. Humph! He may have something to do with the matter. Do you know where he was on that night?"

"Yes. Juliet and he went to the Marlow Theatre to see a melodrama by a new playwright."

"Ha!" said Jennings half to himself, "and the Marlow Theatre is not far from Rexton. I'll make a note of that. Had they a box?"

"I believe so. It was sent by the man who wrote the play."

"Who is he?"

"I can't say. One of that lot who play at being poets in Octagon House. A set of idiots. But what do you make of all this, Jennings?"

"I think with you that Mrs. Octagon and her cub of a son are trying to stop the marriage by bringing you into the matter of the crime. Were you down there on that night?"

"Yes," said Cuthbert with hesitation, and to Jennings' surprise, "I did not intend to say anything about it, as my uncle asked me to hold my tongue. But since things have come to this pass, you may as well know that I was there—and about the time of the murder too."

Jennings sat up and stared. "Great heavens! Mallow, why didn't you tell me this the other night?"

"You might have arrested me then and there," retorted Cuthbert. "I promised my uncle to hold my tongue. But now—"

"You will tell me all. My dear fellow, make a clean breast of it."

"Rest easy, you shall learn everything. You know that the house at the back of Rose Cottage has been deserted for something like twenty years more or less."

"Yes. You told me about it the other night."

"Caranby ran a fifteen-feet wall round it and the inside is a regular jungle. Well, the house is supposed to be haunted. Lights have been seen moving about and strange noises have been heard."

"What kind of noises?"

"Oh, moans and clanking chains and all that sort of thing. I heard indirectly about this, through Juliet."

"Where did she hear the report?"

"From Miss Loach's cook. A woman called Pill. The cook asserted that the house was haunted, and described the noises and the lights. I don't believe in spooks myself, and thought some tricks were being played, so one day I went down and had a look."

"That day I was there?" asked Jennings, recalling Cuthbert's presence.

"Before that—a week or two. I saw nothing. The house is rotting and nothing appeared to be disturbed. I examined the park and found no footmarks. In fact, there wasn't a sign of anyone about."

"You should have gone at night when the ghost was larking."

"That's what Caranby said. I told him when he came back to London. He was very annoyed. You know his romance about that house—an absurd thing it is. All the same, Caranby is tender on the point. I advised him to pull the house down and let the land out for building leases. He thought he would, but asked me to go at night and stir up the ghost. I went on the night of the murder, and got into the grounds by climbing the wall. There's no gate, you know."

"At what time?"

"Some time between ten and eleven. I'm not quite sure."

"Good heavens! man, that is the very hour the woman was killed!"

"Yes. And for that reason I held my tongue; particularly as I got over the wall near the cottage."

"Where do you mean?"

"Well, there's a field of corn nearly ready to be cut near the cottage. It's divided from the garden by a fence. I came along the foot-path that leads from the station and jumped the fence."

"Did you enter Miss Loach's grounds?"

"No. I had no right to. I saw a light in the basement, but I did not take much notice. I was too anxious to find the ghost. Well, I ran along the fence—on the field-of-corn side, remember, and got over the wall. Then

I dodged through the park, scratching myself a lot. I could find nothing. The house seemed quiet enough, so after a quarter of an hour I had enough of it. I got out over the wall on the other side and came home. I caught a cold which necessitated my wearing a great-coat the next day. So there you have my ghost-hunting, and a fine fool I was to go."

"I wish you had told me this before, Mallow."

"If I had, you would have thought I'd killed the old woman. But I tell you now, as I want this matter sifted to the bottom. I refused to speak before, as I didn't wish to be dragged into the case."

"Did you see anything in the cottage?"

"Not a thing. I saw no one—I heard no sound."

"Not even a scream?"

"Not even a scream," said Mallow; "had I heard anything I should have gone to see what was the matter."

"Strange!" murmured Jennings, "can't you tell the exact time?"

"Not to a minute. It was shortly after ten. I can't say how many minutes. Perhaps a quarter of an hour. But not suspecting anything was going to happen, I didn't look at my watch."

Jennings looked thoughtfully at the carpet. "I wonder if the assassin escaped that way," he murmured.

"Which way?"

"Over the wall and through the park. You see, he could not have gone up the lane or through the railway path without stumbling against that policeman. But he might have slipped out of the front door at half-past ten and climbed as you did over the wall to cross the park and drop over the other. In this way he would elude the police."

"Perhaps," said Cuthbert disbelievingly; "but it was nearly eleven when I left the park. If anyone had been at my heels I would have noticed."

"I am not so sure of that. The park, as you say, is a kind of jungle. The man might have seen you and have taken his precautions. Moreover," added the detective, sitting up alertly, "he might have written to Miss Saxon saying he saw you on that night. And she—"

"Bosh!" interrupted Mallow roughly, "he would give himself away."

"Not if the letter was anonymous."

"Perhaps," said the other again; "but Basil may have been about the place and have accused me."

"In that case he must explain his reason for being in the neighborhood at that hour. But he won't, and you may be sure Miss Saxon, for his sake, will hold her tongue. No, Mallow. Someone accuses you to Miss Saxon—Basil or another. If we could only make her speak—"

Cuthbert shook his head. "I fear it's impossible."

"Why not let me arrest you," suggested Jennings, "and then, if at anytime, she would speak."

"Hang it, no!" cried Mallow in dismay, "that would be too realistic, Jennings. I don't want it known that I was hanging about the place on that night. My explanation might not be believed. In any case, people would throw mud at me, considering I am engaged to the niece of the dead woman."

"Yes! I can see that. Well," Jennings rose and stretched himself. "I must see what Susan has to say"; he glanced at his watch; "she should be here in a few minutes."

A silence ensued which was broken by Jennings. "Oh, by the way," he said, taking some papers out of his pocket, "I looked up the Saul case."

"Well, what about it?" asked Cuthbert indolently

Jennings referred to his notes. "The Saul family" he said, "seem to have been a bad lot. There was a mother, a brother and a daughter—"

"Emilia!"

"Just so. They were all coiners. Somewhere in Hampstead they had a regular factory. Others were mixed up in the matter also, but Mrs. Saul was the head of the gang. Then Emilia grew tired of the life—I expect it told on her nerves. She went on the concert platform and met Caranby. Then she died, as you know. Afterwards the mother and brother were caught. They bolted. The mother, I believe, died—it was believed she was poisoned for having betrayed secrets. The brother went to jail, got out years afterwards on ticket-of-leave, and then died also. The rest of the gang were put in jail, but I can't say what became of them."

Cuthbert shrugged his shoulders. "This does not help us much."

"No. But it shows you what an escape your uncle had from marrying the woman. I can't understand—"

"No more can Caranby," said Mallow, smiling; "he loved Miss Loach, but Emilia exercised a kind of hypnotic influence over him. However, she is dead, and I can see no connection between her and this crime."

"Well," said Jennings soberly, "it appears that some other person besides the mother gave a clue to the breaking up of the gang and the whereabouts of the factory. Supposing that person was Selina Loach, who hated Emilia for having taken Caranby from her. One of the gang released lately from prison may have killed the old lady out of revenge."

"What! after all these years?"

"Revenge is a passion that grows with years," said Jennings grimly; "at all events, I intend to go on ferreting out evidence about this old coining case, particularly as there are many false coins circulating now. I should not be surprised to learn that the factory had been set up again; Miss Loach may have known and—"

"This is all supposition," cried Mallow. "I can't see the slightest connection between the coiners and this murder. Besides, it does not explain why Juliet hints at my being implicated."

Jennings did not reply. "There's the bell, too," he murmured, his eyes on the ground, "that might be explained." He looked up briskly. "I tell you what, Mallow, this case may turn out to be a bigger thing than either of us suspect."

"It's quite big enough for me as it is," retorted Cuthbert, "although I don't know what you mean. All I desire is to get to the root of the matter and marry Juliet. Find Miss Loach's assassin, Jennings, and don't bother about this dead-and-gone coining case."

"There's a connection between the two," said Jennings, obstinately; "it's impossible to say how the connection comes about, but I feel that a discovery in one case entails a discovery in the other. If I can prove that Miss Loach was killed by one of the old coiners—"

"What will happen then?"

"I may stumble on the factory that is in existence now."

He would have gone on to explain himself more fully, but that Mallow's man entered with the information that a young person was waiting and asked for Mr. Jennings. Mallow ordered the servant to admit her, and shortly Susan Grant, nervous and blushing, entered the room.

"I am glad to see you," said Jennings, placing a chair for her. "This is Mr. Mallow. We wish to ask you a few questions."

"I have seen Mr. Mallow before," said Susan, gasping and flushing.

"At Rose Cottage?" said Mallow inquiringly.

"No. When I was with Senora Gredos as parlor-maid."

"Senora Gredos?" said Jennings, before Cuthbert could speak. "Do you mean Maraquito?"

"I have heard that her name was Maraquito, sir," said Susan calmly. "A lame lady and fond of cards. She lives in—"

"I know where she lives," said Cuthbert, flushing in his turn. "I went there occasionally to play cards. I never saw you."

"But I saw you, sir," said the girl fervently. "Often I have watched you when you thought I wasn't, and—"

"One moment," said Jennings, interrupting. "Let's us get to the pith of the matter at once. Where did you get Mr. Mallow's portrait?"

"I don't want to say," murmured the girl.

"But you must say," said Mallow angrily. "I order you to confess."

"I kept silent for your sake, sir," she said, her eyes filled with tears, "but if you must know, I took the portrait from Senora Gredos' dressing-room when I left her house. And I left it on your account, sir," she finished defiantly.

X

The Parlor-Maid's Story

On hearing the confession of the girl, both men looked at one another in amazement. How could Cuthbert's photograph have come into the possession of Senora Gredos, and why had Susan Grant stolen it? And again, why did she hint that she had held her tongue about the matter for the sake of Mallow? Jennings at once proceeded to get at the truth. While being examined Susan wept, with an occasional glance at the bewildered Cuthbert.

"You were with Maraquito as parlor-maid?"

"With Senora Gredos? Yes, sir, for six months."

"Do you know what went on in that house?"

Susan ceased her sobs and stared. "I don't know what you mean," she said, looking puzzled. "It was a gay house, I know; but there was nothing wrong that I ever saw, save that I don't hold with cards being played on Sunday."

"And on every other night of the week," muttered Jennings. "Did you ever hear Senora Gredos called Maraquito?"

"Sometimes the gentlemen who came to play cards called her by that name. But she told her maid, who was my friend, that they were old friends of hers. And I think they were sorry for poor Senora Gredos, sir," added Miss Grant, naively, "as she suffered so much with her back. You know, she rarely moved from her couch. It was always wheeled into the room where the gambling took place."

"Ah. You knew that gambling went on," said Jennings, snapping her up sharply. "Don't you know that is against the law?"

"No, sir. Do you know?"

Cuthbert could not restrain a laugh. "That's one for you, Jennings," said he, nodding, "you often went to the Soho house."

"I had my reasons for saying nothing," replied the detective hastily. "You may be sure I could have ended the matter at once had I spoken to my chief about it. As it was, I judged it best to let matters remain as they were, so long as the house was respectably conducted."

"I'm sure it was conducted well, sir," said Susan, who appeared rather indignant. "Senora Gredos was a most respectable lady."

"She lived alone always, I believe?"

"Yes, sir." Then Susan hesitated. "I wonder if she had a mother?"

"Why do you wonder?"

"Well, sir, the lady who came to see Miss Loach—"

"Mrs. Herne?"

"I heard her name was Mrs. Herne, but she was as like Senora Gredos as two peas, save that she was older and had gray hair."

"Hum!" said Jennings, pondering. "Did you ever hear Senora Gredos speak of Mrs. Herne?"

"Never, sir. But Mrs. Pill—the cook of Miss Loach—said that Mrs. Herne lived at Hampstead. But she was like my old mistress. When I opened the door to her I thought she was Senora Gredos. But then the scent may have made me think that."

Jennings looked up sharply. "The scent? What do you mean?"

"Senora Gredos," explained Susan quietly, "used a very nice scent—a Japanese scent called Hikui. She used no other, and I never met any lady who did, save Mrs. Herne."

"Oh, so Mrs. Herne used it."

"She did, sir. When I opened the door on that night," Susan shuddered, "the first thing I knew was the smell of Hikui making the passage like a hairdresser's shop. I leaned forward to see if the lady was Senora Gredos, and she turned her face away. But I caught sight of it, and if she isn't some relative of my last mistress, may I never eat bread again."

"Did Mrs. Herne seem offended when you examined her face?"

"She gave a kind of start—"

"At the sight of you," said Jennings quickly.

"La, no, sir. She never saw me before."

"I'm not so sure of that," muttered the detective. "Did you also recognize Mr. Clancy and Mr. Hale as having visited the Soho house?"

"No, sir. I never set eyes on them before."

"But as parlor-maid, you must have opened the door to—"

"Just a moment, sir," said Susan quickly. "I opened the door in the day when few people came. After eight the page, Gibber, took my place. And I hardly ever went upstairs, as Senora Gredos told me to keep below. One evening I did come up and saw—" here her eyes rested on Cuthbert with a look which made him turn crimson. "I wish I had never come up on that night."

"See here, my girl," said Mallow irritably, "do you mean to say—"

"Hold on, Mallow," interposed Jennings, "let me ask a question." He turned to Susan, now weeping again with downcast eyes. "Mr. Mallow's face made an impression on you?"

"Yes, sir. But then I knew every line of it before."

"How was that?"

Susan looked up surprised. "The photograph in Senora Gredos' dressing-room. I often looked at it, and when I left I could not bear to leave it behind. It was stealing, I know," cried Miss Grant tearfully, "and I have been brought up respectably, but I couldn't help myself."

By this time Cuthbert was the color of an autumn sunset. He was a modest young man, and these barefaced confessions made him wince. He was about to interpose irritably when Jennings turned on him with a leading question. "Why did you give that photograph to—"

"Confound it!" cried Mallow, jumping up, "I did no such thing. I knew Maraquito only as the keeper of the gambling house. There was nothing between—"

"Don't, sir," said Susan, rising in her turn with a flush of jealousy. "I saw her kissing the photograph."

"Then she must be crazy," cried Mallow: "I never gave her any occasion to behave so foolishly. For months I have been engaged, and—" he here became aware that he was acting foolishly in talking like this to a love-sick servant, and turned on his heel abruptly. "I'll go in the next room," said he, "call me when you wish for my presence, Jennings. I can't possibly stay and listen to this rubbish," and going out, he banged the door, thereby bringing a fresh burst of tears from Susan Grant. Every word he said pierced her heart.

"Now I've made him cross," she wailed, "and I would lay down my life for him—that I would."

"See here, my girl," said Jennings, soothingly and fully prepared to make use of the girl's infatuation, "it is absurd your being in love with a gentleman of Mr. Mallow's position."

Miss Grant tossed her head. "I've read Bow-Bells and the Family Herald, sir," she said positively, "and many a time have I read of a governess, which is no more than a servant, marrying an earl. And that Mr. Mallow isn't, sir."

"He will be when Lord Caranby dies," said Jennings, hardly knowing what to say, "and fiction isn't truth. Besides, Mr. Mallow is engaged."

"I know, sir—to Miss Saxon. Well," poor Susan sighed, "she is a sweet young lady. I suppose he loves her."

"Devotedly. He will be married soon."

"And she's got Miss Loach's money too," sighed Susan again, "what a lucky young lady. Handsome looks in a husband and gold galore. A poor servant like me has to look on and keep her heart up with the Church Service. But I tell you what, sir," she added, drying her eyes and apparently becoming resigned, "if I ain't a lady, Senora Gredos is, and she won't let Mr. Mallow marry Miss Saxon."

"But Mr. Mallow is not in love with Senora Gredos."

"Perhaps not, sir, but she's in love with him. Yes. You may look and look, Mr. Jennings, but lame as she is and weak in the back and unable to move from that couch, she loves him. She had that photograph in her room and kissed it, as it I saw with my own eyes. I took it the last thing before I went, as I loved Mr. Mallow too, and I was not going to let that Spanish lady kiss him even in a picture."

"Upon my word," murmured Jennings, taken aback by this vehemence, "it is very strange all this."

"Oh, yes, you gentlemen don't think a poor girl has a heart. I couldn't help falling in love, though he never looked my way. But that Miss Saxon is a sweet, kind, young lady put upon by her mother, I wouldn't give him up even to her. But I can see there's no chance for me," wept Susan, "seeing the way he has gone out, banging the door in a temper, so I'll give him up. And I'll go now. My heart's broken."

But Jennings made her sit down again. "Not yet, my girl," he said firmly, "if you wish to do Mr. Mallow a good turn—"

"Oh, I'll do that," she interrupted with sparkling eyes, "after all, he can't help giving his heart elsewhere. It's just my foolishness to think otherwise. But how can I help him, sir?"

"He wants to find out who killed Miss Loach."

"I can't help him there, sir. I don't know who killed her. Mrs. Herne and Mr. Clancy and Mr. Hale were all gone, and when the bell rang she was alone, dead in her chair with them cards on her lap. Oh," Susan's voice became shrill and hysterical, "what a horrible sight!"

"Yes, yes," said Jennings soothingly, "we'll come to that shortly, my girl. But about this photograph. Was it in Senora Gredos' dressing-room long?"

"For about three months, sir. I saw it one morning when I took up her breakfast and fell in love with the handsome face. Then Gibber told me the gentleman came to the house sometimes, and I went up the stairs against orders after eight to watch. I saw him and found him more good-looking than the photograph. Often did I watch him and envy Senora Gredos the picture with them loving words. Sir," said Susan, sitting up stiffly, "if Mr. Mallow is engaged to Miss Saxon and doesn't love Senora Gredos, why did he write those words?"

"He did not write them for her," said Jennings doubtfully, "at least I don't think so. It is impossible to say how the photograph came into the possession of that lady."

"Will you ask him, sir?"

"Yes, when you are gone. But he won't speak while you are in the room."

Susan drooped her head and rose dolefully. "My dream is gone," she said mournfully, "though I was improving myself in spelling and figures so that I might go out as a governess and perhaps meet him in high circles."

"Ah, that's all Family Herald fiction," said Jennings, not unkindly.

"Yes! I know now, sir. My delusions are gone. But I will do anything I can to help Mr. Mallow and I hope he'll always think kindly of me."

"I'm sure he will. By the way, what are you doing now?"

"I go home to help mother at Stepney, sir, me having no call to go out to service. I have a happy home, though not fashionable. And after my heart being crushed I can't go out again," sighed Susan sadly.

"Are you sorry to leave Rose Cottage?"

"No, sir," Susan shuddered, "that dead body with the blood and the cards will haunt me always. Mrs. Pill, as is going to marry Thomas Barnes and rent the cottage, wanted me to stay, but I couldn't."

Jennings pricked up his ears. "What's that? How can Mrs. Pill rent so expensive a place."

"It's by arrangement with Miss Saxon, sir. Mrs. Pill told me all about it. Miss Saxon wished to sell the place, but Thomas Barnes spoke to her and said he had saved money while in Miss Loach's service for twenty years—"

"Ah," said Jennings thoughtfully, "he was that time in Miss Loach's service, was he?"

"Yes, sir. And got good wages. Well, sir, Miss Saxon hearing he wished to marry the cook and take the cottage and keep boarders, let him rent it with furniture as it stands. She and Mrs. Octagon are going back to town, and Mrs. Pill is going to have the cottage cleaned from cellar to attic before she marries Thomas and receives the boarder."

"Oh. So she has a boarder?"

"Yes, sir. She wouldn't agree to Thomas taking the cottage as her husband, unless she had a boarder to start with, being afraid she and Thomas could not pay the rent. So Thomas saw Mr. Clancy and he is coming to stop. He has taken all the part where Miss Loach lived, and doesn't want anyone else in the house, being a quiet man and retired."

"Ah! Ah! Ah!" said Jennings in three different tones of voice. "I think Mrs. Pill is very wise. I hope she and Thomas will do well. By the way, what do you think of Mr. Barnes?"

Susan did not leave him long in doubt as to her opinion. "I think he is a stupid fool," she said, "and it's a good thing Mrs. Pill is going to marry him. He was guided by Miss Loach all his life, and now she's dead, he goes about like a gaby. One of those men, sir," explained Susan, "as needs a woman to look after them. Not like that gentleman," she cast a tender glance at the door, "who can protect the weakest of my sex."

Jennings having learned all he could, rose. "Well, Miss Grant," he said quietly, "I am obliged to you for your frank speaking. My advice to you is to go home and think no more of Mr. Mallow. You might as well love the moon. But you know my address, and should you hear of anything likely to lead you to suspect who killed Miss Loach, Mr. Mallow will make it worth your while to come to me with the information."

"I'll do all I can," said Susan resolutely, "but I won't take a penny piece, me having my feelings as other and higher ladies."

"Just as you please. But Mr. Mallow is about to offer a reward on behalf of his uncle, Lord Caranby."

"He that was in love with Miss Loach, sir?"

"Yes. On account of that old love, Lord Caranby desires to learn who killed her. And Mr. Mallow also wishes to know, for a private reason. I expect you will be calling to see Mrs. Pill?"

"When she's Mrs. Barnes, I think so, sir. I go to the wedding, and me and Geraldine are going to be bridesmaids."

"Then if you hear or see anything likely to lead to a revelation of the truth, you will remember. By the way, you don't know how Senora Gredos got that photograph?"

"No, sir, I do not."

"And you think Mrs. Herne is Senora Gredos' mother?"

"Yes, sir, I do."

"Thank you, that will do for the present. Keep your eyes open and your mouth closed, and when you hear of anything likely to interest me, call at the address I gave you."

"Yes, sir," said Susan, and took her leave, not without another lingering glance at the door behind which Mallow waited impatiently.

When she was gone, Jennings went into the next room to find Cuthbert smoking. He jumped up when he saw the detective. "Well, has that silly girl gone?" he asked angrily.

"Yes, poor soul. You needn't get in a wax, Mallow. The girl can't help falling in love with you. Poor people have feelings as well as rich."

"I know that, but it's ridiculous: especially as I never saw the girl before, and then I love only Juliet."

"You are sure of that?"

"Jennings"—

"There—there, don't get angry. We must get to the bottom of this affair which is getting more complicated every day. Did you give that photograph to Senora Gredos?"

"To Maraquito. No, I didn't. I gave it to Juliet."

"You are certain?"

"Positive! I can't make out how it came into Maraquito's house."

Jennings pondered. "Perhaps Basil may have given it to her. It is to his interest on behalf of his mother to make trouble between you and Miss Saxon. Moreover, if it is as I surmise, it shows that Mrs. Octagon intended to stop the marriage, if she could, even before her sister died."

"Ah! And it shows that the death of Miss Loach gave her a chance of asserting herself and stopping the marriage."

"Well, she might have hesitated to do that before, as Miss Loach might not have left her fortune to Juliet if the marriage did not take place."

Cuthbert nodded and spoke musingly: "After all, the old woman liked me, and I was the nephew of the man who loved her in her youth. Her heart may have been set on the match, and she might have threatened to leave her fortune elsewhere if Mrs. Octagon did not agree. Failing this, Mrs. Octagon, through Basil, gave that photograph to Maraquito in the hope that Juliet would ask questions of me—"

"And if she had asked questions?" asked Jennings quickly.

Cuthbert looked uncomfortable. "Don't think me a conceited ass," he said, trying to laugh, "but Maraquito is in love with me. I stayed away from her house because she became too attentive. I never told you this, as no man has a right to reveal a woman's weakness. But, as matters are so serious, it is right you should know."

"I am glad I do know. By the way, Cuthbert, what between Miss Saxon, Susan Grant and Maraquito, you will have a hard time."

"How absurd!" said Mallow angrily. "Juliet is the only woman I love and Juliet I intend to marry."

"Maraquito will prevent your marriage."

"If she can," scoffed Cuthbert.

Jennings looked grave. "I am not so sure but what she can make mischief. There's Mrs. Herne who may or may not be the mother of this Spanish demon—"

"Perhaps the demon herself," ventured Mallow.

"No!" said the detective positively. "Maraquito can't move from her couch. You know that. However, I shall call on Mrs. Herne at Hampstead. She was a witness, you know? Keep quiet, Mallow, and let me make inquiries. Meantime, ask Miss Saxon when she missed that photograph."

"Can you see your way now?"

"I have a slight clue. But it will be a long time before I learn the truth. There is a lot at the back of that murder, Mallow."

XI

On the Track

Professor Le Beau kept a school of dancing in Pimlico, and incessantly trained pupils for the stage. Many of them had appeared with more or less success in the ballets at the Empire and Alhambra, and he was widely known amongst stage-struck aspirants as charging moderately and teaching in a most painstaking manner. He thus made an income which, if not large, was at least secure, and was assisted in the school by his niece, Peggy Garthorne. She was the manager of his house and looked after the money, otherwise the little professor would never have been able to lay aside for the future. But when the brother of the late Madame Le Beau—an Englishwoman—died, his sister took charge of the orphan. Now that Madame herself was dead, Peggy looked after the professor out of gratitude and love. She was fond of the excitable little Frenchman, and knew how to manage him to a nicety.

It was to the Dancing Academy that Jennings turned his steps a few days after the interview with Susan. He had been a constant visitor there for eighteen months and was deeply in love with Peggy. On a Bank Holiday he had been fortunate enough to rescue her from a noisy crowd, half-drunk and indulging in horse-play, and had escorted her home to receive the profuse thanks of the Professor. The detective was attracted by the quaint little man, and he called again to inquire for Peggy. A friendship thus inaugurated ripened into a deeper feeling, and within nine months Jennings proposed for the hand of the humble girl. She consented and so did Le Beau, although he was rather rueful at the thought of losing his mainstay. But Peggy promised him that she would still look after him until he retired, and with this promise Le Beau was content. He was now close on seventy, and could not hope to teach much longer. But, thanks to Peggy's clever head and saving habits, he had—as the French say—"plenty of bread baked" to eat during days of dearth.

The Academy was situated down a narrow street far removed from the main thoroughfares. Quiet houses belonging to poor people stood on either side of this lane—for that it was—and at the end appeared the Academy, blocking the exit from that quarter. It stood right in the middle of the street and turned the lane into a blind alley, but a narrow right-of-way passed along the side and round to the back where the street began again under a new name. The position of the place was quaint, and often it had been intended to remove the obstruction, but the owner, an eccentric person of great wealth, had hitherto refused to allow it to be pulled down. But the owner was now old, and it was expected his heirs would take away the building and allow the lane to run freely through to the other street. Still it would last Professor Le Beau's time, for his heart would have broken had he been compelled to move. He had taught here for the last thirty years, and had become part and parcel of the neighborhood.

Jennings, quietly dressed in blue serge with brown boots and a bowler hat, turned down the lane and advanced towards the double door of the Academy, which was surmounted by an allegorical group of plaster figures designed by Le Beau himself, and representing Orpheus teaching trees and animals to dance. The allusion was not complimentary to his pupils, for if Le Beau figured as Orpheus, what were the animals? However, the hot-tempered little man refused to change his allegory and the group remained. Jennings passed under it and into the building with a smile which the sight of those figures always evoked. Within, the building on the ground floor was divided into two rooms—a large hall for the dancing lessons and a small apartment used indifferently as a reception-room and an office. Above, on the first story, were the sitting-room, the dining-room and the kitchen; and on the third, under a high conical roof, the two bedrooms of the Professor and Peggy, with an extra one for any stranger who might remain. Where Margot, the French cook and maid-of-all-work, slept, was a mystery. So it will be seen that the accommodation of the house was extremely limited. However, Le Beau, looked after by Peggy and Margot, who was devoted to him, was extremely well pleased, and extremely happy in his light airy French way.

In the office was Peggy, making up some accounts. She was a pretty, small maiden of twenty-five, neatly dressed in a clean print gown, and looking like a dewy daisy. Her eyes were blue, her hair the color of ripe corn, and her cheeks were of a delicate rose. There was something pastoral about Peggy, smacking of meadow lands and milking time. She should have been a shepherdess looking after her flock rather than a girl toiling in a dingy office. How such a rural flower ever sprung up amongst London houses was a mystery Jennings could not make out.

And according to her own tale, Peggy had never lived in the country. What with the noise of fiddling which came from the large hall, and the fact of being absorbed in her work, Peggy never heard the entrance of her lover. Jennings stole quietly towards her, admiring the pretty picture she made with a ray of dusky sunlight making glory of her hair.

"Who is it?" he asked, putting his hands over her eyes.

"Oh," cried Peggy, dropping her pen and removing his hands, "the only man who would dare to take such a liberty with me. Miles, my darling pig!" and she kissed him, laughing.

"I don't like the last word, Peggy!"

"It's Papa Le Beau's favorite word with his pupils," said Peggy, who always spoke of the dancing-master thus.

"With the addition of darling?"

"No, that is an addition of my own. But I can remove it if you like."

"I don't like," said Miles, sitting down and pulling her towards him, "come and talk to me, Pegtop."

"I won't be called Pegtop, and as to talking, I have far too much work to do. The lesson will soon be over, and some of the pupils have to take these accounts home. Then dejeuner will soon be ready, and you know how Margot hates having her well-cooked dishes spoilt by waiting. But why are you here instead of at work?"

"Hush!" said Miles, laying a finger on her lips. "Papa will hear you."

"Not he. Hear the noise his fiddle is making, and he is scolding the poor little wretches like a game-cock."

"Does a game-cock scold?" asked Jennings gravely. "I hope he is not in a bad temper, Peggy. I have come to ask him a few questions."

"About your own business?" asked she in a lower tone.

Jennings nodded. Peggy knew his occupation, but as yet he had not been able to tell Le Beau.

The Frenchman cherished all the traditional hatred of his race for the profession of "mouchard," and would not be able to understand that a detective was of a higher standing. Miles was therefore supposed to be a gentleman of independent fortune, and both he and Peggy decided to inform Le Beau of the truth when he had retired from business. Meanwhile, Miles often talked over his business with Peggy, and usually found her clear way of looking at things of infinite assistance to him in the sometimes difficult cases which he dealt with. Peggy knew all about the murder in Crooked Lane, and how Miles was dealing with the matter. But even she had not been able to suggest a clue to the assassin, although she was in full possession of the facts. "It's about this new case I wish to speak," said Jennings. "By the way, Peggy, you know that woman Maraquito I have talked of?"

"Yes. The gambling-house. What of her?"

"Well, she seems to be implicated in the matter."

"In what way?"

Jennings related the episode of the photograph, and the incident of the same perfume being used by Mrs. Herne and Maraquito. Peggy nodded.

"I don't see how the photograph connects her with the case," she said at length, "but the same perfume certainly is strange. All the same, the scent may be fashionable. Hikui! Hikui! I never heard of it."

"It is a Japanese perfume, and Maraquito got it from some foreign admirer. It is strange, as you say."

"Have you seen Mrs. Herne?"

"I saw her at the inquest. She gave evidence. But I had no conversation with her myself."

"Why don't you look her up? You mentioned you had her address."

"I haven't it now," said Jennings gloomily. "I called at the Hampstead house, and learned that Mrs. Herne had received such a shock from the death of her friend, Miss Loach, that she had gone abroad and would not return for an indefinite time. So I can do nothing in that quarter just now. It is for this reason that I have come here to ask about Maraquito."

"From Papa Le Beau," said Peggy, wrinkling her pretty brows. "What can he know of this woman?"

"She was a dancer until she had an accident. Le Beau may have had her through his hands."

"Maraquito, Maraquito," murmured Peggy, and shook her head. "No, I do not remember her. How old is she?"

"About thirty, I think; a fine, handsome woman like a tropical flower for coloring."

"Spanish. The name is Spanish."

"I think that is all the Spanish about her. She talks English without the least accent. Hush! here is papa."

It was indeed the little Professor, who rushed into the room and threw himself, blowing and panting, on the dingy sofa. He was small and dry, with black eyes and a wrinkled face. He wore a blonde wig which did not match his yellow complexion, and was neatly dressed in black, with an old-fashioned swallow-tail coat of blue. He carried a small fiddle and spoke volubly without regarding the presence of Miles.

"Oh, these cochons of English, my dear," he exclaimed to Peggy, "so steef—so wood-steef in the limbs. Wis 'em I kin do noozzn', no, not a leetle bit. Zey would make ze angils swear. Ah, mon Dieu, quel dommage I haf to teach zem."

"I must see about these accounts," said Peggy, picking up a sheaf of papers and running out. "Stay to dejeuner, Miles."

"Eh, mon ami," cried papa, rising. "My excuses, but ze pigs make me to be mooch enrage. Zey are ze steef dolls on the Strasburg clock. You are veil—ah, yis—quite veil cheerup."

The Professor had picked up a number of English slang words with which he interlarded his conversation. He meant to be kind, and indeed liked Miles greatly. In proof of his recovered temper, he offered the young man a pinch of snuff. Jennings hated snuff, but to keep Papa Le Beau in a good temper he accepted the offer and sneezed violently.

"Professor," he said, when somewhat better, "I have come to ask you about a lady. A friend of mine has fallen in love with her, and he thought you might know of her."

"Eh, wha-a-at, mon cher? I understands nozzin'. Ze lady, quel nom?"

"Maraquito Gredos."

"Espagnole," murmured Le Beau, shaking his wig. "Non. I do not know ze name. Dancers of Spain. Ah, yis—I haf had miny—zey are not steef like ze cochon Englees. Describe ze looks, mon ami."

Jennings did so, to the best of his ability, but the old man still appeared undecided. "But she has been ill for three years," added Jennings. "She fell and hurt her back, and—"

"Eh—wha-a-at Celestine!" cried Le Beau excitedly. "She did fall and hurt hersilf—eh, yis—mos' dredfil. Conceive to yoursilf, my frien', she slip on orange peels in ze streets and whacks comes she down. Tree year back—yis—tree year. Celestine Durand, mon fil."

Jennings wondered. "But she says she is Spanish."

Le Beau flipped a pinch of snuff in the air. "Ah, bah! She no Spain."

"So she is French," murmured Jennings to himself.

"Ah, non; by no means," cried the Frenchman unexpectedly. "She no French. She Englees—yis—I remembers. A ver' fine and big demoiselle. She wish to come out at de opera. But she too large—mooch too large. Englees—yis—La Juive."

"A Jewess?" cried Jennings in his turn.

"I swear to you, mon ami. Englees Jewess, mais oui! For ten months she dance here, tree year gone. Zen zee orange peels and pouf! I see her no mores. But never dance—no—too large, une grande demoiselle."

"Do you know where she came from?"

"No. I know nozzin' but what I tell you."

"Did you like her?"

Le Beau shrugged his shoulders. "I am too old, mon ami. Les femmes like me not. I haf had mes affairs—ah, yis. Conceive—" and he rattled out an adventure of his youth which was more amusing than moral.

But Jennings paid very little attention to him. He was thinking that Maraquito-Celestine was a more mysterious woman than he had thought her. While Jennings was wondering what use he could make of the information he had received, Le Beau suddenly flushed crimson. A new thought had occurred to him. "Do you know zis one—zis Celestine Durand? Tell her I vish money—"

"Did she not pay you?"

Le Beau seized Jennings' arm and shook it violently. "Yis. Tree pound; quite raight; oh, certainly. But ze four piece of gold, a louis—non—ze Englees sufferin—"

"The English sovereign. Yes."

"It was bad money—ver bad."

"Have you got it?" asked Jennings, feeling that he was on the brink of a discovery.

"Non. I pitch him far off in rages. I know now, Celestine Durand. I admire her; oh, yis. Fine womans—a viecked eye. Mais une—no, not zat. Bad, I tell you. If your frien' love, haf nozzin' wis her. She gif ze bad money, one piece—" he held up a lean finger, and then, "Aha! ze bell for ze tables. Allons, marchons. We dine—we eat," and he dashed out of the room as rapidly as he had entered it.

But Jennings did not follow him. He scribbled a note to Peggy, stating that he had to go away on business, and left the Academy. He felt that it would be impossible to sit down and talk of trivial things—as he would have to do in the presence of Le Beau—when he had made such a discovery. The case was beginning to take shape. "Can Maraquito have anything to do with the coiners?" he asked himself. "She is English—a Jewess—Saul is a Jewish name. Can she be of that family? It seems to me that this case is a bigger one than I imagine. I wonder what I had better do?"

It was not easy to say. However, by the time Jennings reached his home—he had chambers in Duke Street, St. James'—he decided to see Maraquito. For this purpose he arrayed himself in accurate evening dress. Senora Gredos thought he was a mere idler, a man-about-town. Had she known of his real profession she might not have welcomed him so freely to her house. Maraquito, for obvious reasons, had no desire to come into touch with the authorities.

But it must not be thought that she violated the law in any very flagrant way. She was too clever for that. Her house was conducted in a most respectable manner. It was situated in Golden Square, and was a fine old mansion of the days when that locality was fashionable. Her servants were all neat and demure. Maraquito received a few friends every evening for a quiet game of cards, so on the surface no one could object to that. But when the doors were closed, high play went on and well-known people ventured large sums on the chances of baccarat. Also, people not quite so respectable came, and it was for that reason Scotland Yard left the house alone. When any member of the detective staff wished to see anyone of a shady description, the person could be found at Maraquito's. Certainly, only the aristocracy of crime came here, and never a woman. Maraquito did not appear to love her own sex. She received only gentlemen, and as she was an invalid and attended constantly by a duenna in the form of a nurse, no one could say anything. The police knew in an underhand way that the Soho house was a gambling saloon, but the knowledge had not come officially, therefore no notice was taken. But Maraquito's servants suspected nothing, neither did the gossips of the neighborhood. Senora Gredos was simply looked upon as an invalid fond of entertaining because of her weariness in being confined to her couch.

Jennings had appointed a meeting with Mallow in this semi-respectable establishment, and looked round when he entered the room. It was a large apartment, decorated in the Adams style and furnished as a luxurious drawing-room. At the side near the window there was a long table covered with green baize. Round this several gentlemen in evening dress were standing. Others played games of their own at separate small tables, but most of them devoted themselves to baccarat. Maraquito held the bank. Her couch was drawn up against the wall, and the red silk curtains of the window made a vivid background to her dark beauty.

She was, indeed, a handsome woman—so much of her as could be seen. Half-sitting, half-reclining on her couch, the lower part of her frame was swathed in eastern stuffs sparkling with gold threads. She wore a yellow silk dress trimmed about the shoulders with black lace and glittering with valuable jewels. Her neck and arms were finely moulded and of a dazzling whiteness. Her small head was proudly set on her shoulders, and her magnificent black hair smoothly coiled in lustrous tresses above her white forehead. Her lips were full and rich, her eyes large and black, and her nose was thin and high. The most marked feature of her face were the eyebrows, which almost met over her nose. She had delicate hands and beautiful arms which showed themselves to advantage as she manipulated the cards. From the gorgeous coverlet her bust rose like a splendid flower, and for an invalid she had a surprising color. She was indeed, as Jennings had remarked, like a tropical flower. But there was something sensual and evil about her exuberance. But not a whisper had been heard against her reputation. Everyone, sorry for the misfortune which condemned this lovely woman to a sickbed, treated her with respect. Maraquito, as some people said, may have been wicked, but no anchorite could have led, on the face of it, a more austere life. Her smile was alluring, and she looked like the Lurline drawing men to destruction. Fortunes had been lost in that quiet room.

When Jennings entered, Maraquito was opening a fresh pack of cards, while the players counted their losses or winnings and fiddled with the red chips used in the game. On seeing the newcomer, Senora Gredos gave him a gracious smile, and said something to the pale, thin woman in black who stood at the head of her couch. The nurse, or duenna—she served for both—crossed to Jennings as he advanced towards the buffet, on which stood glasses and decanters of wine.

"Madame wishes to know why you have not brought Mr. Mallow."

"Tell madame that he will be here soon. I have to meet him in this place," said the detective to the duenna, and watched the effect of the message on Maraquito.

Her face flushed, her eyes brightened, but she did not look again in Jennings' direction. On the contrary, she gave all her attention to the game which was now in progress, but Jennings guessed that her thoughts were with Mallow, and occasionally he caught her looking for his appearance at the door. "How that woman loves him," he thought, "I wonder I never noticed it before. Quite an infatuation." For a time he watched the players staking large amounts, and saw the pile of gold at Maraquito's elbow steadily increasing. She seemed to have all the luck. The bank was winning and its opponents losing, but the play went on steadily for at least half an hour. At the end of that time a newcomer entered the room. Jennings, who had glanced at his watch, quite expected to see Cuthbert. But, to his surprise, he came face to face with Lord Caranby.

"I did not expect to see you here," said the detective.

"I come in place of my nephew. He is unwell," said Caranby; "present me to Senora Gredos, if you please, Mr. Jennings."

XII

JENNINGS ASKS QUESTIONS

W ill you play, Lord Caranby?" asked Maraquito, when the introduction had been accomplished.

"Pardon me, not at present: in a little time," said the old nobleman, with a polite bow and his eyes on the beautiful face.

"As you like," she answered carelessly; "everyone who comes here does just as he pleases. Is your nephew coming?"

"I fear not. He is unwell."

Maraquito started. "Unwell. Nothing serious, I hope?"

"A slight cold."

"Ah! Everyone has colds just now. Well, Lord Caranby, I hope to have a conversation with you later when someone else takes the bank."

Caranby bowed and moved away slowly, leaning on his cane. Jennings, who was beside him, threw a glance over his shoulder at Senora Gredos.

Maraquito's face was pale, and there was a frightened look in her eyes. Catching Jennings' inquisitive look she frowned and again addressed herself to the game. Wondering why Lord Caranby should produce such an effect, Jennings rejoined him at the end of the room, where they sat on a sofa and smoked. "Have you been here before?" asked the detective.

"No," answered the other, lighting his cigar, "and it is improbable that I shall come again. My reason for coming—" he broke off—"I can tell you that later. It is sufficient to say that it has to do with your conduct of this case."

"Hush!" whispered Jennings quickly, "my profession is not known here."

"I fear it will be if these two have tongues in their heads."

The detective glanced towards the door and saw Hale enter with Clancy at his heels. Jennings had not seen them since the inquest on the body of Miss Loach, when they had given their evidence with great grief and frankness. He was annoyed at meeting them here, for although he had seen them in Maraquito's salon before, yet at that time they had not known his profession. But since the inquest the knowledge was common property, and doubtless they would tell Senora Gredos if they had not done so already. Jennings' chances of learning what he wished would therefore be slight, as everyone is not willing to speak freely before an officer of the law.

"It can't be helped," said Jennings with a shrug; "and, in any case, Maraquito is too anxious to stand well with the police to make any trouble about my coming here."

Caranby did not reply, but looked steadily at the two men who were walking slowly up the room. Hale was slender, tall, and dark in color, with a nose like the beak of an eagle. He was perfectly dressed and had even an elegant appearance. His age might have been forty, but in the artificial light he looked even younger. Clancy, on the other hand, wore his clothes with the air of a man unaccustomed to evening dress. He was light in color, with weak blue eyes and a foolish expression about his slack mouth. Jennings wondered why a man like Hale should connect himself with such a creature. The men nodded to Senora Gredos, who took little notice of them, and then repaired to the buffet. Owing to the position of the detective and Caranby, the new arrivals did not them. Nor for the present was the detective anxious to attract their notice. Indeed, he would have stolen away unperceived, but that he wished to question Hale as to the whereabouts of Mrs. Herne.

"It is a long time since I have seen you," said Caranby, removing his eyes from the newcomers, and addressing the detective; "you were not an—er—an official when we last met."

"It is three years ago," said Jennings; "no. I had money then, but circumstances over which I had no control soon reduced me to the necessity of earning my living. As all professions were crowded, I thought I would turn my talents of observation and deduction to this business."

"Do you find it lucrative?"

Jennings smiled and shrugged his shoulders again. "I do very well," he said, "but I have not yet made a fortune."

"Ah! And Cuthbert told me you wished to marry."

"I do. But when my fortune will allow me to marry, I don't know."

Caranby, without raising his voice or looking at his companion, supplied the information. "I can tell you that," said he, "when you learn who killed Miss Loach."

"How is that?"

"On the day you lay your hand on the assassin of that poor woman I shall give you five thousand pounds."

Jennings' breath was taken away. "A large sum," he murmured.

"She was very dear to me at one time," said Caranby with emotion. "I would have married her but for the machinations of her sister."

"Mrs. Octagon?"

"Yes! She wanted to become my wife. The story is a long one."

"Cuthbert told it to me."

"Quite right," said Caranby, nodding, "I asked him to. It seems to me that in my romance may be found the motive for the death of Selina Loach."

The detective thought over the story. "I don't quite see—"

"Nor do I. All the same—" Caranby waved his hand and abruptly changed the subject. "Do you know why I came here to-night?"

"No. I did not know you ever came to such places."

"Nor do I. My life is a quiet one now. I came to see this woman you call Maraquito."

"What do you call her?" asked Jennings alertly.

"Ah, that I can't tell you. But she is no Spaniard."

"Is she a Jewess by any chance?"

Caranby turned to look directly at his companion. "You ought to be able to tell that from her face," he said, "can you not see the seal of Jacob impressed there—that strange look which stamps a Hebrew?"

"No," confessed Jennings, "that is, I can see it now, but I came here for many a long day before I did guess she was a Jewess. And then it was only because I learned the truth."

"How did you learn it?"

The detective related details of his visit to Monsieur Le Beau and the discovery that Maraquito Gredos was one and the same as Celestine Durand. Caranby listened attentively. "Yes, that is all right," he said, "but her name is Bathsheba Saul."

"What?" said Jennings, so loud that several people turned to look.

"Hush!" said Caranby, sinking his voice, "you attract notice. Yes, I made Cuthbert describe the appearance of this woman. His description vaguely suggested Emilia Saul. I came here to-night to satisfy myself, and I have no doubt but what she is the niece of Emilia—the daughter of Emilia's brother."

"Who was connected with the coining gang?"

"Ah, you heard of that, did you? Exactly. Her father is dead, I believe, but there sits his daughter. You see in her the image of Emilia as I loved her twenty years ago."

"Loved her?" echoed Jennings, significantly.

"You are right," responded Caranby with a keen look. "I see Cuthbert has told you all. I never did love Emilia. But she hypnotized me in some way. She was one of those women who could make a man do what pleased her. And this Bathsheba—Maraquito—Celestine, can do the same. It is a pity she is an invalid, but on the whole, as she looks rather wicked, mankind is to be congratulated. Were she able to move about like an ordinary woman, she would set the world on fire after the fashion of Cleopatra. You need not mention this."

"I know how to hold my tongue," said Jennings, rather offended by the imputation that he was a chatterer, "can I come and see you to talk over this matter?"

"By all means. I am at the Avon Hotel."

"Oh, and by the way, will you allow me to go over that house of yours at Rexton?"

"If you like. Are you a ghost-hunter also?"

"I am a detective!" whispered Jennings quietly, and with such a look that Caranby became suddenly attentive.

"Ah! You think you may discover something in that house likely to lead to the discovery of the assassin."

"Yes I do. I can't explain my reasons now. The explanation would take too long. However, I see Senora Gredos is beckoning to you. I will speak to Hale and Clancy. Would you mind telling me what she says to you?"

"A difficult question to answer," said Caranby, rising, "as a gentleman, I am not in the habit of repeating conversations, especially with women. Besides, she can have no connection with this case."

"On the face of it—no," replied Jennings doubtfully, "but there is a link—"

"Ah, you mean that she is Emilia's niece."

"Not exactly that," answered Jennings, thinking of the photograph. "I will tell you what I mean when we next meet."

At this moment, in response to the imperative beckoning of Maraquito's fan, Caranby was compelled to go to her. The couch had been wheeled away from the green table, and a gentleman had taken charge of the bank. Maraquito with her couch retreated to a quiet corner of the room, and had a small table placed beside her. Here were served champagne and cakes, while Lord Caranby, after bowing in his old-fashioned way, took a seat near the beautiful woman. She gazed smilingly at Lord Caranby, yet there was a nervous look in her eyes.

"I have heard of you from Mr. Mallow," she said flushing.

"My nephew. He comes here at times. Indeed," said Caranby gallantly, "it was his report of your beauty that brought me here to-night."

Maraquito sighed. "The wreck of a beauty," said she bitterly, "three years ago indeed—but I met with an accident."

"So I heard. A piece of orange peel."

The woman started. "Who told you that?"

"I heard it indirectly from a professor of dancing. You were a dancer, I believe?"

"Scarcely that," said Senora Gredos, nervously playing with her fan; "I was learning. It was Le Beau who told you?"

"Indirectly," responded Caranby.

"I should like to know," said Maraquito deliberately, "who has taken the trouble to tell you this. My life—the life of a shattered invalid—can scarcely interest anyone."

"I really forget to whom I am indebted for the information," said Lord Caranby mendaciously, "and a lady of your beauty must always interest men while they have eyes to see. I have seen ladies like you in Andalusia, but no one so lovely. Let me see, was it in Andalusia or Jerusalem?" mused Lord Caranby.

"I am a Spanish Jewess," said Maraquito, quickly and uneasily, "I have only been in London five years."

"And met with an accident a year or two after you arrived," murmured Caranby; "how very sad."

Maraquito did not know what to make of the ironical old gentleman. It seemed to her that he was hostile, but she could take no offence at what he said. Moreover, as he was Mallow's uncle, she did not wish to quarrel with him. With a graceful gesture she indicated a glass of champagne. "Will you not drink to our better acquaintance?"

"Certainly," said Caranby without emotion, and sipped a few drops of the golden-colored wine. "I hope to see much of you."

"I reciprocate the hope," said Maraquito radiantly, "and I'll tell you a secret. I have been consulting specialists, and I find that in a few months I shall be able to walk as well as ever I did."

"Excellent news," said Caranby, "I hope you will."

"And, moreover," added Maraquito, looking at him from behind her fan; "I shall then give up this place. I have plenty of money, and—"

"You will go back to Spain?"

"That depends. Should I leave my heart in England—"

"How I envy the man you leave it with."

Maraquito looked down moodily. "He doesn't care for my heart."

"What a stone he must be. Now I—upon my word I feel inclined to marry and cut my nephew out of the title."

"Your nephew," stammered Maraquito, with a flash of her big eyes.

"You know him well, he tells me," chatted Caranby garrulously, "a handsome fellow is Cuthbert. I am sure the lady he is engaged to thinks as much, and very rightly too."

"Miss Saxon!" cried Maraquito, breaking her fan and looking furious.

"Ah!" said Caranby coolly, "you know her?"

"I know of her," said Maraquito bitterly. "Her brother Basil comes here sometimes, and said his sister was engaged to—but they will never marry—never!" she said vehemently.

"How can you tell that?"

"Because the mother objects to the match."

"Ah! And who told you so? Mr. Basil Saxon?"

"Yes. He does not approve of it either."

"I fear that will make little difference. Mallow is set on the marriage. He loves Miss Saxon with all his heart."

Maraquito uttered a low cry of rage, but managed to control herself with an effort. "Do you?" she asked.

Caranby shrugged his thin shoulders. "I am neutral. So long as Cuthbert marries the woman he loves, I do not mind."

"And what about the woman who loves him?"

"Miss Saxon? Oh, I am sure—"

"I don't mean Miss Saxon, and he will never marry her—never. You know that Mr. Mallow is poor. Miss Saxon has no money—"

"Pardon me. I hear her aunt, Miss Loach, who was unfortunately murdered at Rexton, has left her six thousand a year."

Senora Gredos turned quite pale and clenched her hands, but she managed to control herself again with a powerful effort and masked the rage she felt under a bland, false smile.

"Oh, that makes a difference," she said calmly. "I hope they will be happy—if they marry," she added significantly.

"Oh, that is quite settled," said Caranby.

"There's many a slip between the cup and the lip," said Maraquito viciously. "Yonder is Mr. Saxon. Tell him to come to me."

Caranby bowed and crossed the room to where Basil was talking with a frowning face to Hale. "Don't bother me," he was saying, "it will be all right now that the will has been read."

"For your own sake I hope it will be all right," replied Hale, and Caranby caught the words as he came up. After giving his message, he sauntered round, watching the play, and seemingly listened to no one. But all the time he kept his ears open to hear what Hale and Clancy were talking about.

The two men were in a corner of the room, and Clancy was expostulating angrily with Hale. They held their peace when Caranby drifted near them, he saw that they were on their guard. Looking round, he espied Jennings playing at a side table, and crossed to him.

"Permit me to take your place," said Caranby, and added in a low tone, "watch Hale and Clancy!"

Jennings seized the idea at once and surrendered the chair to the old nobleman. Then he lighted a cigarette and by degrees strolled across the room to where the two were again talking vigorously. "I tell you if Basil is pressed too hard he will—" Clancy was saying, but shut his mouth as he saw Jennings at his elbow. The detective came forward with a smile, inwardly vexed that he had not been able to hear more. As he advanced he saw Clancy touch Hale on the arm.

"How are you?" said Jennings, taking the initiative, "we met at that inquest, I believe."

"Yes," said Hale, polite and smiling, "I remember, Mr. Jennings! I had seen you here before, but I never knew your calling."

"I don't tell it to everyone," said Jennings, "How do you do, Mr. Clancy? I hope you are well. An amusing place this."

"I need amusement," said Clancy, again assuming his silly smile, "since the death of my dear friend. By the way, have you found out who killed her, Mr. Jennings?"

"No. I fear the assassin will never be discovered." Here the two men exchanged a glance. "I am engaged on other cases. There was only one point I wished to learn in connection with Miss Loach's death."

"What is that?" asked Hale calmly.

"Was Mrs. Herne in Miss Loach's bedroom on that night?"

"I forget," said Clancy before Hale could speak.

"That's a pity," resumed Jennings. "You see from the fact of the bell having been sounded, it struck me that the assassin may have been concealed in the bedroom. Now if Mrs. Herne was in that room, she might have noticed something."

"I don't think she did," said Hale hastily. "Mrs. Herne and I left early, owing to Clancy here having offended her. Besides, Mrs. Herne told all she knew at the inquest."

"All save that point."

"The question was not asked," said Clancy.

"No. I should like to ask Mrs. Herne now, but it seems she has gone away from Hampstead."

"I don't care if she has," grumbled Clancy, "I hated Mrs. Herne. She was always quarrelling. Did you call to see her?"

"Yes, but I could not learn where she was. Now, as you are her lawyer, Mr. Hale, you may know."

"She is at Brighton," replied Hale readily, "at the Metropolitan Hotel, but she returns to Hampstead in a week."

Jennings was secretly astonished at his question being thus answered, as he was inclined to suspect the men. However, he took a note of the address, and said he would attend to the matter. "But, to tell you the truth, it is useless," he said. "The assassin will never be discovered. Moreover, there is no reward, and I should only work for no wages. You stay at Rose Cottage now, I believe, Mr. Clancy?"

"I do. Mrs. Pill has taken the place. Who told you?"

"I heard from Susan Grant. She was witness, if you remember. And has Mrs. Pill married Barnes yet?"

"I can't say," said Clancy, looking keenly at the detective. "I am not yet a boarder. I move in after a fortnight. I expect the marriage will take place before then. Susan Grant told you that also?"

"She did. But I don't expect I'll see her again. Well, gentlemen, I must go away. I hope you will be lucky."

Jennings moved away and saw from the eager manner in which the two men began to converse that he was the subject of the conversation. He looked round for Caranby, but could not see him. When he was out of the house, however, and on the pavement lighting a cigarette, he felt a touch on his arm and found Caranby waiting for him. The old gentleman pointed with his cane to a brougham! "Get in," he said, "I have been waiting to see you. There is much to talk about."

"Maraquito?" asked Jennings eagerly.

"She has something to do with the matter. Love for Cuthbert has made her involve herself. How far or in what way I do not know. And what of Clancy and Hale?"

"Oh, I have put them off the scent. They think I have given up the case. But they and Maraquito are connected with the matter somehow. I can't for the life of me see in what way though."

"There is another woman connected with the matter—Mrs. Octagon."

"What do you mean?" asked Jennings quickly.

"I saw her enter Maraquito's house a few moments before you came down."

XIII

Juliet at Bay

Caranby's reply took away Jennings' breath. The case was one of surprises, but he was not quite prepared for such an announcement. He was in the brougham and driving towards the Avon Hotel with the old nobleman before he found his tongue.

"What can Mrs. Octagon have to do with Maraquito?" he asked amazed.

"Ah! that is the question," replied Caranby, affording no clue.

"I did not even know she was acquainted with her."

"Perhaps she gambles."

"Even if she did, Maraquito's salon would hardly be the place she would choose for her amusement. Moreover, Maraquito does not receive ladies. She has no love for her own sex."

"What woman has?" murmured Caranby, ironically. Then he added after a pause, "You know that Mrs. Octagon was present when Emilia fell from the plank in the Rexton house?"

"Yes. She gave evidence at the inquest I understand. But Selina did not, if Cuthbert informed me rightly."

"Selina was ill in bed. She could not come. Afterwards she went abroad. I have often wondered," added Caranby, "why Selina didn't seek me out when death broke my engagement to Emilia. She loved me, and her father being dead, there would have been no bar to our marriage. As it was, she threw over her American and dedicated herself to a hermit's life at Rexton."

"You never saw her again?"

"Never. I started to travel, and came to London only at rare intervals. I did write to Selina, asking her to see me, but she always refused, so I became philosophic and took to celibacy also."

"Very strange," murmured Jennings, his thoughts elsewhere, "but this does not explain Mrs. Octagon's visit to the house."

"I am not so sure of that, if you mean Maraquito's house. Mrs. Octagon may know, as I do, that Maraquito is the niece of Emilia."

"Are you sure of that?" asked the detective eagerly.

"As sure as I am that she is no Spaniard, nor even a Spanish Jewess, as she claims to be. She doesn't even know the language. Her name, to fit a woman, should terminate in a feminine manner. She should be called Maraquita, not Maraquito. That little grammatical error doubtless escaped her notice. But as I was saying, Maraquito—we will still call her so—may have sent for Mrs. Octagon."

"Mrs. Octagon, so far as I have seen, is not the woman to obey such a call," said Jennings grimly.

"Maraquito may have compelled her to come."

"For what reason?"

"Well, you see, Emilia was said by Isabella Loach—Mrs. Octagon that is—to have fallen from the plank. But Mrs. Octagon may have pushed her off."

"May have murdered her in fact."

"Quite so. Isabella loved me, and was, and is, a very violent woman. It may be that she pushed Emilia off the plank, and Maraquito, through her dead father, may have learned the truth. This would give her a hold over Mrs. Octagon."

"But Selina may have killed Emilia. That would explain her hermit life, inexplicable in any other way."

"No," said Caranby in a shaking voice, "I am sure the woman I loved would never have behaved in that way. Isabella killed Emilia—if it was a murder—and then threatened to denounce Selina unless she gave up the idea of marrying me. And that," added Caranby, as though struck with a new idea, "may be the cause why Selina never answered my letter, and always refused to see or marry me. She may have been—no, I am sure she was—under the thumb of Isabella. Now that Selina is dead, Isabella is under the thumb of Maraquito."

"This is all theory," said Jennings impatiently.

"We can only theorize in our present state of uncertainty," was the reply of the nobleman. "But my explanation is a reasonable one."

"I do not deny that. But why should Maraquito send for Mrs. Octagon?"

"Why?" echoed Caranby in surprise, "in order to stop the marriage with Cuthbert. Maraquito loves Cuthbert and hates Juliet. I daresay this is the solution of Mrs. Octagon's strange behavior since the death. It is Maraquito who is stopping the marriage by threatening to denounce Mrs. Octagon for the murder of her aunt. Juliet knows this, and hence her reticence."

"It might be so," murmured Jennings, more and more perplexed. "But Miss Saxon won't be reticent with me. I'll see her to-morrow."

"What means will you use to make her speak?"

"I'll tell her that Cuthbert may be arrested for the crime. You know he was about the place on the night of the murder."

"Yes. He went down to look after a possible ghost. But I hope you will not bring Cuthbert into the matter unless it is absolutely necessary. I don't want a scandal."

"Rest easy, Lord Caranby. I have the complete control of this affair, and I'll only use Cuthbert's presence at Rexton to make Miss Saxon speak out. But then, she may not be keeping silence for Cuthbert's sake, as she can't possibly know he was at Rexton on that night. My own opinion is that she is shielding her brother."

"Do you suspect him?" asked Caranby quickly.

"He may not be guilty of the crime, but he knows something about it, I am sure." Here Jennings related how Clancy had said Basil would speak out if pressed too hard. "Now Basil, for some reason, is in difficulties with Hale, who is a scoundrel. But Basil knows something which Hale and Clancy wish to be kept silent. Hale has been using threats to Basil, and the young man has turned restive. Clancy, who is by no means such a fool as he looks, warned Hale to-night. Therefore I take it, that Basil has some information about the murder. Miss Saxon knows he has, and she is shielding him."

"But Clancy, Hale and Mrs. Herne were all out of the house when the woman was stabbed," said Caranby, "they cannot have anything to do with it."

"Quite so, on the face of it. But that bell—" Jennings broke off. "I don't think those three are so innocent as appears. However, Mrs. Herne is coming back to her Hampstead house next week; I'll see her and put questions."

"Which she will not answer," said Caranby drily. "Besides, you should have put them at the inquest."

"The case had not developed so far. I had not so much information as I have now," argued Jennings.

"Did you examine Mrs. Herne at the inquest?"

"No; she gave her evidence." Jennings hesitated. "She also wore a veil when she spoke, and refused to raise it on account of weak eyes. By the way, do you notice that Maraquito uses a strong scent?"

"Yes. Clancy and Hale also use it."

"Ha!" said Jennings, surprised. "I never knew that. Decidedly, I am growing stupid. Well, Mrs. Herne uses that scent also. It is a rare scent."

Then Jennings told what Susan Grant had said. "Now I think there is some significance in this scent which is connected with the association of Clancy, Hale, Maraquito and Mrs. Herne."

"But Mrs. Herne doesn't know Maraquito."

"I am not so sure of that. Susan Grant thinks she may be Maraquito's mother, she is so like her in an elderly way. Did you know this Mrs. Saul?"

"No. I knew the brother who came to speak to me after the death of his sister, and who afterwards was put in jail for coining. His wife I never met. I never even heard of her. But Maraquito takes after her father in looks and he was like Emilia."

"It is a difficult matter to unravel," said Jennings. "I think Mrs. Herne refused to raise her veil at the inquest so that the likeness between her and Maraquito might not be observed. I was there, and if Mrs. Herne is what I say, she would have been put on her guard by Maraquito. Though to be sure," added Jennings in a vexed tone, "Maraquito did not know then, and perhaps does not know now, that I am a detective."

"Clancy and Hale will enlighten her," said Caranby, as the vehicle stopped, "will you not come in?"

"Not to-night. I will do myself the honor of calling on you later, when I have more to say. At present I am going to sort out what evidence I have. To-morrow I'll call on Miss Saxon."

"Call on Mrs. Octagon," were Caranby's parting words, "believe me, she knows the truth, but I'll tell you one thing. Maraquito did not kill Miss Loach, for the death of Selina has given Juliet enough money to marry Cuthbert, independent of Mrs. Octagon's wishes, and Maraquito would never have brought that about."

"Yet all the same Miss Saxon will not marry."

Caranby made a gesture to show that the matter was beyond his comprehension, and ascended the steps of the hotel. Jennings, deep in thought, walked away, wondering how he was to disentangle the skein which Fate had placed in his hand to unravel.

That night the detective surveyed the situation. So far as he could see, he seemed no further advanced than he had been at the inquest. Certainly he had accumulated a mass of evidence, but it threw no light on the case. From Caranby's romance, it seemed that the dead woman had been connected with the Saul family. That seemed to link her with Maraquito, who appeared to be the sole surviving member. In her turn,

Maraquito was connected in some underhand way with Mrs. Octagon, seeing that the elder woman came by stealth to the Soho house. Mrs. Octagon was connected with the late Emilia Saul by a crime, if what Caranby surmised was correct, and her daughter was forbidden to marry Mallow, who was the nephew of the man who had been the lover both of Miss Loach and Emilia Saul. Hale and Clancy were playing some game with Basil Saxon, who was the son of Mrs. Octagon, and he was associated with Maraquito. Thus it would seem that all these people were connected in various ways with the dead woman. But the questions were: Had one of them struck the fatal blow, and if so, who had been daring enough to do so?

"Again," murmured Jennings, "who touched that bell? Not the assassin, who would scarcely have been fool enough to call anyone to examine his work before he had time to escape. Certainly it may have been a woman! Yes! I believe a man killed Miss Loach, for some reason I have yet to learn, and a woman, out of jealousy, wishing to get him into the grip of the law, touched the bell so that witnesses might appear before the assassin could escape. But who struck the blow?"

This was a difficult question. It could not have been Basil Saxon, for he was at the Marlow Theatre on that night with his sister. Cuthbert had no motive, and Jennings quite believed his explanation as to his exploration of the park between the hours of ten and eleven. Hale, Clancy and Mrs. Herne were all out of the house before the blow had been struck, and, moreover, there was no reason why they should murder a harmless old lady. Maraquito confined to her couch could not possibly have anything to do with the crime. Mrs. Octagon did hate her sister, but she certainly would not risk killing her. In fact, Jennings examining into the motives and movements of those mentioned, could find no clue to the right person. He began to believe that the crime had been committed by someone who had not yet appeared—someone whose motive might be found in the past of the dead woman. Say a member of the Saul family.

But Maraquito was the sole surviving member, and on the face of it was innocent. As yet Jennings did not know whether Mrs. Herne was her mother, in spite of the resemblance which Susan claimed to have seen. Also, Caranby said that Maraquito resembled her father, and the features of the Saul family were so strongly marked that it was impossible the elder Saul could have married a woman resembling him.

"Though, to be sure, he might have married a relative," said Jennings, and went to bed more perplexed than ever.

Next day, before calling at the "Shrine of the Muses," he went to Scotland Yard, and there made inquiries about the rumor of false coins being in circulation. These appeared to be numerous and were admirably made. Also from France and Russia and Italy came reports that false money was being scattered about. The chief of the detective staff possessed these coins of all sorts, and Jennings was forced to own that they were admirable imitations. He went away, wondering if this crime could be connected in any way with the circulation of false money. "Maraquito is a member of the Saul family, who appear to have been expert coiners," said Jennings, on his way to Kensington, "and, according to Le Beau, she gave him a false sovereign. I wonder if she keeps up the business, and if Clancy and Hale, together with Mrs. Herne, this supposititious mother, have to do with the matter. That unfinished house would make an admirable factory, and the presence of the ghosts would be accounted for if a gang of coiners was discovered there. But there is a fifteen-feet wall round the house, and the park is a regular jungle. Cuthbert examined the place by day and night and could see nothing suspicious. I wonder if Miss Loach, living near the place, learned that a gang was there. If so, it is quite conceivable that she might have been murdered by one of them. But how the deuce did anyone enter the house? The door certainly opened at half-past ten o'clock, either to let someone in or someone out. But the bell did not sound for half an hour later. Can there be any outlet to that house, and is it connected with the unfinished mansion of Lord Caranby, used as a factory?"

This was all theory, but Jennings could deduce no other explanation from the evidence he had collected. He determined to search the unfinished house, since Caranby had given him permission, and also to make an inspection of Rose Cottage, though how he was to enter on a plausible excuse he did not know. But Fate gave him a chance which he was far from expecting. On arriving at the "Shrine of the Muses" he was informed that Miss Saxon had gone to Rexton. This was natural enough, since she owned the cottage, but Jennings was inclined to suspect Juliet from her refusal to marry Cuthbert or to explain her reason, and saw something suspicious in all she did. He therefore took the underground railway at once to Rexton, and, alighting at the station, went to Crooked Lane through the by-path, which ran through the small wood of pines. On looking at the cottage he saw that the windows were open, that carpets were spread on the lawn, and that the door was ajar. It seemed that Mrs. Pill was indulging in the spring cleaning alluded to by Susan Grant.

At the door Jennings met Mrs. Pill herself, with her arms bare and a large coarse apron protecting her dress. She was dusty and untidy and cross. Nor did her temper grow better when she saw the detective, whom she recognized as having been present at the inquest.

"Whyever 'ave you come 'ere, sir?" asked she. "I'm sure there ain't no more corpses for you to discover."

"I wish to see Miss Saxon. I was told she was here."

"Well, she is," admitted Mrs. Pill, placing her red arms akimbo, "not as I feel bound to tell it, me not being in the witness-box. She 'ave come to see me about my rent. An' you, sir?"

"I wish to speak to Miss Saxon," said Jennings patiently.

Mrs. Pill rubbed her nose and grumbled. "She's up in the attics," said she, "lookin' at some dresses left by pore Miss Loach, and there ain't a room in the 'ouse fit to let you sit down in, by reason of no chairs being about. 'Ave you come to tell me who killed mistress?"

"No! I don't think the assassin will ever be discovered."

"Ah, well. We're all grass," wailed Mrs. Pill; "but if you wish to see Miss Saxon, see her you will. Come this way to the lower room, an' I'll go up to the attics."

"Let me go, too, and it will save Miss Saxon coming down," said Jennings, wishing to take Juliet unawares.

"Ah, now you speaks sense. Legs is legs when stairs are about, whatever you may say," said Mrs. Pill, leading the way, "an' you'll excuse me, Mr. Policeman, if I don't stop, me 'avin' a lot of work to do, as Susan's gone and Geraldine with 'er, not to speak of my 'usbin' that is to be, he havin' gone to see Mrs. Herne, drat her!"

"Why has he gone to see Mrs. Herne?" asked Jennings quickly.

"Arsk me another," said the cook querulously, "he's a secret one is Thomas Barnes, whatever you may say. He comes and he goes and makes money by 'is doin's, whatever they may be. For not a word do I 'ear of 'is pranks. I've a good mind to remain Pill to the end of my days, seein' as he keeps secrets."

Jennings said no more, but secretly wondered why Thomas had gone to visit Mrs. Herne. He determined to call on that lady at once and see if he could learn what message Thomas had taken her and from whom.

But he had not much time for thought as Mrs. Pill opened a door to the right of a narrow passage and pushed him in. "An' now I'll go back to my dustin'," said the cook, hurrying away.

Jennings found himself face to face with Juliet. She was standing on a chair with her hand up on the cornice. As soon as she saw him she came down with rather a white face. The room was filled with trunks and large deal boxes, and some were open, revealing clothes. Dust lay thick on others apparently locked, and untouched for many years. The light filtered into the dusty attic through a dirty window, and the floor was strewn with straw and other rubbish. Miss Saxon did not know the detective and her face resumed its normal color and expression.

"Who are you and what do you want?" she asked, casting a nervous look at the cornice.

Jennings removed his hat. "I beg your pardon," he said politely. "Mrs. Pill showed me up here when I asked to see you."

"She had no right," said Juliet, looking at her dress, which was rather dusty, "come downstairs and tell me who you are."

She appeared anxious to get him out of the room, and walked before him out of the door. As she passed through Jennings contrived to shut it as though her dress had caught the lower part. Then he lightly turned the key. He could hear Juliet fumbling at the lock. "What is the matter?" she called through.

"The lock has got hampered in some way," said Jennings, rattling the key, "one moment, I'll look at it carefully."

As he said this he made one bound to the chair upon which she had been standing and reached his hand to the cornice at which she had looked. Passing his hand rapidly along it came into contact with an object long and sharp. He drew it down. It was a brand-new knife of the sort called bowie. Jennings started on seeing this object, but having no time to think (for he did not wish to rouse her suspicions), he slipped the knife in his vest and ran again to the door. After a lot of ostentatious fumbling he managed to turn the key again and open the door. Juliet was flushed and looked at him angrily. But she cast no second look at the cornice, which showed Jennings that she did not suspect his ruse.

"Your dress caught the door and shut it," he explained, "the lock seems to be out of order."

"I never knew it was," said Juliet, examining it; "it always locked easy enough before."

"Hum," thought Jennings, "so you have been here before and you have kept the door locked on account of the knife probably," but he looked smilingly at the girl all the time.

"I am sorry," he said, when she desisted from her examination.

"It's my fault," said Juliet unsuspiciously, and closed the door. She led the way along the passage and down the stairs. "Who are you?" she asked, turning round half way down.

"I am a friend of Mallow's," said the detective.

"I have never met you?"

"Yet I have been to your house, Miss Saxon. Perhaps my name, Miles Jennings, may—"

The girl started with a cry. "You are a detective!" she gasped.

XIV

Mrs. Octagon Explains

The young girl leaned against the wall, white, and with closed eyes. Alarmed by her appearance, Jennings would have assisted her, but she waved him off and staggered down the stairs. By a powerful effort she managed to subdue her feelings, and when in the hall turned to him with a sickly smile. "I am glad to see you," she said. "Mr. Mallow has often spoken to you of me. You are his friend, I know."

"His best friend, in spite of the difference in our position."

"Oh," Juliet waved that objection aside, "I know you are a gentleman and took up this work merely as a hobby."

"I fear not," smiled Jennings. "To make money."

"Not in a very pleasant way. However, as you are Mr. Mallow's friend, I am glad you have this case in hand," she fixed her eyes on the detective. "Have you discovered anything?" she asked anxiously.

"Nothing much," replied Jennings, who rapidly decided to say nothing about his discovery of the knife. "I fear the truth will never be found out, Miss Saxon. I suppose you have no idea?"

"I," she said, coloring, "what put such a thing into your head? I am absolutely ignorant of the truth. Did you come to ask me about—"

"That amongst other things," interrupted Jennings, seeing Mrs. Pill's bulky figure at the door. "Can we not talk in some quieter place?"

"Come downstairs," said Juliet, moving, "but the rooms are unfurnished as Mrs. Pill is cleaning them. The house is quiet enough."

"So I see," said the detective, following his companion down to the basement, "only yourself and Mrs. Pill."

"And my mother," she answered. "We came here to see about some business connected with the letting of the cottage. My mother is lying down in the old part of the house. Do you wish to see her?"

"No. I wish to see you."

By this time they had entered the sitting-room in which the crime had been committed. The carpets were up, the furniture had been removed, the walls were bare. Jennings could have had no better opportunity of seeking for any secret entrance, the existence of which he suspected by reason of the untimely sounding of the bell. But everything seemed to be in order. The floor was of oak, and there was—strangely enough—no hearth-stone. The French windows opened into the conservatory, now denuded of its flowers, and stepping into this Jennings found that the glass roof was entirely closed, save for a space for ventilation. The assassin could not have entered or escaped in that way, and there was no exit from the room save by the door.

"Would you like to see the bedroom?" asked Juliet sarcastically. "I see you are examining the place, though I should have thought you would have done so before."

"I did at the time," replied Jennings calmly, "but the place was then full of furniture and the carpets were down. Let me see the bedroom by all means."

Juliet led the way into the next room, which was also bare. There was one window hermetically sealed and with iron shutters. This looked out on to a kind of well, and light was reflected from above by means of a sheet of silvered tin. No one could have got out by the window, and even then, it would have been difficult to have climbed up the well which led to the surface of the ground. The floor and walls had no marks of entrances, and Jennings returned to the sitting-room completely baffled. Then Juliet spoke again. "I cannot help wondering what you expect to find," she observed.

"I thought there might be a secret entrance," said Jennings, looking at her keenly, "but there seems to be none."

Miss Saxon appeared genuinely astonished and looked round. "I never heard of such a thing," she said, puzzled. "And what would a quiet old lady like my aunt need with a secret entrance?"

"Well, you see, the assassin could not have sounded that bell and have escaped by the front door. Had he done so, he would have met Susan Grant answering the call. Therefore, he must have escaped in some other way. The windows of both rooms are out of the question."

"Yes. But I understood that the assassin escaped at half-past ten."

"According to the evidence it looks like that. But who then sounded the bell?"

Juliet shook her head. "I can't say," she said with a sigh. "The whole case is a mystery to me."

"You don't know who killed Miss Loach? Please do not look so indignant, Miss Saxon. I am only doing my duty."

The girl forced a smile. "I really do not know, nor can I think what motive the assassin can have had. He must have had some reason, you know, Mr. Jennings."

"You say 'he.' Was the assassin then a man?"

"I suppose so. At the inquest the doctor said that no woman could have struck such a blow. But I am really ignorant of all, save what appeared in the papers. I am the worst person in the world to apply to for information, sir."

"Perhaps you are, so far as the crime is concerned. But there is one question I should like to ask you. An impertinent one."

"What is it?" demanded the girl, visibly nervous.

"Why do you refuse to marry Mallow?"

"That is very impertinent," said Juliet, controlling herself; "so much so that I refuse to reply."

"As a gentleman, I take that answer," said Jennings mildly, "but as a detective I ask again for your reason."

"I fail to see what my private affairs have to do with the law."

Jennings smiled at this answer and thought of the knife which he had found. A less cautious man would have produced it at once and have insisted on an explanation. But Jennings wished to learn to whom the knife belonged before he ventured. He was sure that it was not the property of Juliet, who had no need for such a dangerous article, and he was equally sure that as she was shielding someone, she would acknowledge that she had bought the weapon. He was treading on egg-shells, and it behooved him to be cautious. "Very good," he said at length, "we will pass that question for the present, though as Mallow's friend I am sorry. Will you tell me to whom you gave the photograph of Mallow which he presented to you?"

"How do you know about that?" asked Miss Saxon quickly. "And why do you ask?"

"Because I have seen the photograph."

"That is impossible," she answered coldly; "unless you were in this house before the death of my aunt."

"Ah! then it was to Miss Loach you gave it," said Jennings, wondering how Maraquito had become possessed of it.

"It was; though I do not recognize your right to ask such a question, Mr. Jennings. My late aunt was very devoted to Mr. Mallow and anxious that our marriage should take place. He gave me the photograph—"

"With an inscription," put in the detective.

"Certainly," she rejoined, flushing, "with an inscription intended for me alone. I was unwilling to part with the photograph, but my aunt begged so eagerly for it that I could not refuse it."

"How did she see it in the first instance?"

"I brought it to show her after Mr. Mallow gave it to me. May I ask where you saw it?"

Jennings looked at her with marked significance. "I saw it in the house of a woman called Maraquito."

"And how did it get there?"

"I can't tell you. Do you know this woman?"

"I don't even know her name. Who is she?"

"Her real name is Senora Gredos and she claims to be a Spanish Jewess. She keeps a kind of gambling salon. To be plain with you, Miss Saxon, I really did not see the photograph in her house. But a girl called Susan Grant—"

"I know. My late aunt's parlor-maid."

"Well, the photograph was in her box. I found it when the servants insisted on their boxes being searched. She confessed that she had taken it from her last mistress, who was Senora Gredos. As you gave it to Miss Loach, I should be glad to know how it came into the possession of this woman."

"I really can't tell you, no more than I can say why Susan took it. What was her reason?"

"Mr. Mallow is a handsome man—" began Jennings, when she stopped him with a gesture.

"Do you mean to say—no, I'll never believe it."

"I was not going to say anything against Mallow's character. But this foolish girl cherished a foolish infatuation for Mallow. She saw him at Senora Gredos' house—"

"Ah!" said Juliet, turning pale. "I remember now. Basil mentioned that Cuthbert gambled, but he did not say where."

"Mallow gambled a little at Maraquito's, as did your brother. The only difference is that Mallow could afford to lose and your brother could not. Are you sure you never heard the name of Maraquito?"

"Quite sure," said Juliet, meeting his gaze so calmly that he saw she was speaking the truth. "Well, I understand how you got the photograph, but how did this woman get it? I never heard my aunt mention her, either as Maraquito or as Senora Gredos."

"Was your aunt open with you?"

"Perfectly open. She had nothing in her life to conceal."

"I am not so sure of that," murmured the detective. "Well, I cannot say how Maraquito became possessed of this photograph."

Juliet shrugged her shoulders. "In that case we may dismiss the matter," she said, wiping her dry lips; "and I can't see what the photograph has to do with this crime."

"I can't see it myself, but one never knows."

"Do you accuse Mr. Mallow?"

"Supposing I did. I know Mr. Mallow was near this place on the night of the murder and about the hour."

Juliet leaned against the wall and turned away her face. "It is not true. What should bring him there?"

"He had business connected with the unfinished house at the back owned by Lord Caranby. But I don't suppose anyone saw him."

"How do you know he was here then?" asked Juliet, gray and agitated.

"He confessed to me that he had been here. But we can talk of that later—"

Juliet interposed. "One moment," she cried, "do you accuse him?"

"As yet I accuse no one. I must get more facts together. By the way, Miss Saxon, will you tell the where you were on that night?"

"Certainly," she replied in a muffled voice, "at the Marlow Theatre with my brother Basil."

"Quite so. But I don't think the play was to your liking."

"What do you mean by that?"

"Well," said Jennings slowly, and watching the changing color of her face, "in your house you do not favor melodrama. I wonder you went to see this one at the Marlow Theatre."

"The writer is a friend of ours," said Juliet defiantly.

"In that case, you might have paid him the compliment of remaining till the fall of the curtain."

Juliet trembled violently and clung to the wall. "Go on," she said faintly.

"You had a box, as I learned from the business manager. But shortly after eight your brother left the theatre: you departed after nine."

"I went to see an old friend in the neighborhood," stammered Juliet.

"Ah, and was that neighborhood this one, by any chance? In a hansom—which I believe you drove away in—one can reach this place from the Marlow Theatre in a quarter of an hour."

"I—I—did not come here."

"Then where did you go?"

"I decline to say."

"Where did your brother go?"

"He did not tell me. Did the manager inform you of anything else?"

"He merely told me that you and your brother left the theatre as I stated. You decline to reveal your movements."

"I do," said Juliet, clenching her hands and looking pale but defiant. "My private business can have nothing to do with you. As you seek to connect me with this case, it is your business to prove what you say. I refuse to speak."

"Will your brother refuse?"

"You had better ask him," said Miss Saxon carelessly, but with an effort to appear light-hearted. "I don't inquire into my brother's doings, Mr. Jennings."

"Yet you heard about his gambling."

"I don't see what that has to do with the matter in hand. Do you accuse me and Basil of having killed my aunt?"

"I accuse no one, as yet," said Jennings, chagrined at her reticence, "I said that before. Did you not speak with your aunt on that night?"

"No," said Juliet positively. "I certainly did not."

Jennings changed his tactics, and became apparently friendly. "Well, Miss Saxon, I won't bother you any more. I am sure you have told me all you know." Juliet winced. "Have you any idea if the weapon with which the crime was committed has been discovered?"

"That is a strange question for a detective to ask."

"A very necessary one. Well?"

"I know nothing about it," she said in an almost inaudible voice.

"Do you know Mrs. Herne?"

"I have met her once or twice here."

"Did you like her?"

"I can hardly say. I did not take much notice of her. She appeared to be agreeable, but she was over-dressed and used a perfume which I disliked."

"Had you ever met anyone using such a perfume before?"

"No. It was strong and heavy. Quite a new scent to me. The odor gave me a headache!"

"Was Mrs. Herne a great friend of your aunt's?"

"I believe so. She came here with Mr. Hale and Mr. Clancy to play."

"Hale," said Jennings, "I forgot Hale. Does he still retain your business, Miss Saxon?"

"No. I have given over the management of my property to our own lawyer. Mr. Hale was quite willing."

"Does your brother Basil still make a friend of Mr. Hale?"

"I don't know," said Juliet, changing color again. "I do not ask about Basil's doings. I said that before. Hark," she added, anxious to put an end to the conversation, "my mother is coming."

"I should like to see Mrs. Octagon," said Jennings.

"She will be here in a few minutes. I shall tell her," and Juliet, without a look, left the room, evidently glad to get away.

Jennings frowned and took out the knife at which he looked. "She knows a good deal about this affair," he murmured. "Who is she shielding? I suspect her brother. Otherwise she would not have hidden the knife. I wonder to whom it belongs. Here are three notches cut in the handle—there is a stain on the blade—blood, I suppose."

He got no further in his soliloquy, for Mrs. Octagon swept into the room in her most impressive manner. She was calm and cool, and her face wore a smile as she advanced to the detective. "My dear Mr. Jennings," she said, shaking him warmly by the hand, "I am so glad to see you, though I really ought to be angry, seeing you came to my house so often and never told me what you did."

"You mightn't have welcomed me had you known," said he dryly.

"I am above such vulgar prejudices," said Mrs. Octagon, waving her hand airily, "and I am sure your profession is an arduous one. When Juliet told me that you were looking into this tragic death of my poor sister I was delighted. So consoling to have to do with a gentleman in an unpleasant matter like this. Why have you come?"

This last question was put sharply, and Mrs. Octagon fastened her big black eyes on the calm face of the detective. "Just to have a look at the house," he said readily, for he was certain Juliet would not report their conversation to her mother.

Mrs. Octagon shrugged her shoulders. "A very nice little house, though rather commonplace in its decoration; but my poor sister never did have much taste. Have you discovered anything likely to lead to the discovery of her assassin?"

"I am ashamed to say I am quite in the dark," replied Jennings. "I don't suppose the truth will ever be discovered."

The woman appeared relieved, but tried to assume a sad expression. "Oh, how very dreadful," she said, "she will lie in her untimely grave, unavenged. Alas! Alas!"

But Jennings was not mystified by her tragic airs.

He was certain she knew something and feared lest it should come to his knowledge. Therefore he resolved to startle her by a blunt question. "I never knew you were acquainted with Maraquito!"

Mrs. Octagon was not at all taken aback. "I don't know such creatures as a rule," she said calmly. "What makes you think I do?"

"I saw you enter her house one night."

"Last night," said Mrs. Octagon coolly. "Yes. Maraquito, or Senora Gredos, or whatever she calls herself, told me you had just gone. I saw her in a little room off the salon where the play went on."

The detective was surprised by this ready admission, and at once became suspicious. It would seem that Mrs. Octagon, expecting such a question, was uncommonly ready to answer it. "May I ask why you went to see this woman?" he demanded.

An innocent woman would have resented this question, but Mrs. Octagon ostentatiously seized the opportunity to clear herself, and thereby increased Jennings' suspicions. "Certainly," she said in an open manner and with a rather theatrical air, "I went to beg my son's life from this fair siren."

"What on earth do you mean?"

"Basil," said Mrs. Octagon, in her deep, rich voice, "is too fond of this fair stranger—Spanish, is she not?"

"She says she is," said the cautious Jennings.

Mrs. Octagon shot a glance of suspicion at him, but at once resumed her engaging manner. "The foolish boy loves her," she went on, clasping her hands and becoming poetical, "his heart is captured by her starry eyes and he would wed her for her loveliness. But I can't have that sort of thing," she added, becoming prosaic, "so I went and told her I would denounce her gambling salon to the police if she did not surrender my son. She has done so, and I am happy. Ah, Mr. Jennings, had you a mother's heart," she laid her hand on her own, "you would know to what lengths it will lead a woman!"

"I am glad your son is safe," said Jennings, with apparent cordiality, though he wondered how much of this was true. "Maraquito is not a good wife for him. Besides, she is a cripple."

"Yes," said Mrs. Octagon tragically, "she is a cripple."

Something in the tone of her voice made Jennings look up and created a new suspicion in his heart. However, he said no more, having learned as much as was possible from this tricky woman. "I must go now," he said, "I have examined the house."

Mrs. Octagon led the way upstairs. "And have you any clue?"

"None! None! I wish you could assist me."

"I?" she exclaimed indignantly, "no, my sister and I were not friends, and I will have nothing to do with the matter. Good-day," and Mrs. Octagon sailed away, after ushering the detective out of the door.

Jennings departed, wondering at this change of front. As he passed through the gate a fair, stupid-looking man entered. He nodded to Jennings, touching his hat, and at the same time a strong perfume saluted the detective's nostrils. "Thomas Barnes uses Hikui also," murmured Jennings, walking away. "Humph! Is he a member of the gang?"

XV

A Dangerous Admission

Jennings had once witnessed a drama by Victorien Sardou, entitled—in the English version—Diplomacy. Therein a woman was unmasked by means of a scent. It seemed to him that perfume also played a part in this case. Why should Clancy, Mrs. Herne, Hale, Maraquito and Thomas use a special odor? "I wonder if they meet in the dark?" thought the detective, "and recognize each other by the scent. It seems very improbable, yet I can't see why they use it otherwise. That women should use perfumes, even the same perfume, is right enough. They love that sort of thing, but why should men do so, especially a man in the position of Thomas? I'll follow up this clue, if clue it is!"

The conversation with Juliet convinced Jennings that she knew of something connected with the matter, but was determined to hold her tongue. The fact that this knife was in her possession showed that she was aware of some fact likely to lead to the detection of the assassin. She might have found it when she came after the death to Rose Cottage, but in that case, had she nothing to conceal, she would have shown it to the police. Instead of this, she hid it in the attic. Jennings congratulated himself on his dexterity in securing this piece of evidence. There was no doubt in his mind that this was the very knife with which Miss Loach had been stabbed.

"And by a man," thought Jennings. "No woman would have such a weapon in her possession; and if she bought one to accomplish a crime, she would purchase a stiletto or a pistol. It would take a considerable exercise of muscle to drive this heavy knife home."

Jennings considered that the only person who could make Juliet speak was Cuthbert. It was true that she already had declined to make a confidant of him, but now, when there was a chance of his being arrested—as Jennings had hinted—she might be inclined to confess all, especially if it was Cuthbert she was shielding. But the detective fancied her brother might be the culprit. On the night of the murder, both had left the Marlow Theatre, which was near Rexton, and Juliet declined to say where they went. It might be that both had been on the spot about the time of the commission of the crime. Again, unless

Miss Loach had admitted her assailant, he must have had a latch-key to let himself in. From the fact that the poor woman had been found with the cards on her lap in the same position in which Susan had left her, Jennings was inclined to think that the assassin had struck the blow at once, and then had left the house at the half hour. But how had he entered? There did not appear to be any secret entrance, and no one could enter by the windows; nor by the door either without a latch-key. The further Jennings examined into the matter, the more he was puzzled. Never had he undertaken so difficult a case. But the very difficulty made him the more resolute to unravel the mystery.

For two or three days he went about, asking for information concerning the coining, and reading up details in old newspapers about the exploits of the Saul family. Also, he went occasionally to the salon of Senora Gredos. There he constantly met Hale and Clancy. Also Basil came at times. That young man now adopted a somewhat insolent demeanor towards the pair, which showed that he was now out of their clutches and no longer had cause to fear them. Jennings felt sure that Basil could explain much, and he half determined to get a warrant out for his arrest in the hope that fear might make him confess. But, unfortunately, he had not sufficient information to procure such a thing, and was obliged to content himself with keeping a watch on young Saxon. But the man sent to spy reported nothing suspicious about Basil's doings.

In this perplexity of mind Jennings thought he would see Cuthbert and relate what he had discovered. Also he hoped that Mallow might interview Juliet and learn the truth from her. But an inquiry at Mallow's rooms showed that he had gone out of town for a few days with his uncle, and would not be back for another two. Pending this return, Jennings sorted his evidence.

Then he was surprised to receive a letter from Mrs. Herne, stating that she had returned to her place at Hampstead, and asking him to call. "I understand from Mr. Clancy," wrote Mrs. Herne, "that you wish to see me in connection with the death of my poor friend. I shall be at home to-morrow at four." Then followed the signature, and Jennings put away the note with a rather disappointed feeling. If he was right in suspecting Mrs. Herne, she certainly felt little fear, else she would have declined to see him. After all, his supposition that the two women and the four men formed a gang of coiners, who worked in the unfinished house, might turn out to be wrong. "But I'll see Mrs. Herne and have a long talk with her," said Jennings to himself. "And then I'll show the knife to Cuthbert Mallow. Also I may examine the unfinished house. If coiners have been there, or are there, I'll soon find out. Mallow hunting for ghosts, probably, made only a cursory examination. And I'll take Drudge to Hampstead with me."

Drudge was a detective who adored Jennings and thought him the very greatest man in England. He was usually employed in watching those whom his superior suspected, and Jennings could always rely on his orders being honestly executed. In this instance Drudge was to wait some distance from the house of Mrs. Herne until Jennings came out again. Then on the conversation which had taken place would depend further orders. The man was silent and lean, with a pair of sad eyes. He followed Jennings like a dog and never spoke unless he was required to answer a question.

Mrs. Herne did not possess a house of her own, which struck the detective as strange, considering she appeared to be a wealthy woman. She always wore costly dresses and much jewellery, yet she was content with two rooms, one to sit in and the other to sleep in. Certainly the sitting-room (which was all Jennings saw) was well furnished, and she apparently thoroughly appreciated the luxuries of life. There was a bow-window which commanded a fine prospect of the Heath, and here Mrs. Herne was seated. The blinds were half-way down, so that the brilliant sunlight could not penetrate into the somewhat dusky room. When the detective entered Mrs. Herne excused the semi-darkness. "But my eyes are somewhat weak," she said, motioning him to a seat. "However, if you wish for more light—" she laid her hand on the blind-cord.

"Not on my account," said Jennings, who did not wish to appear unduly suspicious. "I am quite satisfied."

"Very well, then," replied Mrs. Herne, resuming her seat and crossing her delicate hands on her lap. "We can talk. I am at your orders."

She was arrayed in a blue silk dress of a somewhat vivid hue, but softened with black lace. She had a brooch of diamonds at her throat, a diamond necklace round it, bracelets set with the same gems and many costly rings. Such a mass of jewelry looked rather out of place in the daylight, but the twilight of the room made the glitter less pronounced. Jennings thought that Mrs. Herne must have Jewish blood in her veins, seeing she was so fond of gems. Certainly she was very like Maraquito, even to having eyebrows almost meeting over her thin high nose. But these, as was her hair, were gray, and her skin lacked the rich coloring of the younger woman. Jennings rapidly took in the resemblance, and commenced the conversation, more convinced than ever that there was some bond of blood between Mrs. Herne and Senora Gredos. This belief helped him not a little.

"I daresay Mr. Clancy told you why I wished to see you?"

Mrs. Herne nodded in a stately way. "Yes. You wish to know if I was in the bedroom of my friend on that evening. Well, I was. I went in for a few minutes to take off my cloak and hat, and then I went in again to resume them."

"Did you see anyone in the room?"

"No. Had there been anyone I should certainly have seen the person. But there is no place where anyone could hide."

"Not even a cupboard?"

"There was a wardrobe, for Miss Loach disliked cupboards, as she thought clothes did not get sufficiently aired in them. A wardrobe, and of course anyone might have hid under the bed, but I did not look. And I don't think," added Mrs. Herne, examining her rings, "that anyone was about. Miss Loach was always very suspicious, and searched the house regularly."

"Did she, then, anticipate anyone hiding—a burglar, for instance?"

"Yes, I think she did. Her nature was warped from certain events which happened in her early life, and she suspected everyone."

"Was she on bad terms with anyone?"

"No. She never quarrelled. I am the quarrelsome person," said the lady, smiling. "I quarrelled with Mr. Clancy, who is a rude man. But we have made it up since, as he has apologized. It was Mr. Clancy who told me of your wish to see me. Do you want to ask anything else?"

"If you do not mind."

"On the contrary, I am anxious to afford you all the information in my power. Nothing would give me more satisfaction than to see the murderer of my dear friend brought to justice."

She spoke with great feeling, and there was an unmistakable ring of truth about her speech. Jennings began to think he must be wrong in suspecting her to have anything to do with the death. All the same, he was on his guard. It would not do to let Mrs. Herne, clever as she was, pull wool over his eyes. "Have you any idea who killed Miss Loach?" he asked.

"No. She was quite well on that evening, and did not anticipate death in any way—least of all in a violent form. Mr. Hale, Mr. Clancy and myself would have been with her till nearly midnight had I not quarrelled with Mr. Clancy. As it was, Mr. Hale escorted me home about half-past nine, and I understand Mr. Clancy left about ten. When Miss Loach was not playing whist or bridge she never cared about having anyone in her house. She was rather a misanthrope."

"Did she expect anyone that evening?"

"No. At all events, she said nothing about expecting anyone."

"Did she expect her nephew?"

"Mr. Basil Saxon?" said Mrs. Herne, looking surprised. "Not that I am aware of. She did not mention his name. To be sure, they were on bad terms, and she had forbidden him the house. No, I do not think she expected him."

"Do you know the cause of the quarrel?"

"It had something to do with money. I believe Miss Loach helped Mr. Saxon, who was rather extravagant, but she grew weary of his demands and refused to help him further. He lost his temper and said things which forced her to order him out of the house."

"Did he utter any threats?"

"Miss Loach never said that he did. Mr. Jennings," remarked the old lady, bending her brows, "is it possible you suspect that young man?"

"No. I suspect no one at present. But I am bound to make inquiries in every direction, and of course, if Mr. Saxon is of a passionate temper, he might wish to avenge himself for being forbidden the house."

"He has a temper," said Mrs. Herne, thoughtfully, "but I never saw it exhibited, though I met him once at Miss Loach's. She said he had a lot of bad blood in him, but that may have been because she hated her sister, Isabella Octagon."

"Did she hate her?"

"Yes. And I think she had cause. Mrs. Octagon behaved very badly in connection with some romantic episode of the past."

"I fancy I know about that," said Jennings quickly, then added, "You are fond of perfumes?"

"What a strange question," laughed Mrs. Herne. "Yes, I am. Do you like this scent. It is called Hikui, and was given to me by a dear friend who received it from a Japanese attache."

"From a friend or relative?"

Mrs. Herne frowned. "What do you mean by that?"

Jennings shrugged his shoulders. "Oh, nothing. Only you are very like a lady called Senora Gredos."

"Maraquito," said Mrs. Herne unexpectedly. "Of course I am. Her father was my brother."

"You are then her aunt?"

"Naturally. But the fact is, I do not proclaim the relationship, as I do not approve of Maraquito's gambling. Of course the poor thing is confined to her couch and must have something to amuse her. All the same, gambling on a large scale is against my principles. But, if asked, I do not disown the relationship. Now you understand why I am like Maraquito."

"I understand," hesitated Jennings, "you belong to a Spanish family?"

"Spanish Jews. I am a Jewess, so is Maraquito."

"Do you speak Spanish?"

"Yes. Do you wish to speak it with me?"

"Unfortunately I do not know the language," said Jennings, profoundly regretting the fact. "And your niece?"

"She does not speak it. She was brought up in England."

"In that case she should ask you if her name is masculine or feminine, Mrs. Herne?"

The old lady started. "I should like to know what you mean?"

"Senora Gredos' Christian name should be Maraquita, not Maraquito!"

"Really. I never gave the matter a thought. I will tell her about it if you like. I said she did not speak Spanish! She has led a strange life. At one time she wished to dance and took the name of Celestine Durand. She was taught by a professor of dancing called Le Beau, who lives in Pimlico, but while learning she slipped in the street and became the wreck you see her."

Certainly Mrs. Herne was very frank, and spoke the truth, as all this bore out the statements of Le Beau and Lord Caranby. "Her maiden name was Saul, I believe," said Jennings, thinking Mrs. Herne would deny this promptly.

To his astonishment she did nothing of the sort. "My maiden name is Saul," she said gravely. "But as Maraquito is the daughter of my unfortunate brother, her true name is the same—not her maiden name, you understand. I do not know how you learned this, but—"

"Lord Caranby paid a visit to Maraquito's salon and recognized that she was a Saul from her likeness to Emilia, with whom—"

"With whom he was in love," finished Mrs. Herne, crossing her hands; "that painful story is well known to me. Emilia was my sister."

"Lord Caranby never told me she had one," said Jennings.

"Lord Caranby does not know the history of our family."

"Save what appeared in the papers," put in the detective.

Mrs. Herne flushed through her sallow skin. "It is not well bred of you to refer to the misfortunes of my family," she said; "my mother and brother were unlucky. They were innocent of this charge of coining, brought against them by an enemy."

"The evidence was very plain, Mrs. Herne."

"Ah!" she flashed out, "you have been looking up the case. Why?"

"From what Lord Caranby said—"

"He has no right to say anything," cried Mrs. Herne, rising and speaking vehemently; "he loved my sister, and she lost her life at that dreadful house. I was abroad at the time, and had only just married. My husband was a jeweller. We cut ourselves off from the family when the misfortune came. Only of late years did I recognize Maraquito when she came to me for assistance. Her father died and she had no money. I helped her to pay for her dancing—"

"Oh," said Jennings, recalling the false money, "you paid."

"Have you anything to say on that point?" she asked haughtily.

"No! No! I merely congratulate you on your generosity."

"I could not allow my own niece to starve. I helped her, and then she met with the accident. After that—"

"You assisted her to start this gambling-house."

"By no means. Mr. Hale found the money for that. He is in love with Maraquito. But you can understand why I do not proclaim my relationship with her. The past of our family is too painful. I became acquainted with Miss Loach through Mrs. Octagon—she was then the wife of Mr. Saxon—when I went to inquire into my sister's death. I liked Miss Loach and frequently went to see her. Now that she is dead I shall leave England. I have arranged to do so next week, and you will not see me here again. That is why I gave you this chance of making inquiries."

"I am much obliged," said Jennings quite believing her story, since she told it so earnestly: "but does Maraquito love Hale?"

"No. She loves Mr. Mallow, Lord Caranby's nephew."

"She has a rival in Miss Saxon," said the detective.

Mrs. Herne turned red. "My niece fears no rival," she said haughtily. "Miss Saxon shall never be the wife of Mr. Mallow."

Jennings shrugged his shoulders. "I do not see how she can stop the affair."

"Oh yes, she can. The mother is on her side."

"Ah! I thought there was some work of that kind."

"Hear me!" cried Mrs. Herne, imposing silence with a gesture. "Basil Saxon is in love with Maraquito and she can twist the poor fool round her finger. She agrees to send him away if Mrs. Octagon stops this most absurd marriage."

"Which she has done."

"And which she will continue to do," said Mrs. Herne decisively; "the mother does not wish Basil to marry my niece, though she is quite as good as they if not better."

"Well," drawled Jennings, rising, "I now know why Mrs. Octagon has acted in this way. There's no more to be said."

"Are there any further questions you wish to ask me? Remember I go abroad forever next week. You will never see me again."

"I think I have asked you everything. By the why," Jennings balanced his hat between two forefingers, "I suppose your niece's complaint is incurable?"

"She thought so until lately. But she has consulted a specialist, who tells her she will walk again in a few months."

"Then I suppose since she has made money through Hale's gambling-house she will marry him out of gratitude."

"She will marry Mallow," said Mrs. Herne, closing her mouth firmly.

"Lord Caranby may object."

"His objections will be overcome," she replied, with a crafty smile.

"In what way? I am not curious, but—"

"I have my own opinion of that, Mr. Jennings."

"Well, I should like to know how the obstinate objections of a firm old man like Caranby are to be overcome."

"Ah, now you wish to know too much," said Mrs. Herne, laughing and moving towards the center of the room. "I refuse to tell you that. But if you are friendly with Miss Saxon, tell her to give up Mr. Mallow. Otherwise—"

"Otherwise," echoed Jennings, curious to know why she paused.

"She will lose what is dearest to her."

"Humph! I wonder what that can be. Had you not better threaten Miss Saxon personally, Mrs. Herne?"

"I have no need to, Maraquito will do that. With my niece as an enemy, Miss Saxon has no chance of gaining the prize she desires."

"But you reckon without the feelings of Mr. Mallow. He loves—"

"He does not—he does not!" cried Mrs. Herne, pressing one hand to her heart and speaking fiercely; "he loves Maraquito. And is she not worthy to be loved? Is she—go—go." Mrs. Herne waved her hand. "I have told you everything you asked, and more. Should you require further information about Maraquito's love, I refer you to herself."

"Oh, I am not interested enough in the matter to ask her," said the detective, and bowing to the lady who had sunk on the sofa, took his departure. A strange idea occurred to him, suggested by the agitation of Mrs. Herne.

When he met Drudge, who was partaking of a glass of gin, he gave him instructions to watch the Hampstead house and follow Mrs. Herne when she came out. Then having posted his spy—for Drudge was nothing else—Jennings hurried back to town. That same evening he sent a wire to Cuthbert to the address given by the servant, asking him to come up to town next morning.

At eleven Jennings presented himself and found Cuthbert waiting for him, rather surprised and agitated. "Why did you wire me in so peremptory a manner?" asked Mallow; "have you discovered anything?"

"Yes! I am sorry to break your holiday. By the way, you have been at Brighton. Did you stop at the Metropolitan?"

"Yes. I and Uncle Caranby have been there for a few days."

"Did you see Mrs. Herne there?"

"No. Why do you ask?"

"For a reason I'll tell you later." Jennings glanced round the room and his eyes became fixed on a trophy of arms. "You are fond of these sort of things?" he demanded.

"Yes, in a way. Yonder are war-spears, revolvers, swords, and—"

"I see—I see. Here is an empty space. What was here?"

"By Jove, I never noticed that before. I forget!"

"Perhaps this will supply the gap," said Jennings, and held out the knife. "Do you recognize this?"

"Certainly. There are three notches in the handle. It is my knife. Did you take it off the wall?"

XVI

Juliet's Story

Instead of answering, Jennings looked at Mallow. "It was the merest chance I glanced at the wall and saw that one of the arms which form that trophy was missing. It was also a chance that I suggested the blank space might be filled up with this knife. Are you sure it is your property?"

Mallow with a puzzled expression took the weapon in his hand and examined it closely. "It is mine," he admitted, "on the butts of my revolvers you will find I carve these notches. I also did so on this bowie, which I bought in New York when I went on my last big-game shoot to the Rockies. I marked my things in this way so that the other fellows should not use them by mistake. I brought back this knife, and although it is not a pretty ornament, I fixed it up on the wall yonder. I used it to cut up game. But if you did not take it off the wall—and I confess I never missed it until you drew my attention to the fact that it was missing—where did you get it?"

Jennings scarcely knew what to say. Cuthbert talked of the matter in so easy a manner that it was impossible to think he had killed Miss Loach. Also he was not the sort of man to murder an inoffensive old woman, the more especially as he—on the face of it—had no motive to commit so brutal an act, or to jeopardize his neck. Struck by his friend's silence, Mallow looked up suddenly. Whether he read the truth in Jennings' eyes or the recollection of Jennings' profession brought the Crooked Lane crime into his mind, it is impossible to say. But he suddenly grew pale and dropped the knife with a look of abhorrence.

"Yes," said Jennings, in reply to his mute inquiry, "that is the knife that was used to stab Miss Loach."

"This knife?" said Mallow, with a gasp, "but how the dickens," he used a stronger word, "did my knife come to be used in that way?"

"I should like you to explain that," said the detective icily.

"Good heavens, Jennings, you don't think—"

"What am I to think," said Jennings coldly, "I swear I never suspected you, Mallow. To own the truth, I don't suspect you now, but for your own sake—for your own safety, explain how that knife came to be in Miss Loach's house."

"I can't say," cried Cuthbert, vehemently, "really I can't. I swear I never missed it until you drew my attention to the blank left in the trophy of arms yonder." He flung himself into a seat, and passed his hand through his hair with a bewildered air. "Surely, Jennings, you do not think me guilty of killing that poor wretch?"

Jennings stretched out his hand, which Mallow grasped. "There is my answer," said the detective, "of course I don't suspect you. The mere fact that you own the knife is yours shows me that you are innocent. But the fact that this particular weapon was used reveals to me the strange behavior of Miss Saxon—her motive, I mean."

Cuthbert jumped up. "What has Juliet to do with this?" he asked.

"I went to see her," explained Jennings rapidly, "and was shown up to the attic of Rose Cottage by Mrs. Pill. Miss Saxon was standing on a chair with her hand on the cornice. I managed to place my hand in the same place—it matters not how—and there I found that."

"This knife?" Cuthbert, still bewildered, took up the formidable weapon. "But how did she become possessed of it?"

"You must ask her that."

"I? Why did you not ask her yourself?"

"She would have lied to me—for your sake."

"For my sake? Do you mean to say she thinks I am guilty?"

"Yes, I do," said Jennings decisively.

"It's an infernal lie! I don't believe Juliet would think me such a blackguard unless she did not love me—and she does love me."

"Of course," interposed Jennings swiftly, "so much so that she has concealed this knife so as to—as she thinks—save you. Now, can you not see why she asked you to proceed no further in the case for your—own sake. I thought she was shielding her brother. It is you she believes guilty—"

"And therefore will not marry me?"

"No. I don't think for one moment she cares about that. When a woman loves a man she will stick to him through thick and thin. If he is a regular Cain, she will marry him. Bless the whole sex, they are the staunchest of friends when they love. No, Mallow, in some way Mrs. Octagon has learned that you have killed her—"

"But I never did—I never did. I told you everything."

"What you told me may have been told to Mrs. Octagon with

additions. She thinks you guilty, and therefore has threatened to denounce you unless Juliet gives you up. She has done so, therefore Mrs. Octagon holds her bitter tongue."

"But her reason for wishing to break off the marriage."

"We discussed that before. In the first place, you are Caranby's nephew and she hates him. In the second, she and Basil want the fingering of the six thousand a year left by Miss Loach. Should you marry Miss Saxon, they know well you will look after her interests, therefore they don't wish the match to take place. I am not quite sure if this is Basil's plan, or if he knows so much, but I am quite certain that the scheme is of Mrs. Octagon's concoction. But now you can see why Miss Saxon behaved so strangely."

"She has no right to take up such a position," cried Cuthbert, with a fierce look. "She should have been plain with me and have accused me to my face."

"Do you think a woman cares to accuse the man she loves? Besides, Mrs. Octagon may have forced her to keep silence, so as to make the matter more difficult for you. The only way in which you can clear up matters is to see Miss Saxon and insist on an explanation."

"And if she won't give it?"

"I think she will this time," said Jennings with a grim smile. "By now she must have discovered her loss, and she knows well enough that the knife is in my possession. Already she knows that I threatened to arrest you—"

"But you would never do that."

"I would if it meant the clearing of your character. I tell you, Mallow, you are in danger. There is a conspiracy against you, and the using of your knife to kill that old woman proves it. To prepare the ground for an accusation, someone stole it. You must fight, man, or your enemies may bring about your arrest, in spite of all I can do."

Mallow dropped into his seat, flushed and angry.

"I have no enemies," he muttered, trying to collect his wits.

"Yes, you have, and of the worst kind. Two women are against you."

"Two women? Mrs. Octagon, I know, hates me as Caranby's nephew and because she wants to handle this money. But the other?"

"Maraquito Gredos."

"Bosh! She loves me. I am sure she has worried me enough."

"Of course she loves," said Jennings satirically. "She loves you so deeply that she would see you on the scaffold rather than let you marry

Miss Saxon. That is why Mrs. Octagon went the other night to see her. Mrs. Herne gave a different version, but—"

"How do you know Mrs. Octagon went to see Maraquito?"

"Your uncle saw her. Sit down, Mallow." Jennings gently pushed back the astonished man into his seat. "Listen while I tell you all I have discovered lately."

Mallow listened in silence, and saw very truly that Maraquito would stick at nothing to gain her ends. However, he made no remark. "Now," went on Jennings, "it may be that Maraquito hired someone to kill Miss Loach and is trying to put the blame on you so that she may entangle you in her net. It will be either the gallows or marriage with you. Of course she could not kill the woman herself, but her aunt, Mrs. Herne—"

"She was out of the house an hour before the blow was struck."

"Quite so," rejoined Jennings dryly, "but she may have come back again. However, the main point is, that Maraquito in some way is working with Mrs. Octagon on this basis to prevent your marriage. In this way they have impressed Miss Saxon that you are guilty, and they have shown her this knife. This evidence she retained in order to save you and at the price of her marriage."

"It might be so," said Mallow, dazed with this view of the case. "I certainly seem to be in a hole. If I could see Juliet—but her mother prevents me."

"I have a plan to bring you together. I am engaged to a girl called Miss Garthorne. She is the niece of an old dancing master who taught Maraquito—"

"Le Beau?"

"The same. Well, I learn from Peggy—that is Miss Garthorne's name—that she was at school for a few months with Miss Saxon. Peggy, in spite of her poverty, has had a good education, thanks to Le Beau, who loves her like a father. Hence, in spite of the difference in rank, she was brought into contact with Miss Saxon."

"Yes! Yes! I see. But the scheme?"

"Well, Peggy must write to Miss Saxon and ask her to come and see her at the Pimlico Academy. As Miss Saxon was great friends with Peggy, she will come. Then you can talk to her there and learn the truth. Find out who gave her the knife. She will answer, especially if you tell her that, owing to my finding the knife, I am inclined to have you arrested. You understand?"

"Yes," said Cuthbert, a new fire in his eyes, and drawing himself up firmly. "I'll get at the truth somehow, and Juliet will not leave that Academy until I learn it. I have had more than enough of this kind of thing. But how did the knife leave my rooms?"

"Who has called to see you within the last month?"

"Oh, dozens of people."

"Has Mrs. Octagon?"

"No. She never liked me enough to pay me a visit. But Basil—"

"Ha!" cried Jennings, slapping his knee. "I believe Basil may have taken it. He is working with his mother to stop the marriage, and—"

"Stop—stop!" interposed Mallow, coloring, "you are accusing Juliet's mother and brother of being accomplices to a crime. Basil is a fool and Mrs. Octagon is not a nice woman, but I don't think either would kill a woman in cold blood."

Jennings had his own opinion about this. Mrs. Octagon—as was proved by her early history—was capable of doing much, when number one was in question, and Basil was an irresponsible, hysterical fool. In a moment of rage he might have—"But no," said Jennings, breaking off this train of thought. "I can't see the truth. Miss Saxon knows it. You must ask her. Be careful, for your life may depend upon it."

"Bunkum!" said Mallow roughly, "I am not afraid."

"Then you ought to be," said Jennings quickly, "you were down at Rose Cottage on that night and the knife is yours. Certainly you have no motive, but Mrs. Octagon and Maraquito will soon find one, if you don't fall in with their wishes. However, you know what you have to do," and Jennings rose to take his leave, first slipping the knife into his pocket.

"Wait a bit," said Cuthbert, rising. "I'll do what you say. Just drop me a line when the meeting is to be. But I want to tell you—At the Metropolitan Hotel at Brighton I met with my bank manager."

"What of that?"

"He happens to be the manager of the bank where Miss Loach kept her money and where Juliet keeps it now."

"Well," said Jennings, becoming suddenly attentive.

"He didn't tell secrets," went on Mallow, "but we got talking of Basil, and the manager hinted that Basil had had a lucky escape."

"From what?"

"I can't say. The manager—French, his name is—refused to speak more openly, and of course he couldn't. But if Miss Loach had not died,

Basil would have got into trouble. He didn't put the matter exactly in these words, but I gathered as much."

"Humph!" said Jennings, his eyes on the carpet, "that supplies a motive for Basil killing the old woman."

"Nonsense, Basil would not kill anything. He is a coward."

"When a rat is in the corner it fights," said the detective significantly. "Basil may have been between the devil, represented by Miss Loach, and the deep sea, which we may call Hale. He may have—"

"No! No! No!" said Mallow, "nothing will ever persuade me that Basil is guilty."

Jennings looked doubtful. He had his own opinion as to young Saxon's capability for crime. "However, the whole case is so perplexing that I fear to name any particular person," said he, taking his hat. "Now I shall see Miss Garthorne and get her to write to Miss Saxon."

Apparently there was no difficulty about this, for in three days he wrote to Mallow, telling him to come to Pimlico on Friday at four o'clock. Juliet was surprised when she received an invitation from an old schoolfellow of whom she had lost sight for years. However, owing to her troubles, she felt the need of some sympathetic soul in whom she could safely confide, and knowing Peggy was one of those rare friends who could keep her own counsel, Juliet readily agreed to pay the visit. She arrived at the Academy shortly before three o'clock, and the two girls had a long talk of their old days. Also Juliet told some of her difficulties—but not all—to Peggy. "And I don't know how things will turn out," said Miss Saxon disconsolately, "everything seems to be wrong."

"They will continue to be wrong unless you act wisely," said Peggy.

"In what way should I act?"

"Stick to Mr. Mallow. He loves you and you love him. I do not see why you should surrender your life's happiness for the sake of your family. Of course you have not told me all," and Peggy looked at her inquiringly.

Juliet shuddered. "I dare not tell you all," she said faintly. "I have to think of other people."

"Think of Mr. Mallow first."

"I am thinking of him."

"Then it is on his account you keep silence."

Juliet nodded. "I must hold my tongue. If you could advise me—"

"My dear," said clear-headed Miss Garthorne, rather impatiently, "I can't advise unless I know all, and you will not trust me."

"I have to consider others," repeated Juliet obstinately; "if Cuthbert knew what I feel—"

"Why don't you tell him? See here, Juliet, you are keeping something back from me. On my part, I have kept something back from you. But I see it is necessary to speak plainly. Juliet, I am engaged."

"Oh, I am so glad," cried Miss Saxon, embracing her friend. "Is he nice?"

"I think so; but I am not sure if you will be of that opinion."

"Do I know him?" asked Juliet, opening her eyes widely.

"You do. Not very well, perhaps, but you know him."

"What is his name?"

"I'll tell you that after you have seen Mr. Mallow."

Miss Saxon rose with rather an offended look. "I have no intention of seeing Mr. Mallow."

"Supposing he was here, would you consent to an interview?"

"I don't dare—I dare not! If he asked questions!—what do you mean?"

"Nothing," said Peggy briskly. "We have joined issue, as the lawyers say. I advise you to speak out and you refuse."

"I don't understand all this. Is Cuthbert here?"

"Yes. To be plain with you, Juliet, a person I know arranged that I should write to you and that Mr. Mallow should meet you here."

Juliet looked annoyed. "Who is interfering with my private business?"

"Someone who can help you."

"No one can help me," retorted Juliet.

"Oh, yes, and the advice of this person is that you should tell the truth to Mr. Mallow."

"Who is this person?"

"I'll tell you that after you have seen Mr. Mallow. He is in the room below."

"This interfering person you refer to?"

"No, Mr. Mallow. Will you come downstairs and see him?"

Juliet drew back as Peggy opened the door. "I dare not."

"In that case you will have to consent to the arrest of Mr. Mallow."

Juliet shrieked. "Cuthbert arrested! For what?"

"For the murder of Miss Loach."

"It is not true—it is not true," gasped Juliet. "Oh, Peggy, what does it all mean? How do you come to know—?"

"Because I'm engaged to Miles Jennings."

"The detective! The man who behaved so badly to me?"

"I don't know what you call behaving badly," said Miss Garthorne in an offended way. "Miles wishes to help you out of your difficulties, and you will not allow him. No! Don't ask questions. I refuse to answer. Miles told me all about the case and I know everything—"

"Then you know that he came the other day to Rose Cottage and—"

"I know everything," said Peggy, leaving the room; "and if you are wise you will come with me."

When Peggy disappeared, Juliet hesitated. She really could not speak to Cuthbert, and resolved to steal out of the trap into which she had been inveigled by the treacherous Peggy. On the other hand, things were becoming so serious that she knew she would have to speak out sooner or later, especially as Cuthbert was in danger of arrest. But even if she confessed all, could she save him? "I should only make matters worse," thought Juliet, descending the stairs, "he'll thank me some day for holding my tongue. I'll go."

So she arranged, but meantime Peggy had informed the waiting Mallow of Juliet's strange behavior. Determined to make her speak, and anxious to arrive at some understanding, Cuthbert waited at the foot of the stairs. Juliet, coming down, ran straight into his arms, and turned white.

"You!" she gasped, retreating, "you are here after all."

"Did you not hear Miss Garthorne tell you so?" asked Cuthbert.

"Peggy is behaving very wickedly."

"It is you who are behaving badly," said Mallow bluntly, "you know much about this case and you are keeping me in the dark."

"It is for your own good," murmured Juliet.

"You should allow me to be the best judge of that. Come in here," and Cuthbert drew her towards the open door of the dancing-room, "tell me what you know and how it affects me."

The room was large and bare and empty. At one end there was a kind of dais on which was placed a few chairs. The young man walked up to this and turned to beckon Juliet, for whom he placed a chair. She still lingered at the door and seemed disposed to fly.

"Juliet, if you go now, all is over," he said determinedly.

"Cuthbert, how can you?"

"Because I mean what I say. Things can't go on like this. You think of your brother—of your mother. You never give a thought to me."

Juliet came up the room hurriedly. "I am thinking of you all the time, Cuthbert," she said angrily, "I keep silence for your good."

"In what way?"

"This murder—" she began. Then her voice died away, "you know—"

"I know that Miss Loach was murdered, but who did it I don't know."

"Oh," Juliet dropped into a chair, "are you innocent?"

"Surely you never thought me guilty?"

"I—I—don't think you are, and yet—"

"You are going to accuse me of having been on the spot?"

Juliet could restrain herself no longer. "I saw you myself," she burst out; "I was there also."

XVII

JULIET'S STORY CONTINUED

C uthbert was so surprised by this admission that astonishment held him silent for a moment. He never expected to hear that Juliet herself had been on the spot. Seeing this, she went on quickly. "Now you can understand why I held my tongue. You were at Rose Cottage on that night. You have enemies who know you were there. I have been threatened should I insist on our engagement being fulfilled that you will be arrested. Therefore I kept away and held my tongue."

"But if you had told me this long ago—"

"How could I?" she cried vehemently. "Could I come and say to you, I believe you are a murderer?"

"Did you believe that, Juliet?" he asked in a grieved tone.

"Yes and no," she faltered. "Oh, Cuthbert, you know how I love you. I could not bring myself to think you were guilty—and yet the proofs are so strong. You were at Rose Cottage at a quarter to eleven—"

"No. I was there at a quarter past ten."

"I tell you I saw you at a quarter to eleven. You were getting over the wall into the park. Then there was the knife—your knife."

"How did you know it was mine?"

"By the notches. You told me you always cut three notches on the handle of any weapon you possessed. One day when mother and I came to afternoon tea at your place you showed me some of your weapons— the knife amongst them. One knife is much like another, and I would not have noticed but for the notches and for the fact that I saw you on that night. I hid the knife and Mr. Jennings—"

"He found it," said Mallow. "Quite so. He told me he did. When you left the attic he contrived to—"

"Then the closing of the door was a trick," said Juliet in an agitated tone. "I might have guessed that. He took the knife. He has threatened to arrest you, so Miss Garthorne says."

"She says rightly," replied Mallow, thinking it best to make use of all he knew, so as to force her to speak freely. "But of course, if you can explain—"

"Explain!" she cried wildly and sinking into a chair. "What can I explain? That I saw you climbing that wall, running away apparently from the scene of your crime. That I found the knife by the body?"

"What!" Cuthbert started up and looked at her. "You saw the body?"

"Yes. I was in the house—in the room. I found my aunt dead in her chair, with the cards on her lap, exactly as the parlor-maid saw her. Near her on the floor was the knife. There was blood on the blade. I picked it up—I saw the handle was notched in three places, and then—"

"Then you suspected me."

"No. Not till I saw you outside."

Cuthbert took a turn up and down the dais much perplexed. "Juliet," he said. "I swear to you I never killed this woman."

Juliet flew to him and folded him in her arms. "I knew it—I knew it," she said, "in spite of the letter—"

"What letter?"

"That accusing you and threatening to tell the police about you if I did not break the engagement."

"Who wrote it?"

"I can't say, save that it must have been some enemy."

"Naturally," replied Mallow cynically. "A friend does not write in that way. Have you the letter with you."

"No. It is at home. I never thought of bringing it. But I will show it to you soon. I wish now I had spoken before."

"I wish to heaven you had!"

"I thought it best to be silent," said Juliet, trying to argue. "I feared lest if I spoke to you, this enemy, whosoever he is, might carry out the threat in the letter."

"Is the letter written by a man or a woman?"

"I can't say. Women write in so masculine a way nowadays. It might be either. But why were you at the cottage—"

"I was not. I went to explore the unfinished house on behalf of Lord Caranby. I was ghost-hunting. Do you remember how you asked me next day why I wore an overcoat and I explained that I had a cold—"

"Yes. You said you got it from sitting in a hot room."

"I got it from hunting round the unfinished house at Rexton. I did not think it necessary to explain further."

Juliet put her hand to her head. "Oh, how I suffered on that day," she said. "I was watching for you all the afternoon. When you came I thought you might voluntarily explain why you were at Rexton on the previous night. But you did not, and I believed your silence to be a guilty one. Then, when the letter arrived—"

"When did it arrive?"

"A week after the crime was committed."

"Well," said Cuthbert, rather pained, "I can hardly blame you. But if you loved me—"

"I do love you," she said with a passionate cry. "Have I not proved my love by bearing—as I thought—your burden? Could I do more? Would a woman who loves as I do accuse the man she loves of a horrible crime? I strove to shield you from your enemies."

"I thought you were shielding Basil. Jennings thought so also."

Juliet drew back, looking paler than ever. "What do you know of him."

"Very little," said Cuthbert quickly. "Was he at Rose Cottage on the night in question?"

"No. He was not there. I did not see him."

"Yet he was at the Marlow Theatre with you."

"Yes. He left the theatre before I did."

"Sit down, Juliet, and tell me exactly how you came to be at Rose Cottage on that night and why you went."

Miss Saxon seated herself and told all she knew. "It was this way," she said, with more calmness than she had hitherto shown. "Basil and I went to see this new melodrama written by Mr. Arkwright—"

"What? The man Mrs. Octagon wishes you to marry?"

"Yes. He has written a play to make money. My mother was angry, as she thought such a thing was not worthy of him. He sent her a box. She refused to go, so Basil and I went. But the play was so dull that Basil left early, saying he would come back for me."

"Do you know where he went?"

"No. He did not say. Well, the play became worse instead of better. I was weary to death, so I thought as the theatre was near Rexton, that I would go and see Aunt Selina. Then I hoped to return to the box and meet Basil. I was told the play, being a long one, would not be over till midnight. I left the theatre at a quarter past ten. It took fifteen minutes to drive to the cottage. Then I entered quietly to give aunt a surprise."

"Ah! It was you opening the door that Thomas heard."

"Yes! At half-past ten; I had a latch-key. Aunt Selina loved me very much and wanted me to come and see her whenever I could. So that I could come and go at pleasure without troubling the servants, she gave me a latch-key. I happened to have it in my pocket. I really wished to see her about this quarrel she had with Basil."

"What was this quarrel about?"

Juliet deliberated before replying. "It was a small thing," she said at length. "Aunt Selina was fond of Basil and often gave him money. Mr. Octagon doesn't allow Basil much, and mother has enough to do to make both ends meet. Basil is, I fear, extravagant. I know he gambles, though he never told me where he went—"

"To Maraquito's," said Cuthbert. "I have met him there."

"I know," said Juliet in rather a reproachful tone. "I wish you would not gamble, Cuthbert."

"I have given it up now. I only played for the excitement, but since our engagement I have hardly touched a card. I shall not play for money again. My visits to Maraquito's now are purely in the interests of this case."

"Does she know anything about it?" asked Juliet, astonished.

"Yes," replied Mallow, wondering if the girl knew that Mrs. Octagon had paid a visit to Senora Gredos. "Mrs. Herne, who was your aunt's friend, is the aunt of Senora Gredos."

"I never knew that. But about this quarrel. Basil spent more money than he could afford, poor boy—"

"Young scamp," murmured Cuthbert.

"Don't blame him. He means well," expostulated Juliet. "Well, aunt gave him a lot of money, but he always wanted more. Then she refused. About a week before Aunt Selina died, Basil wanted money, and she declined. They had words and she ordered Basil out of the house. It was to try and make it up between them that I called on that night."

"Are you sure Basil did not go also?"

"I don't think so," said Juliet doubtfully. "He was on bad terms with Aunt Selina and knew he would not be welcomed. Besides, he had not a latch-key. Well, Cuthbert, I reached Rose Cottage at half-past ten and let myself in. I went downstairs quietly. I found Aunt Selina seated in her chair near the fire with the cards on her lap, as though she had been playing 'Patience.' I saw that she was dead."

"Why did you not give the alarm?"

Juliet hesitated. "I thought it best not to," she said faintly.

It seemed to Mallow that she was keeping something back. However, she was very frank as it was, so he thought it best not to say anything. "Well, you saw she was dead?"

"Yes. She had been stabbed to the heart. There was a knife on the floor. I picked it up and saw it was yours. Then I thought—"

"That I had killed her. Thank you, Juliet."

"No, no!" she protested. "Really, I did not believe that at the time. I could not think why you should kill Aunt Selina. I was bewildered at the time and then—" here Juliet turned away her head, "I fancied someone else might have killed her."

"Who?"

"Don't ask me. I have no grounds on which to accuse anyone. Let me tell you what I can. Then you may think—but that's impossible. Cuthbert, ask me no more questions."

Mallow thought her demeanor strangely suspicious, and wondered if she was shielding her mother. Mrs. Octagon, who hated Selina Loach, might have struck the blow, but there was absolutely no proof of this. Mallow decided to ask nothing, as Juliet requested. "Tell me what you will, my dear," he said, "so long as you don't believe me guilty."

"I don't—I don't—really I don't. I picked up the knife and left the room after ten minutes. I stole up the stairs and shut the door so quietly that no one heard. You see, the first time I did not trouble to do that, but when I found that aunt was dead I was afraid lest the servants should come and find me there. I fancied, as I had the knife in my hand and had entered by means of the latch-key, that I might be suspected. Besides, it would have been difficult to account for my unexpected presence in the house at that hour."

"I quite comprehend!" said Mallow grimly. "We can't all keep our heads in these difficult situations. Well?"

"I came out into the garden. I heard the policeman coming down the lane, and knew I could not escape unobserved that way. Then if I took the path to the station I fancied he might see me in the moonlight. I ran across the garden by the wall and got over the fence amongst the corn, where I lay concealed. Then I saw you coming round the corner. You climbed the wall and went into the park. After that I waited till after eleven, when the policeman entered the house, summoned by the servants. I then ran round the field, sheltered from observation by the corn, which, as you know, was then high, and I got out at the further side. I walked to Keighley, the next place to Rexton, and took a cab home. I went straight to bed, and did not see Basil till the next morning. He told me he had come home later, but he did not say where he had been, nor did I ask him."

"But I am sure—unless my watch was wrong, that I climbed the wall at a quarter past ten," insisted Mallow.

"You might have climbed it again at a quarter to eleven."

"No! I climbed it only once. Which way did I come?"

"Along the path from the station. Then you walked beside the fence on the corn side, and jumping over, you climbed the wall."

"Certainly I did that," murmured Mallow, remembering what he had told Jennings. "Did you see my face?"

"No! But I knew you by your height and by the light overcoat you wore. That long, sporting overcoat which is down to your heels. Oh, Cuthbert, what is the matter?"

She might well ask this question, for Mallow had started and turned pale. "Nothing! nothing," he said irritably. "I certainly did wear such an overcoat. I was with Caranby before I went to Rexton, and knowing his room would be heated like a furnace, I took every precaution against cold."

Juliet doubted this, as she knew Mallow did not coddle himself in any way. However, she had seen the overcoat too often to mistake to whom it belonged. Moreover, Cuthbert did not deny that he had jumped the wall in the way she explained. "Well, now you know all, what will you do?" she asked.

"I really can't say," said Mallow, who was trying to conceal his agitation. "I can't think who took the knife out of my room. It was in a trophy of arms on the wall, and I never noticed that it was missing, till Jennings drew my attention to the loss. Certainly Miss Loach was killed with that knife."

"I am positive of that," said Juliet. "There is blood on the handle. But you understand why I kept silence?"

"Yes. But there was really no need. I shall call and see your mother and insist on her giving her consent to our marriage. She has no reason to refuse. Do you know why she objects?"

"No. She simply says she does not wish me to marry you."

"Did you not tell her what you have told me?"

"I did not. What was the use? It was because of my discovery of the knife and seeing you, and receiving that letter, that I refused to marry, and so fell in with my mother's plans."

"Juliet, you are not engaged to Arkwright?"

"No. I am engaged to you and you only. I mean I only pretended that I would not marry you. My mother thought I was obeying her, but I was really shielding you on account of that letter."

"Give me the letter, love, and I'll show it to Jennings."

"No," said Miss Saxon, shrinking back; "get him to drop the case."

"Why?" asked Cuthbert dryly. "I could understand that request when you thought me guilty, but now that you know I am innocent, and that Jennings is aware I was at Rose Cottage on that night, surely there is no bar to his proceeding with the case."

"I do not wish it," faltered Juliet.

Cuthbert looked at her steadily and turned away with a sigh. "You are keeping something from me," he said.

"And you from me," she retorted. "Why did you start when I spoke of the overcoat?"

"Juliet, my own," Cuthbert took her hands earnestly, "there are circumstances in this case which are very strange. Innocent persons may be sacrificed. It is best for you and me to have nothing more to do with the matter. Miss Loach is dead. Who killed her will never be known. Let us marry, dear heart, and leave the case alone."

"I am quite willing. But my mother?"

"I shall persuade her to consent."

"I hope so; but I fear she hates you because you are Lord Caranby's nephew. She hinted as much. I don't know the reason."

"I do," said Mallow calmly, "and I think I may be able to persuade her to see reason. I shall meddle no more with the case."

"What about Mr. Jennings?"

"I will tell him what I have told you, and what you have told me. Then I will point out the futility of looking for a needle in a haystack. He may be inclined to let the case drop. He ought to be weary of it by this time."

Juliet looked wistfully at him. "Can't we be plain with one another?"

"No," said Mallow, shaking his head, "you have your suspicions and I mine. Let us refrain from talking about the matter."

Miss Saxon drew a breath of relief. "I think that is best," she said, and her expression was reflected in the eyes of her lover. "When will you come and see mother?"

"Next week. If her objection is a question of money, you can hand over the whole of that income you have inherited."

"Aunt Selina's six thousand a year! Why?"

"Because I have enough money for us both, and when Caranby dies I shall be almost a millionaire. I don't like you having this money."

"But your reason?"

"I have none that I can tell you. Besides, if we can buy Mrs. Octagon's consent with even six thousand a year—"

"I do not mind," said Juliet. "But now that I know you are really innocent, and I take shame to myself for having doubted you, I am willing to marry you, even though my mother withholds her consent."

"My darling!" Cuthbert folded the girl in his arms and kissed her. "I now know that you truly love me. Indeed, I never doubted you."

"But I doubted myself," said Juliet tearfully. "I should never have suspected you, even though the evidence was so strong."

"You lost your head for the moment," said her lover, "but don't let us talk any more about the matter. I shall pacify Jennings and get him to drop the case. Then we will marry and take a tour round the world so as to forget these unpleasant matters."

"Yes, that is best," said Juliet, and the two walked towards the door.

They should have been completely happy now that all misunderstandings were cleared up, but each wore a gloomy expression. Apparently the shadow of Miss Loach's death still clouded the sunshine of their lives.

XVIII

THE UNEXPECTED HAPPENS

Jennings was at breakfast in his rooms, considering what he should do next in connection with the case. As yet he had not heard from Cuthbert with regard to the interview with Juliet. The detective waited upstairs in Le Beau's sitting-room for the conclusion of the meeting, but when Mallow never appeared he went down. Then he learned from Peggy, who was in the office, that the lovers had been gone for some time "I thought you knew," said Miss Garthorne.

"No," replied Jennings, "I did not know," and then, since he had no further reason to remain, he took his departure also, wondering why Mallow had not come to report the matter.

That same evening he sought out Mallow, but was unable to find him at his accustomed haunts. More perplexed than ever, Jennings, leaving a note at Mallow's rooms, had returned to his own. He could make no new move until he heard from Mallow, and the young man did not appear inclined to give any assistance. Next morning, while at breakfast, he expected his friend, but still there was no appearance of the visitor. A ring came to the door and Jennings thought that this was Cuthbert at last. He was distinctly disappointed when Drudge made his appearance.

"Well," said Jennings sharply, "what is it?"

"I followed the lady you saw, sir."

"Mrs. Herne? Yes."

"She left her house in Hampstead and walked down the hill. There she took a cab. I followed in another. Her cab stopped at the house of Maraquito in Soho. Since then I have been watching the house, but I have not seen Mrs. Herne again."

"She is Senora Gredos' aunt," explained Jennings, "so I expect she is stopping with her."

"No, sir, she isn't. I made friends with a boy called Gibber—"

"Yes. He is a page in the house. Well?"

"I gave him a drink or two," said Drudge, "and a few stamps, as he is a collector. He become friendly with me, and I asked him about the house. He was very frank, but he said nothing about the gambling."

"Humph! I expect he has been told to hold his tongue. Well, did you hear anything at all?"

"I heard that Gibber had never seen Mrs. Herne. He did not even know her name. Now, sir," went on Drudge, laying a finger in the palm of his hand, "if Mrs. Herne was stopping at the Soho house, Gibber would have seen her."

A flash of joy passed across the countenance of Jennings, but he turned away from his underling so that he might not betray the satisfaction he felt. "Mrs. Herne is Maraquito's aunt," he said again.

"No, sir, pardon me. Maraquito hasn't got an aunt. Leastways the aunt, if there is such a person, has never set foot in the house."

"Perhaps Maraquito sees her secretly."

"Well," said Drudge pensively, "she certainly went in by a side door, Mr. Jennings. Do you want me to watch further, sir?"

"Yes. Keep your eye on the Soho house, and should Mrs. Herne reappear, follow her. Anything else?"

"Yes, sir. Mrs. Herne when walking down the hill dropped a small bag."

"Ah! Have you got it?"

"No. She was too sharp for me. I was picking it up when she missed it and came to claim it. But before she reached me I had opened it. Only her handkerchief was inside. I gave it back, and she gave me a shilling. But the queer thing, sir, is the scent."

"What scent?" asked Jennings, looking keenly at the man.

"Oh, a strange strong scent, fit to knock you down, sir."

"Well, and why shouldn't a lady use scent. It is customary."

"It is, sir. My wife uses scent. But this was a queer smell. And then a man shouldn't use scent," burst out Drudge.

"Some men are effeminate enough to do so," said Jennings drily. "But I don't quite understand all this."

"I can tell you what puzzled me at once," said the underling, "after watching Maraquito's house for some time, I put another fellow on, and went to the office. I had to go to see the police about some matter, and I spoke to Inspector Twining of the Rexton district. He had on his desk a handkerchief and a few articles which had just been taken from a man who had been arrested for passing false coins."

"Oh!" Jennings looked very interested, "go on."

"This man was in one of the cells, and he is to be brought before the magistrate this morning. They searched him and took his handkerchief from him."

"It is not customary to do that?"

"No, Sir. But this man—I don't know his name—had two handkerchiefs. The searcher thought that was one too many," said Drudge, with the glimmer of a smile, "and took one."

"Why do you tell me all this?" asked Jennings impatiently.

"Because the handkerchief was scented with the same perfume as the handkerchief of Mrs. Herne I picked up. The moment I smelt it I thought of her coming back for the bag. The scent is so strange and strong that I thought it just as well to mention it to you. You are interested in Mrs. Herne, sir, so if this man uses the same scent—"

"Quite so. You have acted very wisely. Where was the man arrested?"

"At a place near Rexton. He was trying to get a drink and gave a shilling—it was false. The inspector will show it to you, sir. And another queer thing, Mr. Jennings, this man had some rags and a bottle of petroleum on him."

"Humph! Perhaps he intended to set fire to some place. Have you heard of any fire?"

"No, sir, not near Rexton."

"At what time was the man arrested?"

"At nine last night. He is in jail now, and will be brought up this morning on a charge of passing false money."

"I'll look into it, Drudge. It is strange about the scent: but there may be nothing in the matter. The man could easily buy scent of the kind Mrs. Herne uses. Go back to Soho and watch the house. Let me know if Mrs. Herne comes out, and where she goes."

"Yes, sir," said Drudge, and bowed himself out.

When the man was gone Jennings walked up and down his room in a great state of excitement. He was beginning to see the end of the matter. That the scent should be used by a man who was passing false coins confirmed his idea that it was some peculiar sign whereby the members of the gang recognized one another. If Mrs. Herne really was the aunt of Maraquito, this matter implicated her as well as the niece. And Mrs. Herne had been accustomed to go to Rose Cottage, which hinted that Miss Loach had perhaps learned of the existence of the gang and had suffered for her indiscreet curiosity.

"I believe Miss Loach threatened to disclose what she knew. She may have learned that the gang worked in that house from the fact of the ghosts, in which so strongminded an old lady would not believe. I daresay she threatened exposure, and someone killed her. Perhaps

Mrs. Herne herself. No, confound it, she was out of the house. Well, I'll see this man now in jail. I may be able to force him to tell. And I'll call on Lord Caranby to-day, and get permission to search the unfinished house. I am quite sure there is a factory there. I wish Mallow would come and tell me if he has learned anything."

Again there was a ring at the door, and this time Jennings, expecting no one else, certainly hoped to see Cuthbert. But, to his surprise, the servant showed in Lord Caranby. The old gentleman was calm and composed as usual, but Jennings thought he looked ill and frail. The dark circles round his eyes were more pronounced than ever, and he leaned heavily on his cane. He was perfectly dressed as usual, and seemed disposed to be friendly.

"I am glad to see you, Lord Caranby," said the detective, when the old gentleman was accommodated with the chair, "have you had breakfast?"

"Thank you, yes. But I could not eat any," said Caranby, breathing heavily. "Those stairs of yours are trying, Mr. Jennings. I am not so young or so strong as I was."

"You don't look the picture of health, my lord."

"Can you expect a dying man to?"

"Dying—oh, no, you—"

"Dying," insisted Caranby, rapping his stick on the ground. "I know that I have not many months to live, and I sha'n't be sorry when the end comes. I have had a hard time. Cuthbert will soon be standing in my shoes. I suffer from an incurable complaint, Mr. Jennings, and my doctor tells me I shall die soon."

"I am sure Mallow will be sorry," said Jennings, wondering why Caranby, ordinarily the most reticent of men, should tell him all this.

"Yes—yes, Cuthbert is a good fellow. I should like to see him happy and settled with Miss Saxon before I die. But Maraquito will do her best to hinder the match."

"She may soon have enough to do to look after herself," said Jennings grimly. "I shall see that she gets her deserts."

"What do you suspect her of?" asked Caranby hastily.

"I can't tell you yet. I have no proofs. But I am suspicious."

"She is a bad woman," said the old man. "I am certain of that. And she will stop at nothing to marry Cuthbert. But this is not what I came to see you about, Mr. Jennings. You asked my permission to go over my house at Rexton?"

"I did. And I was coming to-day to get the permission confirmed."

"Then I am sorry to say you cannot go over it."

"Why not?" asked Jennings, wondering why Lord Caranby had changed his mind—a thing he rarely did. "I only want to—"

"Yes! Yes!" Caranby waved his hand impatiently, "but the fact is, the house has been burnt down."

"Burnt down—at Rexton!" cried Jennings, jumping from his seat.

"Yes. It caught fire in some way last night, about eight o'clock. There was a high wind blowing, and the house has been burnt to the ground. Not only that, but, as the weather has been dry, the whole of the trees and shrubs and undergrowth in the park have gone likewise. I am informed that everything within the circle of that wall is a heap of ashes. Quite a burning of Rome," chuckled Caranby.

"Do you suspect the house was set on fire?"

"Of course I do. Even though the weather is hot, I don't think this can be a case of spontaneous combustion. Probably some tramp—"

"No," said Jennings decisively, "it is strange you should come to me with this news. One of my men has lately been here, and he tells me that a man was arrested near Rexton last night for passing false money. He had on him a bottle of petroleum and some rags."

"Ah!" said Caranby, quite serene, "so you think—"

"There can be no doubt about it, my lord. This man set fire to the house. People don't carry bottles of petroleum about for nothing."

"But why should he set fire deliberately to my house?"

"At the instance of the Saul family?"

Lord Caranby sat bolt upright. "What do you mean?"

"Humph! It is rather a long story. But this man who was caught used a particular kind of scent called Hikui. Maraquito uses it also, and her aunt, Mrs. Herne."

"Mrs. Herne? She is not Maraquito's aunt."

"She told me herself that she was."

"And I tell you that Emilia, who is dead, was the only aunt Maraquito ever had. Why does Mrs. Herne say this?"

"That is what I am trying to find out. She said that you did not know the whole history of the Saul family."

"I know quite enough," said Caranby gloomily, "the members were abominably wicked. Maraquito's father died after he was discharged from jail for coining; and the mother also."

"Well, my lord, this man, who apparently fired your house, was trying to pass false coins. He uses the same scent as Maraquito does, leaving mysterious Mrs. Herne out of the question."

"Well, and what do you deduce from that?"

"I believe that there is a gang of coiners in existence, of which this man, Clancy, Hale, Maraquito and Mrs. Herne are members. All use the scent Hikui, which probably is a sign amongst them. In what way it is utilized I cannot say, unless they meet one another in the dark, and recognize their confreres by the scent."

"I see. It might be so. But why should this man burn my house?"

Jennings shrugged his shoulders. "I can hardly say. I think the coiners used that house as a factory. But since it is burnt down, that seems impossible. This man may have fired it out of revenge, on account of some row with the gang."

"Or else," said Caranby deliberately, "knowing that you were going to search the house, perhaps it was fired to destroy all traces of the factory. Do you connect this with Selina's death?"

"I do. I believe that she learned of the existence of the factory, and that she threatened to denounce Clancy, Hale and Mrs. Herne. Then, to silence her, she was stabbed."

"But the three you mention were out of the house before the death."

"I know that, and they gave their evidence freely enough at the inquest. I have not yet fitted the pieces of the puzzle into one another, but I am certain the lot are connected from their use of the perfume. Also, as this man who has been caught was passing false money, and as Maraquito and probably Mrs. Herne are surviving members of the Saul family who practised coining, I should not be surprised to find that my theories are correct. But how could anyone know that I intended to go over your house?"

"You asked me in Maraquito's salon. Clancy and Hale were about."

"Humph!" said Jennings, "you see the various parts of the puzzle are fitting together excellently. Probably one of those two overheard."

"Probably. That Hale looks a sly creature and capable of much. I wonder if he is related to the Saul family. He has the same nose."

"And the same eyebrows meeting over the nose," said Jennings. "Mrs. Herne has a similar mark. I am sure she is a relative of Maraquito's."

"If she is her aunt, I give you leave to call me a fool," said Caranby, rising. "I know that Emilia told me she had no sister. What will you do next, Jennings?"

"I shall see this man who fired the house and try to get at the truth. Then I am having Mrs. Herne watched—"

"And Maraquito?"

"She can't move from her couch, so there is no danger of her escaping. But now that the coining factory is destroyed, I shall find it difficult to bring home the crime to anyone. I wish Cuthbert would come."

"Do you expect him?"

"Yes. Listen, Lord Caranby," and Jennings related the episode of the knife, and how he had brought Mallow and Juliet together. "And it seems to me," went on the detective, "that Cuthbert learned something from Miss Saxon which he does not wish to tell me."

"Something to do with Mrs. Octagon."

"Why with her?" demanded Jennings suddenly.

"Oh, because I think Isabella capable of much. She is a fatal woman!"

"What do you mean by that phrase?"

"Isabella exercised a bad influence on my life. But for her I should have married Selina and should not have fallen in with Emilia Saul. I should have been happy, and probably Selina would not have met with her tragic death."

"Do you think the sister has anything to do with it?"

"I can't say. All I know is that whomsoever Isabella came into contact with had trouble. I do well to call her a fatal woman."

"Humph!" said Jennings, "I would rather call Maraquito a fatal woman, as I believe she brought about the death in some way for the double purpose of silencing Miss Loach regarding the factory of coins and of stopping the marriage of her rival with Cuthbert."

Curiously enough, Cuthbert was shown into the room at this moment. So interested had Caranby and Jennings been in their conversation that they had not heard the bell. Mallow looked in good health, but his face wore a worried expression. Without preamble, and after greeting his uncle, he walked up to his friend.

"Jennings," he said calmly, "I have seen Juliet, and she agrees with me that this case should not be gone on with."

"Ah! does she, and on what grounds?"

"Because she has consented to marry me. She intends, at my request, to make over Miss Loach's money to her mother. We have had quite enough dabbling in crime, and we are both sick of it."

"I think you are very wise," said Caranby unexpectedly, "let the case be, Mr. Jennings."

"What did Miss Saxon tell you?" asked the detective irrelevantly.

Mallow sat down and in a calm voice detailed all that he had learned from Juliet. "So you see it throws no light on the subject." Had Mallow mentioned the time at which Juliet asserted she saw him climb over the wall a new light would certainly have been thrown. But he purposely omitted this, and simply said that Juliet had seen him. "I told you I was there, Jennings," he added. "Quite so," said the detective. "Certainly, nothing new has come out."

"Well, then leave the case alone."

"I fear I shall have to, now that the Rexton house has been burnt down," and Jennings related in his turn what had taken place.

Cuthbert listened moodily. "You see," he said, "everything is against us. I only wanted the mystery cleared up so that Juliet might marry me, but now that she wishes to do so, without searching further, I am not going to do anything else."

"Nor I," said Jennings sadly, "nothing is to be learned. The case will remain a mystery to the end of time."

Caranby rose and took Cuthbert's arm. "You young men are faint-hearted," he said, with a shrug.

"If you want my opinion, Mrs. Octagon killed her sister. A fatal woman, I tell you both—a fatal woman."

"And a clever one," said Jennings gloomily, "she has baffled me."

XIX

Susan's Discovery

Although Jennings appeared to acquiesce in Mallow's suggestion that the case should be abandoned, he had not the slightest intention of leaving the matter alone. His professional pride was irritated by the difficulties, and he swore that he would in some way learn the truth. Moreover, the matter did not only deal with the death of Miss Loach, but with the discovery of a coining gang. From various obvious facts connected with the Crooked Lane crime, Jennings made sure that such a gang was in existence, and that the factory had been in the unfinished house. Now that the house was burnt down, it would seem that the coiners had lost their city of refuge, and would probably give up their nefarious trade. As the gang—judging from the number of false coins circulated during the past five years—had been in existence for a long time, it was probable that the members had made sufficient money to retire from so dangerous a business.

"I wonder if the house was set on fire by this arrested man, out of revenge," thought Jennings, as he dressed to go out, "or whether the gang, finding things were growing dangerous since the death of Miss Loach, ordered him to destroy the factory? I can hardly think that, as to preserve the secret, Miss Loach was assassinated. It is not likely that after paying so terrible a price, such destruction would be agreed upon. Certainly the factory may be removed to another place. Humph! I wonder if I can trace it. The best thing for me to do will be to go to Rexton and look at the ruins."

So to Rexton the detective went, and found a large crowd round the wall of the park. This had been broken down in several places so as to admit the fire engines, and Jennings found a policeman on duty who had been one of the first to see the fire, and who had indeed summoned the brigade. On telling his name and position, the man was willing to state all he knew.

"I was on duty about eight o'clock," he said officially. "There was a high wind blowing, but the night was fine and dry. While walking down Crooked Lane, intending to take the path to the station, I saw a light behind the wall of the park. Then a tongue of flame shot up, and it didn't need much cleverness to see that the old house was on fire. Almost before I could collect my wits, sir, the place was in a blaze. You see the dry weather, the heat and the high wind, made everything blaze finely. I signalled for the brigade, and it came up as soon as possible. But as there is no gate in the wall, we had to break it down to get the engines in. There was a large crowd by this time, and we had all the help we needed. By this time the whole house was flaming like a bonfire. When we got the wall down the most part of the house was gone, and the fire had caught the surrounding shrubs, so all we could do was to halt on the edge of the mass and squirt water, in the hope of putting out the flames. But, Lord bless you!" said the officer with good-humored contempt, "you might as well have tried with a child's squirt. As you see, sir, everything is gone within the wall. Leastways, all but that big oak near the wall."

It was as the man said. House, trees, shrubs, even the grass had been swept away by the fierce flames. Within the walls which had secluded the place from the world was a blackened space covered with debris. Where the house had stood was a mound of twisted iron girders, charred beams and broken slates. And everywhere the wind was lifting the fine gray ashes and scattering them abroad, as though in sorrow for the destruction of the previous night. Jennings took all this in at a glance. Policemen were on guard at the various gaps in the wall, as no one was allowed to enter. But the detective, by virtue of his office, walked across the bare expanse with the inspector, and trod under foot the black ashes. There was nothing to be gained, however, by this inspection. All that could be seen were the destroyed park and the mound where the house had been. "What of the cellars?" asked Jennings.

"Well," said Inspector Twining genially, "I suppose there are cellars, but there's nothing in them. The house was shut up for years by a queer nobleman."

"By Lord Caranby," replied the detective. "I know. I suppose the cellars are under that heap. I must get Lord Caranby to allow me to clear it away."

"I expect that will be done, whether or no. Lord Caranby came down and told one of our men that he intended to throw down the wall and let the place as a building site. So when the building begins the heap will soon be cleared away and the cellars laid bare. But there's nothing there," said the inspector again.

"I am not so sure of that."

"What do you mean?"

"Nothing. I have an idea," answered the detective, who did not wish to tell the man how he now began to fancy that the factory for safety had been placed in the cellars. "By the way, did this man who was arrested give his name?"

"No. He refuses to answer any questions. He was, as you know, Mr. Jennings, arrested for trying to pass a bad shilling, but there is no doubt he fired the place. The bottle of petroleum he had in his possession was empty, and—"

"Yes! I heard all that. Where is he now?"

The inspector named a place near Rexton where the man had been incarcerated, pending being brought before the magistrate. "I am going that way," said the inspector. "If you like to come—"

"I'll come," said Jennings. "I intended to see this man. There has been a lot of talk about false coins being passed lately."

Mr. Twining nodded, and began to tell of various cases which had taken place in the district. The two took the train to the place where the police station to which the inspector belonged was situated. It was now after twelve o'clock, and Jennings thought he would have some luncheon before going to the station. But, unexpectedly, a constable seeing the inspector, came hurriedly towards him, saluting as he spoke.

"Please, sir, you're wanted at the station," he said. "A message was sent to Rexton."

"I have just come from Rexton. What is it?"

"That man who was arrested for coining, sir?"

"What about him?" asked the inspector, while Jennings listened with all his ears. He was far from expecting to hear the reply.

"He is dead, sir," said the policeman.

"Dead! What do you mean? He was well enough this morning."

"Well, sir, he's dead now—poisoned!"

"Poisoned!" echoed Jennings, and thought—"Ha! here's an undesirable witness got out of the way." Then he followed in the wake of the inspector, who on hearing the news, hurriedly walked towards the police station. Here they found that the news was true. The constable left in charge of the office was greatly agitated, as it seemed he had been lax in doing his duty. But he made a faithful report.

"It was this way, sir," he said, trying to speak calmly. "A boy of fifteen, very poorly dressed—in rags almost—came crying and asking for the prisoner. He said the prisoner was his father."

"How did he know that, when the prisoner gave no name and was arrested only last night?"

"The boy—Billy Tyke his name is, so I suppose the father is called Tyke also—says his father went out last night. He was always a drunkard, and left the boy to starve. The boy followed him later, and knowing he would be on the burst, went to the public-house, where the man was arrested for passing the bad shilling. There, he was told that his father was in jail, and came here to ask us to let him see him."

"You should have refused and have detained the boy. Well?"

"I was moved by the little chap's tears," said the constable, abashed, "so I let him go into the cell."

"Were you with him?" asked the inspector sharply.

"No, sir. We left them alone for a few minutes. As the boy was so sad and cut up, I thought there would be no harm in doing that. Well, sir, the boy came out again in ten minutes, still crying, and said he would get a lawyer to defend his father. He did not believe his father had passed the money. Then he went away. Later—about half an hour later, we went into the cell and found the man lying groaning, with an empty bottle of whisky beside him. The doctor came and said he thought the man had been poisoned. The man groaned and said the young shaver had done for him. Then he became unconscious and died."

Jennings listened to this statement calmly. He saw again the hand of the coiners. The person who controlled the members evidently thought that the man would blab, and accordingly took precautionary measures to silence him. Without doubt, the man had been poisoned, and the boy had been sent to do it. "What is the boy like?" he asked.

"Billy Tyke, sir?" said the constable, replying on a nod from his chief, to whom he looked for instructions, "a thin boy, fair and with red rims round his eyes—looks half starved, sir, and has a scarred mouth, as though he had been cut on the upper lip with a knife."

Jennings started, but suppressed his emotion under the keen eyes of the observant Twining. He had an idea that he knew who the boy was, but as yet could not be sure. "I'll cut along to the public-house where this man was arrested," said Jennings, "I suppose you'll hold an inquest."

"Certainly, seeing the man has been poisoned." Then the inspector proceeded to rebuke the constable who had performed his duty so ill, and threatened him with dismissal. Jennings left in the midst of the trouble, after getting the inspector to promise that he would report the result of the inquest.

At the public-house—it was the "White Horse," Keighley, an adjoining suburb—Jennings learned that the man who called himself— or rather who was called by his presumed son—Tyke, was not an habitue of the place. Therefore, the boy could not have known that his supposed father was there. Apparently some information had reached the lad, whereby he was able to trace Tyke to the prison, and had carried to him there the bottle of poisoned whisky. Jennings returned to town quite satisfied that he had another clue to the existence of the coiners. Also, he determined to satisfy himself on a point concerning Maraquito, about which he had long been in doubt.

For the next few days Jennings did nothing. He kept away from Mallow, as he did not wish that young man to know that he was still going on with the case. Sometimes he went to Maraquito's place, and learned incidentally that, as there was a chance of her being cured, she was about to give up the gambling salon. Jennings quite expected this information, and assured Hale, who gave it to him, that it was the best thing Maraquito could do. "Sooner or later the police will pounce down on this place," he said.

"As you are a detective, I wonder you haven't stopped it before," said Hale, with an unpleasant smile.

"I had my reasons," said Jennings calmly, "besides, Maraquito has conducted the place quite respectably. I suppose," he added idly, "you will go abroad also?"

"What do you mean by that?" demanded Hale in silky tones.

"Mrs. Herne has gone to the Continent," said Jennings quietly, "and if Senora Gredos gives up this very dangerous business, she may go also. As you will be deprived of two of your friends, Mr. Hale, doubtless you will go also."

"I might. One never knows," replied Hale coolly.

"By the way?" asked Jennings, looking round, "I was admitted by a parlor-maid this evening. Where is Gibber?"

"I believe Senora Gredos has dismissed him for dishonesty."

"Ah, really," replied the detective, who had his own opinion. "So it seems Senora Gredos is getting rid of her household already."

Hale winced under the eye of Jennings and turned away with a shrug. He was apparently glad to get away. Jennings looked after him with a smile. "I'll catch the whole gang," he murmured, and took his departure, having learned what he wished to know—to wit, that Gibber had disappeared.

"Without doubt he was the boy who poisoned Tyke," said Jennings, as he walked home with a cigar for company. "I believe Maraquito is the head of the gang, and the fatal woman that Caranby talks about. She heard that Tyke had been arrested, and sent the boy to poison him lest he should blab. I wonder if it was by her direction that the house was fired. Well, I'll wait. As yet I cannot get a warrant, having nothing but theory to go on. But the nets are being spread, and unless Maraquito and her friends clear out with Mrs. Herne, they will be caught. When they are all in jail there may be some chance of learning who murdered that unfortunate woman in Rose Cottage."

Later on, Jennings received the report of the inquest, which appeared also that evening in the newspapers. It seemed that Tyke had been poisoned with arsenic, administered in the whisky bottle. From his appearance he was a hard drinker, and doubtless the boy had no difficulty in inducing him to drink. Tyke had drank freely—indeed the doctor said he had taken enough to kill three men,—and therefore he had died almost immediately the boy left, and before he had time to speak. The inspector, who wrote to Jennings, stated that the constable who had admitted the boy had been dismissed the force, but the boy himself could not be traced. "I shouldn't be surprised if he had taken refuge in the cellars of the house," said Jennings, "that is, if the factory is there. I must see Caranby and get his permission to remove the rubbish. Only when I have searched the foundation of that house, will my suspicions be set at rest."

Unexpected aid came to help him in this quarter, as Caranby sent a note, stating that the rubbish and debris of the fire would be removed next week, and inviting Jennings to be present. Caranby added that Mallow had resumed his visits to the "Shrine of the Muses," but that Mrs. Octagon still continued hostile. Basil, however, was more friendly. "I daresay," commented Jennings, on reading this last sentence, "he has his own axe to grind over that money."

It was about this time that the detective received a visit from Susan Grant. She looked as neat and timid as usual, and appeared at his rooms one morning with a request for an interview. "I said I would help Mr. Mallow if I could," she said when seated.

"Oh, and have you anything likely to help him,-"

"Not exactly," said Susan, "but I found some old papers of father's."

"I don't quite understand," said the detective, who did not see what the girl's father had to do in the matter.

"Well, it's this way, sir. Father was poisoned five years ago."

"Who poisoned him?"

"That we never knew," explained Susan. "Father's name was Maxwell, but when mother married Mr. Grant she made me take that name. It was supposed that father committed suicide, and mother felt the disgrace dreadful. That was why she married and changed the name. But I don't believe father, when on the point of making us rich, would swallow so much arsenic as he did."

"What's that—arsenic?" said Jennings, recalling the death of Tyke.

"Yes, sir. It was this way. Father was working at Rexton—"

"At Rexton?" said Jennings impatiently, "yes, yes, go on."

"At a house near the railway station which I can point out, mother having seen it when she went to inquire."

"Inquire about what?"

"About father's secret job. He had one he used to go to for three hours every day by agreement with the foreman. Father was very clever and could do all sorts of things. Mother never knew what the job was, but father said it would make us all rich."

"Yes, go on." Jennings looked at her, nursing his chin.

"The other day I came across some papers," said Susan, taking a roll out of her pocket. "And it proved to be plans of father's secret job. And you might have knocked me down with a feather, Mr. Jennings, when I saw on the plans the name of Rose Cottage."

The detective jumped up, greatly excited. "Rose Cottage!" he cried, holding out his hands. "The plans—the plans!"

"I brought them, as I know Miss Saxon who now has Rose Cottage, is engaged to Mr. Mallow—"

"Haven't you got over that nonsense yet?" said Jennings, who was looking eagerly at the plans.

"Yes, I have," replied Miss Grant, confidentially. "I am engaged to a rising young baker who is just a foreman just now, but we hope to save and start a shop. Still, I promised to help Mr. Mallow, and I thought he would like to see those plans. You see, sir, they have to do with Rose Cottage."

"Yes, I do see," almost shouted Jennings, "and I'll bag the whole lot."

"What are you talking about, sir?"

"Ah, I forgot you don't know," said the detective subsiding, "I'll tell you later. But you have made a discovery, Susan. This plan shows a secret entrance into Rose Cottage."

"I know it does, sir, and I thought Miss Saxon would like to see it. I don't know what Miss Loach wanted with a secret entrance, though."

"I fancy I do," said Jennings, rolling up the plans. "Your father was a very clever man, Susan. Too clever for some people. He made this secret entrance when the new wing of the cottage was built five years ago, and those who employed him gave him arsenic by way of a reward. Tyke died of arsenic also, so they are carrying on the same game."

"Oh dear, oh dear!" wept Susan, not hearing the latter part of the sentence. "So father was poisoned after all. Who did it, sir?"

"I can't tell you that," said Jennings, becoming cautious. "You had better say nothing about this, Susan, till I give you leave. You have done Mr. Mallow a great service. These plans may lead to a discovery of the murderer."

"And then Miss Saxon will marry Mr. Mallow."

"Yes. Will you be sorry?"

"No, Mr. Jennings. I am quite satisfied with my baker."

"Then I tell you what, Susan. Lord Caranby has offered a reward for the detection of the murderer. If these plans lead to his detection, you will receive a sufficient sum to set up in business."

XX

BASIL

While Jennings was thus working at the case, and hoping to bring it to a successful issue, Cuthbert was resting in the happy belief that no further steps were being taken. The detective had appeared so despondent when Mallow called with Caranby that the former thought with some show of reason that he meant what he said. Had he known that Jennings was still active he would have been much disturbed.

Agreeably to Cuthbert's suggestion, Juliet had offered the money of Miss Loach to her mother. But Mrs. Octagon refused to be bribed—as she put it—into consenting to the match. In the presence of Mallow himself, she expressed the greatest detestation for him and for his uncle, and told Juliet she would never acknowledge her as a daughter if she married the young man. The poor girl was thus between two fires—that of her love for Cuthbert, and that of her mother's hearty hatred for the Earl and his nephew. Under the circumstances Cuthbert thought it best to remain away from the "Shrine of the Muses" for a time until Mrs. Octagon could be brought to see reason. But she was so obstinate a woman that it was doubtful if she would ever behave in an agreeable manner. Cuthbert returned to his rooms in a rather low state of mind. He knew that Juliet, whatever happened, would remain true to him, and had quite hoped to bribe Mrs. Octagon into consenting by means of the inherited money. But now things seemed more hopeless than ever. Juliet, although not very fond of her mother, was a devoted daughter from a sense of duty, and it would be difficult to bring her to consent to a match against which the elder woman so obstinately set her face.

Certainly Juliet had said she would marry with or without her mother's consent, but now that the consent was withheld with violent words, she seemed inclined to wait. However, if she did not marry Mallow, he knew well that she would marry no one else, least of all the objectionable Arkwright, Cuthbert derived some degree of comfort from this small fact. He wondered if there was any chance of forcing Mrs. Octagon into giving her consent, but after surveying the situation could see no opportunity.

After dinner that night, Cuthbert was thinking of going to see his uncle, who still stopped at the Avon Hotel. When Hale was announced. Mallow was surprised. The lawyer was not a friend of his, and he had no liking for his company. However, he felt a certain curiosity as to the reason of this unexpected visit and welcomed the man with civility. But he did not ask him to have any coffee though it was on the table. Cuthbert held to the traditions of the East regarding bread and salt, and he wished to leave himself free to deal with Hale as an enemy, should occasion arise, as it might. Hale was far too intimate with Maraquito to please the young man. And Maraquito's attentions were far too pressing to make Cuthbert feel comfortable in her presence.

"Well, Mr. Hale," said Mallow coldly, "why have you come?"

The lawyer, who was in an evening suit and dressed with taste and care, took a seat, although not invited to do so. He looked cold and calm, but there was an excited gleam in his large eyes which showed that his calmness masked some emotion, the cause of which Cuthbert could not fathom. "I have come to see you about young Saxon," he said.

"Really," answered Mallow coolly, although surprised, "what can you have to say to me about him."

"He is your friend—"

"Pardon me. I can hardly call him so. We are acquaintances only."

"But you are engaged to his sister," persisted Hale.

Mallow threw away the cigarette he was lighting and jumped up. "I see no reason why Miss Saxon's name should be mentioned, Mr. Hale."

"Don't you, Mr. Mallow? I do."

"Then I object to your mentioning it. State your business and go, Mr. Hale. I have no acquaintance with you."

"I can't state my business unless I mention Miss Saxon's name."

"Then you will please to take yourself off," said Mallow.

Hale smiled coldly, though evidently annoyed. "I think it is to your interest to hear me," he said deliberately, "and to the interest of the lady whom you hope to call your wife."

"Does this business concern Miss Saxon?"

"Indirectly it does. But it rather has to do with her brother."

Mallow frowned. The conversation was taking a turn of which he did not approve. However, he knew well the dangerous ground upon which he stood with regard to the case, and thought it best to hear what his unexpected visitor had to say. "State your business," he said curtly.

"Very good," replied Hale, nursing his silk hat on his knee. "I see you don't offer me coffee or a cigarette."

"We are not friends, sir. And let me remind you that you thrust yourself uninvited on me."

"To do you a service," said Hale quickly. "I think, therefore, that I deserve a better reception."

"Will you please come to the point?" said Mallow coldly, "whatever the service may be, I am quite sure it is two for you if one for me. You are not the man to go out of your way, Mr. Hale, to help anyone."

Hale nodded and smiled grimly. "You are quite right. Now, then, Mr. Mallow, do you know that Basil Saxon was to have inherited the money of my late client, Miss Loach?"

"No, I never knew that. I understood that Miss Loach always intended to leave the money to Miss Saxon."

Hale shook his well-oiled head. "On the contrary, Mr. Saxon was her favorite. In spite of his wild ways she liked him. However, she was also fond of Miss Saxon, and you may thank Miss Loach, Mr. Mallow, for having been the means of forwarding your engagement."

"What do you mean by that?" asked Cuthbert angrily.

"Mrs. Octagon," went on the lawyer deliberately, "would never have consented to Miss Saxon becoming engaged to you had not Miss Loach insisted that she should agree."

"Seeing that Mrs. Octagon hated her sister and was not likely, to be influenced by her, I do not see how that can be."

"Perhaps not. Nevertheless, such is the case. You saw how, when Miss Loach died, Mrs. Octagon seized the first opportunity to place obstacles in the way of your marriage."

"I believe she did that on Maraquito's account, Mr. Hale. I know perfectly well that Mrs. Octagon called on Maraquito."

"Quite so—to ask Maraquito not to let Basil Saxon play beyond his means. Certainly, Maraquito having a strange fancy for you, agreed, on condition that Mrs. Octagon refuse to let Miss Saxon marry you. But, in any case, Mrs. Octagon hates your uncle too much to allow her daughter to become your wife. You will never get Mrs. Octagon's consent unless I help you."

"You!" echoed Mallow, astonished and annoyed. "What possible influence can you have with Mrs. Octagon. I have certainly seen you at her house, but I scarcely think you know her well enough—"

"Oh, yes, I do." Hale rose in his earnestness. "See here, sir; I love Maraquito and I wish to marry her."

"You can, so far as I am concerned,"

"So you say," said Hale bitterly, "but you cannot be ignorant that Maraquito loves you."

"I don't see what that has to do with our conversation," replied Mallow, growing red and restless.

"It has everything to do with the matter. I want to marry Maraquito, as I am rich and deeply in love with her. She would have become my wife long ago but that you crossed her path. Lord knows why she should love a commonplace man like you, but she does."

"Isn't that rather personal?" said Mallow dryly.

"I beg your pardon. But what I wish to say is this. If you marry Miss Saxon and place yourself beyond Maraquito's reach, I will be able to induce her to marry me. Our interests are bound up together. Now, to do this you must have Mrs. Octagon's consent. I can get it."

"In what way?"

"She loves Basil, her son, more than she does herself," went on Hale, paying no attention to the remark. "To save him she would do much."

"To save him from what?"

"Basil;" continued the lawyer, still not noticing the interruption, "is a young fool. He thought himself sure of Miss Loach's money—and he was until a week before she died. Then he came to Rose Cottage and insulted her—"

"I have heard that. She ordered him out of the house."

"She did. Miss Loach was a bitter, acrid old woman when the fit took her. However, Basil insulted her so grossly that she made a new will and left all the money to Miss Saxon. Now it happens that Basil, to supply himself with funds, when his aunt refused to aid his extravagance further, forged her name to a bill—What's the matter?"

"Nothing," said Mallow, who had started from his chair, "only your intelligence is sufficiently unpleasant."

"I can understand that," sneered the lawyer, "since you wish to marry his sister. You don't want a forger for a brother-in-law."

"Who does?" said Cuthbert, not telling that he was thinking of Basil in connection with a still darker crime. "Go on, Mr. Hale."

"The bill fell into my hands. When Miss Saxon got the money she transferred the business to her own lawyer. I had to give the bill up."

"Ah!" said Mallow meaningly, "I see now the hold you had over Basil."

"Yes, that was my hold. I did not want to give up the bill. But it had been met, and as Miss Loach is dead, there was a difficulty in proving the signature to be a forgery. I therefore gave the bill to Miss Saxon. She knew of her brother's guilt—"

"I see—I see," murmured Cuthbert, wondering if she had been shielding Basil as well as him. "My poor girl!"

"She is a brave girl," said Hale, in a voice of reluctant admiration. "She met me and fought for her brother. I gave way, as I did not wish to make trouble. Why, it doesn't matter. However, you see how things stand. Basil is a forger. If his mother knew that he was in danger of being arrested she would consent to your marriage, and then I might marry Maraquito. I have come here to tell you this."

"But if Miss Saxon has the bill, and there is a difficulty of proving the signature, owing to Miss Loach's death, I don't see—"

"Ah, not in this case. But Basil Saxon forged my name also. I hold a forged check. I met it and said nothing about it. Basil, thinking because his sister held the bill that he was out of my power, was most insolent. But I said nothing of the check which he thought I never detected. The more fool he. He must have a fine opinion of my business capacity. However, as the check is only for fifty pounds, he probably thought that it would escape my notice. Well, you see how I can force Mrs. Octagon's hand. What do you say?"

Mallow put his hands to his head quite bewildered by the information.

"You must give me time to think," he said, "but if I consent—"

"You marry Miss Saxon. I ask no reward for my services. All I want is to get you out of my way as regards Maraquito. I will give you the forged check on the day you wed Miss Saxon. I can see," added Hale, rising, "that you are somewhat upset with this news, and no wonder. You never thought Basil was such a scoundrel."

"I thought him a fool, never a knave."

"My dear sir, he is a thoroughly bad man," said Hale cynically, "though I daresay other people are just as bad. However, I will give you a week to think over the matter. Good-night."

"Good-night," said Mallow, touching the bell, but without meeting the gaze of Hale, "I will think over what you have said."

"You will find it to your advantage to do so," replied Hale, and went out of the room at the heels of the servant.

Mallow remained where he was in deep thought. It was terrible to think that the brother of Juliet should be such a scamp. A forger and perhaps something else. Here, indeed, was a motive for Miss Loach to meet with her death at her nephew's hand. Probably on the night in question she threatened to let the law take its course, and then Basil— but at this point of his meditations a ring came at the door. In a few moments Cuthbert heard a step he knew and rose with an agitated air. Basil entered the room.

The young man was carefully dressed as usual in his rather affected way, but his face was pale and he seemed uneasy. "I see you have had a visit from Hale," he said, trying to appear at his ease.

"How do you know that?" asked Mallow abruptly, and declining to see the proffered hand.

"I saw Hale enter a cab as I came up the stairs," said Basil, drawing back; "and even had I not seen him I would know that he has been telling you a lot of lies because you refuse to shake hands."

"Are they lies?"

"Ah, then, he has been talking. He is my enemy. He comes here to do me harm," said Basil, his eyes flashing.

"He came here as your friend," replied Mallow abruptly, "Hale wishes me to marry your sister. He offers to hand over to me a certain check if I marry her."

"I don't know what you are talking about," cried Basil petulantly, and threw himself into a chair, very pale.

"I think you know very well. Why have you come here?"

Basil looked sullen. "I want you to marry Juliet also. And I came to say that I thought I could get my mother to take that money and to withdraw her opposition."

"So that you may have the fingering of the money?"

"Oh, I suppose she will give me some," said Basil airily, and began to roll a cigarette with deft fingers.

Mallow was enraged at this coolness. "Basil, you are a scoundrel!"

"Am I, indeed? Nice words to use to your future relative."

"How do you know I will ever be your relative. Suppose I refuse Hale's demand, and let him proceed on this check?"

Basil's cigarette dropped our of his hand. "I don't know what check you mean," he declared with alarm, "there was a bill—I couldn't help myself. My aunt—"

"Gave you a lot of money and you repaid her by forging her name. But you also forged Hale's name."

"Ah, I know what you mean now. It was only for fifty pounds."

"Had it been for fifty pence the crime is the same," said Mallow vehemently, "why did you not let me help you? I offered to. But you preferred to commit a crime."

"Such a fuss to make," muttered the youth discontentedly, "the bill is in the possession of Juliet, and no steps can be taken on that. If mother accepts this six thousand a year, she will buy the check back from Hale. He's a scoundrel and will do anything for money. Then you can marry Juliet, and I can go abroad for a few years on an income of three thousand. Mother will allow me that."

The coolness of this speech almost took Mallow's breath away. The man did not seem to be at all affected by his crime. So long as he was not found out he appeared to think nothing about the matter. "And I know you will marry Juliet," proceeded Basil, "you love her too well to give her up."

"That is true enough," said Cuthbert, who, having already spared him too long, now determined to punish him, "but I may love her so well that I may not wish to buy her."

"What do you mean by buying her?" demanded Basil sulkily.

"What I say. Is it only to save you that I am to marry Juliet? My marriage must be one of love—"

"She does love you. And I don't see," added Basil complainingly, "why you should jump on a chap for wishing for your happiness—"

"And your own safety."

"Oh, bosh! The bill is destroyed. Juliet put it into the fire, and Hale will sell the check at his own price."

"His price is that I am to marry Juliet."

"So that he can marry Maraquito, I suppose. I know that she loves you and that Hale is crazy about her. It's very hard on me," whined the egotistical youth, "for I want to marry her myself, only mother put her spoke in my wheel."

"Dare you offer yourself to Maraquito, bad as she is, knowing what you are?" cried Mallow, fairly disgusted.

"Oh, the forgeries. What of them? It's nothing." Basil snapped his fingers. "Maraquito won't mind. But I suppose I'll have to give her up on account of that infernal check. Such a small one as it was too. I wish I had made it one hundred and fifty. I could have done so."

In the face of this callous behavior it was sheer wrongdoing to spare the man. "I do not allude to the forgery, though that is bad enough," said Cuthbert, glancing round to see that the door was closed, "but to the murder of your aunt. You killed her."

Basil leaped from his chair with great indignation. "I did not. How dare you accuse me?" he panted.

"Because I have proofs."

"Proofs?" Basil dropped back as though he had been shot.

"Yes. I learned from my man that you took the bowie knife which used to hang on the wall yonder. He saw you take it, and thought you had received my permission. You went to the Marlow Theatre with your sister. You left her in the box and went out after eight o'clock. You went to Rexton to Rose Cottage. After Clancy left the house your aunt admitted you and you killed her—"

"I swear I did not!" said Basil, perfectly white and trembling.

"You did, you liar! Juliet followed you to the cottage."

"Juliet? She did not know I had gone."

"Ah! you see, you were there. Yes, she said she went in order to try and make it up between your aunt and you. But I believe now she went to see if you were committing a crime. I am not aware how much Juliet knows of your wickedness, Basil, but—"

"She knows only about the forgery. I was not at the cottage."

Mallow made a weary gesture. "Why do you tell these falsehoods?" he said with scorn. "Juliet entered the cottage by means of her latch-key. She found Miss Loach dead and the knife on the floor. You dropped it there. She came out and saw a man of my height—which you are, and of my appearance (you are not unlike me at a distance) climbing the wall into the park. He had on alight overcoat—my overcoat. Juliet thought I was the man. I did not say no. But the moment she mentioned the coat I knew it was you. You borrowed the coat from me, and returned it the other day. Now then—"

"Stop! stop!" cried Basil, rising with pale lips and shaking hands, "I admit that I went to Rexton on that night, but I swear I am innocent."

"Pah!" cried Mallow, thinking this was another lie, and a weak one too.

Basil seized him by the arm. "Mallow, I swear by all that I hold most sacred that I did not kill Aunt Selina. I own I took the knife. I wished to frighten her into giving me money. I left the theatre in order to go to Rexton. I thought I might be spotted if I came by the lane. I climbed the wall of the park on the other side after nine, some time after nine. I was crossing when a man chased me. I don't know who it was. I could not see in the bushes, and the night was rather dark at the moment, though clear later. I dropped the knife, it fell out of my pocket, and I scrambled over the wall and bolted."

"Then how did Juliet see you shortly before eleven?"

"I came back for the knife. I thought it might be traced to you and that you might get into trouble. Really I did," said Basil, seeing Mallow make a gesture of dissent. "I came back by the railway path, and along by the corn. Where Juliet could have been, I don't know. I climbed the wall and crossed the park. I could not find the knife where I thought I had dropped it, near the house. I then climbed the opposite wall and got away home. Next day I heard of the death and went down to look for the knife again. I never thought she had been killed with that knife, as no weapon was found. Juliet said nothing to me about the matter—"

"No. Because she thought the knife was mine, as it is, and that I was the man who climbed the wall. I was on the spot. I remember telling you that, when we met in the street, and you were afraid. I see now why you asked me if I had been in the park at night."

"I thought you might have spotted me. When were you there?"

"About twenty minutes past ten."

"Well, then, I was there at ten or a few minutes later. I got away from the man who chased me some time before you came. It was, as you say, at a quarter to eleven when I came back, and by that time I suppose you had gone."

"I went over the opposite wall as you did," said Cuthbert, "we must have run each other very close."

"I expect we were in different parts of the park," said Basil, "but I swear that I am telling you the truth. I said nothing about this, as I was afraid of being arrested. But, if you like, I'll tell that detective Jennings what I told you. He will help me."

"My advice to you is to hold your tongue and keep silent."

"But if I am traced?" stammered Basil.

"I shall say nothing," said Mallow, "and Jennings has dropped the case. I shall get the check from Hale, and you must go abroad. I believe you are innocent."

"Oh, thank you—thank you—"

"But you are a scoundrel for all that. When I get you sent abroad and marry your sister, neither she nor I will have anything to do with you. And if you come back to England, look out."

XXI

AN EXPERIMENT

Next day Cuthbert received a letter from Jennings. It intimated that Maraquito wished to see him that evening. "If you will call at nine o'clock," wrote the detective, "she will be alone. The police have decided to close the gambling-house, and she is making preparations to leave England. I understand she has something to tell you in connection with the death of Miss Loach, which it is as well you should hear. A confession on her part may save you a lot of trouble in the future."

Mallow hesitated to obey this summons. He thought it was strange that Maraquito should get the detective to write to him, as he knew she mistrusted the man. And, apart from this, he had no wish to see Senora Gredos again. Things were now smooth between him and Juliet—comparatively so—and it would not do to rouse the girl's jealousy. Maraquito was a dangerous woman, and if he paid her a solitary visit, he might fall into some snare which she was quite capable of laying. Such was her infatuation, that he knew she would stop at nothing to gain her ends.

On the other hand, Maraquito, to all appearances, knew of something in connection with the case which it behooved him to learn if he wished for peace in the future. So far as Mallow knew, the matter was at an end. He believed that Jennings had shelved the affair, and that no further inquiries would be made. This belief calmed his anxiety, as he greatly desired to save Basil Saxon from arrest. Certainly, the young scamp protested his innocence, and told a plausible tale, but he was such a liar that Mallow could not be satisfied. He might be innocent as he said, yet the facts of the visit to the cottage, the possession of the knife and of the overcoat which he wore when seen by Juliet, hinted at his guilt. Also the forged bill and check might implicate him in the matter. Did Jennings learn of these things, he would certainly arrest Saxon on suspicion, and, for Juliet's sake, Cuthbert did not wish such a thing to happen.

It struck Mallow that Hale might have confided in Maraquito, with whom he was in love. Being unscrupulous, she would probably use this information, and might threaten to denounce Basil, to the subsequent disgrace of Juliet, if Cuthbert refused to marry her. Taking these things into consideration, Mallow decided that it would be best to pay the visit and learn what Maraquito had to say.

It was a wild, blustering evening, rainy and damp. When Mallow stepped out of the door he shivered as the keen wind whistled down the street. Few people were abroad, as they preferred, very sensibly, the comfort of a fireside to the windy, gleaming thoroughfares. Wishing his visit to be as secret as possible, Mallow walked to Soho and turned into Golden Square shortly before the appointed hour. He did not expect a pleasant interview, as Maraquito was an uncivilized sort of woman with little control over her very violent emotions. Altogether, he anticipated a disagreeable quarter of an hour.

He was admitted smilingly by a woman, and noticed with some surprise that Gibber the page was not at his accustomed post. But he put this down to the fact that there was no gambling on this particular evening. The windows of the great salon were dark, and Senora Gredos received him in a small apartment which she used as a sitting-room. Her couch was drawn up close to the fire, and she appeared to be in better health than usual. Standing at the door, Mallow thought she made a pretty picture. She had on a white wrapper trimmed with gold lace, and as usual, wore a profusion of jewelry. Across the lower part of the couch was flung a gorgeous purple coverlet of eastern manufacture, and what with the brilliant colors and the glitter of precious stones, she looked remarkably eastern herself. Mallow noticed particularly how Jewish she was in appearance, and wondered how he could have been so blind as not to have remarked it before. The room looked cheerful and warm, and was welcome after the chilly, dreary streets. Mallow, having taken off his overcoat in the hall, came forward and bowed somewhat formally, but Maraquito was not to be put off with so frigid a greeting. Holding out both hands, she shook his warmly and pointed to a chair near her couch. It was now a few minutes after nine.

"How good of you to come and see me," she said in her deep, rich voice. "The evening was so dull."

"You are not having any play this evening?"

Maraquito shrugged her fine shoulders and unfurled a quite unnecessary fan, which, to keep up her fiction of being a Spanish lady, she always carried. "Some idiot told the police what was going on and I received a notice to close."

"But the police knew long ago."

"Not officially. The police can be silent when it suits. And I always kept things very quiet here. I can't understand why any objection should be made. I suspect that man Jennings told."

"I thought you liked him."

"Oh, I fancied he was a friend of yours and so I made the best of him. But, to tell you the truth, Mr. Mallow, I always mistrusted him. He is much too fond of asking questions for my taste. Then Mr. Hale told me that the man was a detective, so I understood his unwarrantable curiosity. I shall have nothing to do with him in future."

"In that case," said Mallow, anxious to arrive at the truth, "I wonder you employ him to write letters for you."

The woman raised herself on one rounded elbow and looked surprised at this speech. "Really, I don't think I am so foolish," said she dryly. "Why do you say that?"

Mallow looked puzzled. "Jennings wrote me a letter, asking me to come here this evening at nine. He said you wished to see me."

Maraquito's eyes flashed. "I always wish to see you," she said, sinking her voice to a tender tone, "and I am much obliged that Mr. Jennings' note should have brought you here. But I gave him no authority to write it."

"Have you seen Jennings lately?" asked Cuthbert, more and more puzzled.

"A few nights ago. But he said nothing about you. He simply played cards for a time and then took himself off."

"Are you leaving England?"

"I am. Being an invalid as you see, I have no amusement but card-playing. Now that the Puritan authorities have stopped that, I cannot stay in this dull country to be bored. But who told you?"

"Jennings said you were making preparations to leave."

"In this letter he wrote you?" asked Maraquito, frowning.

"Yes. I am sorry I did not bring the letter with me. But I can show it to you on another occasion. He also said you had something to tell me."

Maraquito fastened her brilliant eyes on his face. "Mr. Jennings seems to know much about my affairs and to take a deep interest in them. But I assure you, I never gave him any authority to meddle."

"Then why did he write and bring me here?"

Senora Gredos frowned and then her face cleared. "The man is such a secretive creature that I don't trust him," she said; "and yet he declared himself to be my friend. He knows I like you, and hinted that he should be glad to bring us together."

"Jennings is a gentleman in spite of his profession," said Mallow in cutting tones. "I scarcely think he would take so great a liberty."

"Is it a liberty?" asked Maraquito softly.

"I consider it to be one. Jennings knows that I am engaged."

"Stop!" she cried, gripping her fan so tightly that her knuckles grew white. "Do you dare to tell me this?"

"Senora—Maraquito—don't let us have a scene. I told you before that I could not give you the love you asked."

"And I told you that I would have that love in spite of your unwillingness," said the woman doggedly. "You have scorned me, and I ought to have sufficient pride to let you go your own way. But I am such an infatuated fool that I am content to let you tread on me."

"I have no wish to do that, but—"

"You do—you do—you do!" she said, vehemently. "Why can you not love me? I would be a better wife than that doll you—"

"Drop that, Maraquito. Leave Miss Saxon's name out of the question."

"I shall talk of Miss Saxon as long as I like," cried Maraquito, snapping the fan and growing flushed. "You scorn me because I am an invalid—"

"I do not. If you were perfectly restored to health I would give you the same answer." Mallow was on his feet by this time. "I think it would be wise of me to go."

But Senora Gredos, stretching out her hand, caught him by the coat convulsively. "No! no! no!" she muttered fiercely. "I did not ask you to come here. I did not send for you. But now that you are here, you will stop. We must understand one another."

"We do understand one another," said Cuthbert, who was growing angry at this unreasonable attitude. "You must know that I am engaged to Miss Saxon!"

"You will never marry her—never!" cried Maraquito passionately; "oh, cruel man, can you not see that I am dying of love for you."

"Maraquito—"

"If I were not chained to this couch," she said between her teeth, "I should go after her and throw vitriol in her face. I would give her cause to repent having lured you from me with her miserable doll's face. Pah! the minx!"

Cuthbert grew really angry. "How dare you speak like this?" he said. "If you were able to attack Miss Saxon in the vile way you say, I should show you no mercy."

"What would you do—what would you do?" she panted.

"Put you in jail. That sort of thing may do abroad but we don't allow it here. I thought you were merely a foolish woman. Now I know you are bad and wicked."

"Cuthbert—Cuthbert."

"My name is Mallow to you, Senora Gredos. I'll go now and never see you again. I was foolish to come here."

"Wait—wait," she cried savagely, "it is just as well that you are here—just as well that we should come to an understanding."

"There can be no understanding. I marry Miss Saxon and—"

"Never, never, never! Listen, I can ruin her—"

"What do you mean?"

"Her brother—"

"Oh, Basil, I know all about that."

Maraquito threw herself back on her couch, evidently baffled. "What do you know?" she demanded sullenly.

"That you are about to accuse him of the death of Miss Loach."

"Yes, I do. He killed her. There is a forged bill in—"

"I know all about that also," said Cuthbert, making a gesture for her to be silent. "If you hope to stop my marriage with Miss Saxon by such means, you have wasted your time," he moved again towards the door. "It is time this interview ended," he said.

"Why did you seek it then?" she flashed out.

"I did not. Jennings wrote, asking me to call and see you. I understood that you had something to say to me."

"I have much—though how that detestable man knew I can't think. But I can disgrace that doll of a girl through her brother."

"No, you cannot. Basil is perfectly innocent of murder."

"You have to prove that," she sneered, her features quivering and one white hand clutching the purple drapery, "and you know—so you say, that Basil is a forger."

"He is a fool. I don't condone his folly, but his sister shall not suffer on his account. The bill to which Miss Loach's name was forged is in the possession of Miss Saxon—in fact I may tell you that Basil himself assured me it had been destroyed."

"Of course he would say that," scoffed Maraquito, her eyes flashing, "but the check to which Hale's name is affixed is not destroyed, and Hale shall proceed on that."

"Hale shall not do so," said Cuthbert resolutely. He did not wish to betray Hale's confidence, as a confession would entail the man's loss of the woman he loved. But it was necessary to stop Maraquito somehow; and Cuthbert attempted to do so in his next words, which conveyed a distinct threat. "And you will not move in the matter."

Maraquito laughed in an evil manner. "Won't I?" she taunted. "I just will. Hale will do what I want, and he will have Basil arrested unless you promise to give up this girl and marry me."

"Hale will do nothing, neither will you," retorted Cuthbert. "I don't care about threatening a woman, but you must not think that you are able to play fast and loose with me."

"How can you hurt me?" asked Maraquito with a scornful smile, although her lips quivered at his tone.

"I can tell Jennings that you are Bathsheba Saul!"

She turned quite pale. "I? My name is Maraquito Gredos."

"It is nothing of the sort. My uncle Lord Caranby came here and recognized you from your likeness to the woman Emilia he was once engaged to. He can state that in court."

"Where is his proof?"

"Proof will be forthcoming when necessary."

"Not to prove that I am Bathsheba Saul. I know nothing of the name."

Cuthbert shrugged his shoulders. He had said what was necessary and, unwilling to speak further, prepared to go. Maraquito saw him slipping from her grasp. Once gone, she knew he would never come back. With a cry of despair she stretched out her hands. "Cuthbert, do not leave me!" she cried in anguish.

"I must leave you. I was foolish to come. But you know now, that if you move in this matter I can move too. I doubt very much, madam, if your past life will bear looking into."

"You coward!" she moaned.

"I know I am a coward," said Mallow uncomfortably; "it is not my way to threaten a woman—I said that before. But I love Juliet so much that at any cost I must protect her."

"And my love counts for nothing."

"I am sorry, Maraquito, but I cannot respond. A man's heart is not his own to give."

"Nor a woman's," she moaned bitterly; "oh, heaven, how I suffer. Help!"

Cuthbert heard footsteps ascending the stairs—the light footsteps of a hasty man. But Maraquito's head had fallen back, her face was as white as snow and her mouth was twisted in an expression of anguish. She seemed to be on the point of death, and moved by her pain—for she really appeared to be suffering, he sprang forward to catch her in his arms. Had he not done so she would have fallen from the sofa. But hardly had he seized her form when she flung her arms round his neck and pressed her mouth to his. Then she threw back her head, not now white, but flushed with color and triumph. "I have you now," she said breathlessly. "I love you—I love you—I will not let you go!"

What Cuthbert would have done it is hard to say. Apparently Maraquito was determined to hold him there. But at this moment Jennings appeared at the door. On seeing him arrive so unexpectedly, Maraquito uttered a cry of rage and dismay, and released Mallow. "Send him away—send him away!" she cried, pointing to Jennings, who looked cold and stern. "How dare he come here."

"I come on an unpleasant errand," said Jennings, stepping forward. "I want you, Mallow!"

Cuthbert, who had moved forward, stopped. "Why do you want me?"

Jennings placed his hand on the young man's shoulder. "I arrest you on the charge of murdering Selina Loach!"

Maraquito uttered a shriek, and Cuthbert's face grew red. The latter spoke first. "Is this a jest?" he asked harshly.

"You will not find it so."

"Let me pass. I refuse to allow you to arrest me."

Jennings still continued to keep his hand on Cuthbert's shoulder, whereupon the young man flung it aside. At the same moment Jennings closed with him, and a hand-to-hand struggle ensued. Maraquito, with straining eyes, watched the fight. With stiffened muscles the two reeled across the room. Cuthbert was almost too amazed to fight. That Jennings should accuse him and attack him in this way was incredible. But his blood was up and he wrestled with the detective vigorously. He was an excellent athlete, but Jennings was a west-country-man and knew all that was to be known about wrestling. With a quick twist of his foot he tripped up his opponent, and in a minute Cuthbert was lying on his back with Jennings over him. The two men breathed hard. Cuthbert struggled to rise, but Jennings held him down until he was suddenly dragged away by Maraquito, who was watching the fight eagerly. There she stood in the centre of the room which she had reached with a bound.

"I thought so," said Jennings, releasing Mallow and rising quickly.

Maraquito threw a small knife at Cuthbert's feet. "Kill him—kill him!" she said with hysterical force.

"There is no need to," said the detective, feeling his arms, which were rather sore. "Mallow, I beg your pardon for having fought you, but I knew you would not lend yourself to a deception, and the only way in which I could force this lady to show that she was able to walk was by a feigned fight."

"Then you don't intend to arrest me?" said Mallow, rising and staring.

"Never had any idea of doing so," rejoined Jennings coolly. "I wished to learn the truth about Mrs. Herne."

"Mrs. Herne!"

"Or Maraquito Gredos or Bathsheba Saul. She has a variety of names, my dear fellow. Which one do you prefer?" he asked, turning to the discovered woman.

Maraquito looked like the goddess of war. Her eyes flashed and her face was red with anger. Standing in a striking attitude, with one foot thrust forward, her active brain was searching for some means of escape. "I don't know what you mean by calling me these names!"

"I mean that you are to be arrested. You are Mrs. Herne. Your accident was merely a sham to avert suspicion."

"Mrs. Herne is my aunt."

"Pardon me, no. The only aunt you ever had was Emilia Saul, who died in Caranby's house. In our interview at Hampstead you betrayed yourself when we talked of Mallow. I had you watched. You were seen to enter this house, and out of it Mrs. Herne never came. Your servants do not know Mrs. Herne—only their invalid mistress."

Maraquito, seeing her danger, panted with rage, and looked like a trapped animal. "Even if this is true, which I deny," she said in a voice tremulous with rage, "how dare you arrest me, and for what?"

"For setting that boy Gibber to poison the man who called himself Tyke. The lad has left your service—which means he is in hiding."

"I know nothing about this," said Maraquito, suddenly becoming cool. "Do you mean to arrest me now?"

"I have the warrant and a couple of plain-dress detectives below. You can't escape."

"I have no wish to escape," she retorted, moving towards a door which led into an inner room. "I can meet and dispose of this ridiculous charge. The doctor told me that a sudden shock might bring back my strength. And that it has done. I am not Mrs. Herne—I am not Bathsheba Saul. I am Maraquito Gredos, a Spanish lady—"

"Who doesn't know her own language," said Jennings.

"I pass over your insults," said the woman with dignity. "But as you intend to take me away, will you please let me enter my bedroom to change my dress?"

Jennings drew aside and permitted her to pass. "I am not afraid you will escape," he said politely. "If you attempt to leave you will fall into the hands of my men. They watch every door."

Maraquito winced, and with a last look at the astounded Mallow, passed into the room. When she shut the door Mallow looked at Jennings. "I don't know what all this means," he said.

"I have told you," replied Jennings, rather impatiently, "the letter I sent you was to bring you here. The struggle was a feigned one on my side to make Maraquito defend you. I knew she would never let you be worsted if she could help; exactly as I knew you would never consent to play such a trick on her."

"Certainly not. With all her faults, she loves me."

"So well that she will kill Juliet Saxon rather than see her in your arms. Don't frown, Mallow, Maraquito is a dangerous woman, and it is time she was laid by the heels. You don't know what I have found out."

"Have you learned who killed Miss Loach?"

"No. But I am on the way to learn it. I'll tell you everything another time. Meanwhile, I must get this woman safely locked up. Confound her, she is a long time."

"She may have escaped," said Mallow, as Jennings knocked at the door.

"I don't see how she can. There are men at the front door and at a secret entrance she used to enter as Mrs. Herne." He knocked again, but there was no reply. Finally Jennings grew exasperated and tried to open the door. It was locked. "I believe she is escaping," he said, "help me, Mallow."

The two men put their shoulders to the door and burst it in. When they entered the bedroom it was empty. There was no sign of Maraquito anywhere, and no sign, either, of how she had managed to evade the law.

XXII

THE SECRET ENTRANCE

As may be guessed, Jennings was very vexed that Maraquito had escaped. He had posted his men at the front and back doors and also at the side entrance through which Senora Gredos in her disguise as Mrs. Herne had entered. He never considered for the moment that so clever a woman might have some way of escape other than he had guessed. "Yet I might have thought it," he said, when Cuthbert and he left the house. "I expect that place is like a rabbit-burrow. Maraquito always expected to be taken some day in spite of her clever assumption of helplessness. That was a smart dodge."

"How did you learn that she was shamming?"

"I only guessed so. I had no proof. But when I interviewed the pseudo Mrs. Herne at her Hampstead lodgings, she betrayed so much emotion when speaking of you that I guessed it was the woman herself. I only tried that experiment to see if she was really ill. If she had not moved I should have been done."

"It seems to me that you are done now," said Cuthbert angrily. He was not very pleased at the use Jennings had made of him.

"By no means. Maraquito will take refuge in a place I know of. She does not fancy I am aware of its existence. But I am on my way there now. You can come also if you like."

"No," said Mallow decisively, "so far as I am concerned, I have no further interest in these matters. I told you so the other day."

"Don't you wish to know who killed Miss Loach?"

Mallow hesitated, and wondered how much the detective knew. "Have you any clue to the assassin?" he asked.

Jennings shrugged his shoulders. "I can't say that. But I suspect the coiners have something to do with the matter."

"The coiners?"

"Ah! I know you have not learned much about them. I have no time now to talk, but you will see everything in the papers shortly. I can tell you, Mallow, there's going to be a row."

Mallow, like all young Englishmen, was fond of fighting, and his blood was at once afire to join in, but, on second thoughts, he resolved to stick to his original determination and stay away. It would be better, he thought, to let Jennings carry out his plans unhampered. In order, therefore, to preserve Basil's secret, Mallow nodded to the detective and went home. That night he spent wondering what had become of Maraquito.

Meantime, Jennings, with a dozen men, was on his way to Rexton. It was now after eleven, and the clock struck the half hour as they landed at Rexton Station. The police force of the suburb had been notified of the raid about to be made, and Inspector Twining was on the spot. He guided the party through the side path which terminated near Rose Cottage. The night was dark and rainy, but there were occasional gleams of moonlight. There was no light in the windows of Rose Cottage, and everything appeared to be quiet. Behind loomed the ruins of the unfinished house beneath which was the coining factory.

On the way to the spot Jennings conversed with Twining in low tones and detailed his experience with Maraquito.

"I am quite sure that she has gone to the factory," he said; "she does not think that I know about it. I fancy she will tell her pals that the game is up and the lot will light out for America."

"They may have gone by this time," suggested the inspector.

"I don't think so. Maraquito must have just arrived, if indeed she has come here. Besides, she will never guess that I know how to get into the place, or indeed think that I know of its existence."

"How did you guess?"

"Guess is a good word. I just did guess, Twining. From various facts which there is no time to tell you, I became convinced that there was a factory in existence. Also I fancied that the death of that old lady was connected with the preservation of the secret. But I only got at the hard facts the other day, when a girl called Grant—"

"I remember. She gave evidence at the inquest."

"Precisely. Well, she brought me some plans belonging to her father which she found. He was engaged in a quiet job hereabouts five years ago, and died when it was finished. He was poisoned with arsenic."

"What! like that man Tyke?"

"Yes. The person who runs this show—Maraquito, I think—evidently has a partiality for that extremely painful poison. Well, this workman having constructed the secret entrance, was got out of the way by death, so that the secret might be preserved. And I guess Miss Loach was settled also in case she might give the alarm."

"But if the secret entrance is in the cottage," said Twining, "this old woman may have been aware of its existence."

"Certainly, and was about to split when she was killed. At least, that is my theory."

"She must have been in with the gang."

"I have never been able to fix that," said Jennings thoughtfully. "I know she was a lady and of good birth. Also she had money, although she condemned herself to this existence as a hermit. Why she should let Maraquito and her lot construct a secret entrance I can't understand. However, we'll know the truth to-night. But you can now guess, Twining, how the bell came to be sounded."

"No, I can't," said the inspector, promptly.

"I forgot. You don't know that the secret entrance is in the room where Miss Loach was murdered. Well, one of the gang, after the death, sounded the bell to call attention to the corpse, and then slipped away before Susan Grant could get to the room."

"But why should this person have sounded the bell?"

"That is what I have to find out. There's a lot to learn here."

"Have you any idea who killed Miss Loach?"

"Maraquito, under the disguise of Mrs. Herne."

"Was she Mrs. Herne?"

"Yes. She masqueraded as an invalid who could not leave her couch, but I managed to get at the truth to-night."

"But from the evidence at the inquest, Mrs. Herne was out of the house when the blow was struck."

"Quite so: But we did not know of this secret entrance then. I fancy she came back—"

"But how can you—"

"There's no more time to talk," interrupted Jennings. "We must get to work as soon as possible. Order your men to surround the house."

"And the park also?"

"We have not enough men for that. And I don't think there's any other exit from the factory save that through Rose Cottage. If there was, Maraquito and her two friends would not have played whist so persistently with Miss Loach every night."

"It was three times a week, I think."

"Well, it doesn't matter. Here we are." Jennings opened the garden gate and walked boldly up the path towards the silent house. The men, under the low-spoken directions of Twining, spread themselves round the house so as to arrest any coiner who might attempt escape. Then the detective rang the bell. There was no answer for a few minutes. He rang again.

A window in the cottage was opened cautiously, and the head of Mrs. Pill, in a frilled nightcap of gigantic size, was thrust out. "Is that you, Thomas, coming home at this late hour the worse for drink, you idle wretch, and me almost dead with want of sleep."

"It's a message from your husband, Mrs. Barnes," said Jennings, signing to Twining to keep out of sight. "Come and open the door, and I'll tell you what has happened."

"Oh, lor! is Thomas gone the way of flesh?" wailed Mrs. Barnes, formerly Pill. "Come to the cottage door."

"No. Open this one," said Jennings, who had his own reasons for this particular entrance being made use of. "You know me—"

"Mr. Jennings, as was in the case of my pore, dear, dead lady. Of course I knows you, sir, and the fact as you are police makes me shudder to think as Thomas is jailed for drink. Wait one moment, sir. I'll hurry on a petticoat and shawl. How good of you to come, sir."

When the window shut down, Jennings bent towards the inspector, who was crouching on the other side of the steps. "This woman is innocent," he whispered. "She knows nothing, else she would not admit us so quickly."

"It may be a blind, Jennings. She may have gone to give the gang warning, you know."

"I don't know," retorted the detective sharply. "I am quite sure that Mrs. Barnes doesn't even know her husband Thomas is one of the lot. I don't care if she does give warning either, if your surmise is correct. All our men are round the house, and if any of the gang escape we can collar them."

"That is supposing there isn't another exit from the unfinished house," muttered Twining, anxious to have the last word.

Mrs. Barnes appeared at the door in a brilliant red petticoat, a white woollen shawl, and the cap aforesaid. Her feet were thrust into carpet slippers and she carried a candle. "An' it is good of you, sir, to come 'ere and tell me that Thomas is in jail, he being-"

"We can talk of that inside," said the detective, pushing past her. "I suppose you don't mind my friend coming in."

Mrs. Barnes almost dropped when she saw the second person, especially when she noted the uniform. "It must be murder at least," she wailed, almost dropping the candle in her fright; "lor! do tell me, sir, that Thomas have not murdered anyone."

"Lead us down to the sitting-room and we'll tell you, Mrs. Barnes."

"I can't do that, sir, Mr. Clancy may be 'ome any moment"

"Isn't he at home now?"

"Bless you, no, Mr. Jennings, he being fond of goin' out, not that he's an old man, and why shouldn't he enjoy hisself. Not that a woman could wish for a better lodger, though he only bin 'ere a week or so, he givin' no trouble and havin' a latch-key."

"I want to see Mr. Clancy also," said Jennings impatiently, while Twining turned on the electric light in the hall. "Take us down to the basement."

The woman would have objected again, but from the stern expression on her visitors' faces she judged that it would be wiser to obey. She descended, candle in hand, turning on the lights as she went down. In the sitting-room she paused and faced the detective. "Do tell me what's wrong, sir?" she asked. "Thomas is a fool, but we're newly wed and I shouldn't like anything to 'appen to 'im, though he do take fondly-like to the bottle."

"When did Thomas go out?"

"At eight, and Mr. Clancy at nine, though Mr. Clancy havin' a latch-key, don't give me trouble lettin' him in which Thomas does."

"Ah!" said Jennings, with a side-glance at the inspector, "so your husband goes out often?"

"He do, sir. Three times a week. I 'ave tried to break 'im of these larky 'abits but he won't do what I arsks him. I wish I'd stopped at bein' Pill," wailed Mrs. Barnes, wiping her eyes. "An' if Thomas is drunk and bail bein' required—"

"I don't know if your husband is drunk or sober," interrupted Jennings. "We are on a different errand. Tell me, Mrs. Barnes, do you know if Miss Loach had a secret entrance to this room?"

"Lor no, sir," cried the woman, casting a surprised glance round, "whatever would she 'ave that for, pore dear?"

"The furniture is oddly placed," said Twining.

And indeed it was. Tables and chairs and sofa were ranged in two lines on either side of the room, leaving the middle portion bare. The floor was covered with a Turkey carpet down the centre, but the sides of the floor were without covering. Mrs. Barnes explained this.

"Miss Loach liked to 'ave things straight this way for the night, bein' of tidy 'abits. She thought the floor bein' clear left the 'ousemaid, who was Geraldine, room to sweep and dust thoroughly. Mr. Clancy 'ave the same fancy, though being a man as tidy as ever was."

"Strange Mr. Clancy should be tidy," said Jennings drily. "He certainly is not so in his dress. Now the best thing you can do, Mrs. Barnes, is to go to bed."

"An' leave you 'ere," screeched the cook indignantly. "Why, whatever would Mr. Clancy say, he being respectable."

"Very good then, you can stop here. Stand on one side, Twining, and you, Mrs. Barnes. Both of you stand on the bare floor near the wall."

Considerably surprised, Mrs. Barnes did as she was told, and uttered a cry when she saw the floor begin to move. Jennings, who was pressing a button at the end of the room, stopped. "Take her upstairs, Twining. She will alarm the gang!"

"Alarm who?" cried the cook, struggling with the inspector. "Whatever do you mean? Shame—shame to 'old a defenceless lady. 'Elp!"

But her cries for help were unheeded. Twining bore her up the stairs and summoned one of his men. In a few minutes Mrs. Barnes was safely locked up in her own bedroom in the cottage, a prey to terrors. Poor woman, being innocent, she could not understand the meaning of this midnight visit, nor indeed the mysterious moving of the floor. It had never happened so before within her recollection.

Twining came down with six men, leaving the others to guard the exits from the house and garden. At the door of the sitting-room he stopped at the head of those he was bringing. At his feet yawned a gulf in which steps appeared. The whole of the centre of the floor had disappeared into the wall opposite to the fireplace, and the rough steps led down into a kind of passage that ran in the direction of the unfinished house. "This is the entrance," said Jennings, "it works from a concealed button on the wall. Electricity is used. You see why the sides of the floor are left bare; the carpet has quite disappeared. But we have no time to lose," he jumped down lightly. "Come along men, hurry up."

"As we will be at a disadvantage, we may as well get our barkers out," said the inspector, and the men produced revolvers. Then they went into the burrow at the tail of the intrepid Jennings.

That gentleman stole along the narrow passage: It ran straightly for a few yards and then took a turn to the right. The ground continued to slope for some distance until it terminated in a heavy door of wood. Jennings fancied this might be locked, and felt a pang of disappointment. But it proved to be merely closed to. Apparently the coiners were so sure of their safety that they did not trouble to keep the door locked. The detective opened it gently, and with the men close at his heels stole forward. He held his revolver lightly in his right hand, ready for emergencies. The passage was quite dark, but being narrow, the men had no hesitation in going forward. Some way down, after leaving the door, the passage branched into two ways, for Jennings came against a wall directly ahead. Wondering what this meant, he struck a match, and the blue light revealed one passage running down to the left and another opening up to the right. While the detective hesitated which to take, the darkness was suddenly illuminated with the glare of lamps. From a dozen electric lights at the sides of the passage sprang a white glow. At the further end of the sloping passage appeared the figure of a man. He gave a shout when the figures of the police were revealed in the sudden illumination and vanished suddenly. There was not a moment to be lost. Jennings, crying to his men, dashed ahead. As he neared the end of the burrow, for it was nothing else, a pistol shot rang out and he felt as though his shoulder had been pierced with a red-hot iron. But the wound did not stop him.

"Quick, men—quick! Some stop and guard the double way. They will try and escape that way."

His orders were obeyed with precision, and two men stopped behind, while the rest, with Twining at their head, pressed forward. They ran against another door, but it also was open, as the watching man had not had time to close it. Through this the police poured, and found themselves in a large, dry cellar, brilliantly lighted. On every hand were the evidences of the pursuits of the gang. But no one had time to take in details. The startled and infuriated coiners were fighting for their liberty. In a moment the lights were out, but not before Jennings saw Clancy and Hale at the far end of the cellar, with white faces and levelled revolvers. There were other men also. Shots rang out, but in the darkness everyone fired at random. The coiners strove to force their way to the door, evidently anxious to gain the forked passage, so that they could escape by one of the two exits. Twining uncovered his lantern and flashed the light round. It converted him into a target and he fell, shot through the heart by Hale. The other men made a dash for liberty, but the police also producing their lights, managed to seize them. At last Hale, apparently seeing there was no chance of escaping in the gloom, turned on the electric lights again, and the illumination revealed a cellar filled with struggling men. Jennings made for Clancy, as it struck him that this man, in spite of the foolish look on his face, was the prime agent. Clancy fired and missed. Then he strove to close with Jennings. The latter hammered him over the head with the butt of his revolver. Shouts and oaths came from the infuriated thieves, but the police fought like bulldogs, with tenacious courage, silent and grim.

"Hold them—hold them!" cried Jennings, as he went down.

"I'll do for you this time," said Hale between his teeth, and flung himself forward, but Jennings struggled valiantly. The coiner was over him, and trying to get at his revolver which had fallen in the fight. Jennings waited till he stretched, then fired upward. Hale gave a yell of agony, and throwing up his arms, fell on one side. Wounded, and in great pain, Jennings rose. He had just time to see Clancy in the grip of two policemen, fighting desperately, when his senses left him and he fainted. The shouts and oaths and shots rang out wildly and confusedly as he lost consciousness.

XXIII

A Scamp's History

When Jennings came to himself he was lying on a sofa in the dining-room on the ground-floor of the villa. His shoulder hurt him a trifle, but otherwise he felt well, though slightly weak. The doctor was at his side. It was the same man who had attended to the body of the late occupant of the house.

"Are you feeling better?" said Doctor Slane, when he saw the eyes of the detective open. "You had better remain here for a time. Your men have secured the rascals—all five of them."

"And Twining?" asked Jennings, trying to sit up.

"He is dead—shot through the heart. Clancy killed him."

"Then he'll swing for it," said Jennings in a stronger tone, "we lose a good man in poor Twining. And Hale?"

"You have wounded him severely in the lungs. I fear he will die. We have put him in Mrs. Barnes' room on her bed. The poor woman is wild with grief and terror. I suppose you know her husband was amongst those rascals."

"I thought as much. His going out was merely a blind. But I must get up and look at the factory. Send Atkins to me."

Atkins was the man next in command now that the inspector was dead.

The doctor tried to keep Jennings on his back, but the detective would not listen. "There is much to do," he said, rising unsteadily. "You have bound up my shoulder. I won't lose any more blood."

"You have lost a good deal already."

"It's my business. We detectives have our battles to fight as well as soldiers have theirs. Give me some brandy and send Atkins."

Seeing that the man was resolved, Slane gave him the drink and went out. In a few minutes Atkins entered and saluted. Jennings, after drinking the fiery spirit, felt much better, and was fairly steady on his legs. "Did you see any women amongst the men we took?" he asked.

"No, sir," replied the other, "there were five men. Two are wounded— one slightly, and the other—Hale—severely. He wants to make a confession to you, and I have sent to the office for a clerk to take down his words. Dr. Slane says he will not live till morning."

"He will cheat the law, I suppose," said Jennings, "give me your arm, Atkins. I want to visit the factory."

"Are you strong enough, sir?"

"Quite strong enough. Don't bother," replied the other as a twinge of pain made him wince. "We've made a good haul this time."

"You'll say that, sir, when you see the factory. It is the most complete thing of its kind."

"Tell the clerk when he arrives not to take down Hale's confession till I arrive. I won't be more than a quarter of an hour. Give me your arm when you return."

Atkins departed on his errand, and Jennings sat down, wondering what had become of Maraquito. He made sure she would go to the factory, as being a place of refuge which the police would find hard to discover. But, apparently, she had taken earth in some other crib belonging to the gang. However, he would have all the ports watched, and she would find it hard to escape abroad. Maraquito was so striking a woman that it was no easy matter for her to disguise herself. And Jennings swore that he would capture her, for he truly believed that she had killed Miss Loach, and was the prime mover in the whole business. Hitherto she had baffled him by her dexterity, but when they next met he hoped to get the upper hand.

His underling returned and, resting on his arm, Jennings with some difficulty managed to get down the stairs. The whole house now blazed with light. Formerly the detective had wondered why Miss Loach had been so fond of electric lamps, thinking that as an old lady she would have preferred a softer glow. But now he knew that she required the electricity for the illumination of the factory, and for manipulating the metals required in the manufacture of coins. There was no doubt that she was one of the gang also, but Jennings could not conceive why she should take to such a business. However, the woman was dead and the gang captured, so the detective moved along the narrow passage with a sense of triumph. He never thought that he would be so lucky as to make this discovery, and he knew well that such a triumph meant praise and reward. "I'll be able to marry Peggy now," he thought.

The coiners had been removed to the Rexton cells, and only Hale remained under the charge of Mrs. Barnes and Dr. Slane. The body of Twining lay in the dining-room of the villa. A policeman was on guard at the door of the villa, and two remained at the forked passage. When Jennings arrived here he felt inclined to turn off to the right and explore the other passage, but he was also anxious to see the factory and assure himself of the value of his discovery. He therefore painfully hobbled along, clinging to Atkins, but sustained in his efforts by an indomitable spirit.

"Here you are, sir," said Atkins, turning on the light and revealing the workshop. "A fine plant, isn't it?"

"It is, indeed," said Jennings, glancing up to the rough roof where five or six lamps blazed like suns, "and a nice hiding-place they found. I'll sit here and look round, Atkins."

He dropped into a chair near the bench and stared at the cellar. It was large, and built of rough stones, so that it looked like a prison cell of the Bastille. The floor was of beaten earth, the roof of brick, built in the form of an arch, and the door was of heavy wood clamped with iron. The brilliant illumination enabled Jennings to see everything, even to the minutest detail of the place.

In one corner were three large dynamos, and in another a smelting pot, and many sheets of silver and copper. Also, there were moulds of gutta-percha arranged to hold coins in immersion. On a bench were a number of delicate tools and a strong vice. Jennings also saw various appliances for making coins. On rough deal shelves ranged round the walls stood flasks and jars containing powders, with tools and a great many chemicals. Also there were piles of false money, gold and silver and copper, and devices for sweating sovereigns. In a safe were lumps of gold and silver. Beside it, a bath filled with some particular liquid used in the trade. Electric cells, acids, wooden clips to hold the coins could also be seen. In fact the whole factory was conducted on the most scientific principles, and Jennings could understand how so many cleverly-prepared coins came to be in circulation. There were even moulds for the manufacture of francs and louis.

"I daresay the gang have other places," he said to Atkins, "but this is their headquarters, I fancy. If I can only get some of them to tell the truth we might find the other places."

"Hale wants to confess."

"Yes. But I fancy it is about the murder of Miss Loach. She was apparently killed to ensure the safety of this den. We must root the coiners out, Atkins. Maraquito, who is the head of the business, is at large, and unless we can take her, she will continue to make false money in some other place. However, I have seen enough for the time being. Keep guard over this place till we hear from the Yard tomorrow."

"You'll go home and lie down, sir."

"No. I intend to hear Hale's confession. By to-morrow it will be too late. I wouldn't miss hearing what he has to say for anything."

"But can you keep up, sir?"

"Yes, yes—don't bother," said Jennings, rising, the pain making him testy, "give me your arm, Atkins. By the way, where does the other passage lead to? I have not enough strength to explore."

"It leads to the top of the ground, sir, and comes out into the trunk of a tree."

"What do you mean?"

"Well, sir, it's very clever. There's an old oak near the wall, and the trunk is hollow. All anyone has to do is to climb up through the trunk by means of stairs and drop over the wall. The coiners were making for that when we captured them."

"Humph! Have that place watched. Maraquito may come here to-night after all. It is now one o'clock."

"I don't think she'll come, Mr. Jennings. But we have every point watched. No one can come or go unless we know."

"Come along then," said Jennings, who was growing weak, "let us see Hale. The sooner his confession is written and signed the better."

Not another word did Jennings say till he got on to the ground floor of the villa. But he had been thinking, for when there he turned to the man who supported him. "How is it the oak with the hollow trunk still stands?" he asked.

"Oh, it escaped the fire, sir. Some of the boughs were burnt off but the trunk itself is all right. It is close to the wall too."

"Humph!" said Jennings, setting his teeth with the pain, "give me a sup of brandy out of your flask, Atkins. Now for Hale."

When he arrived in the bedroom where Hale was lying groaning, Jennings had the factitious strength of the spirit. A sleepy-eyed clerk was seated at the table with sheets of paper before him. A lamp was on the table. Mrs. Barnes was crouching in a chair near the bed. When she saw Jennings she flung herself down weeping.

"Oh, sir, I knew no more of this than a babe unborn," she wailed, "I never thought my second was a villing. To think that Thomas—"

"That's all right, Mrs. Barnes, I quite acquit you."

"Not Barnes. Pill I am again, and Mrs. Pill I'll be to the end of my days. To think Thomas should be a blackguard. Pill drank, I don't deny, but he didn't forge and coin, and—"

"Wasn't clever enough, perhaps," said Hale from the bed in a weak voice, "oh, there you are, Jennings. Get that fool out of the room and listen to what I have to tell you. I haven't much time. I am going fast."

Jennings induced Mrs. Pill, as she now insisted on being called, to leave the room. Then he sat down on the bed beside the dying man. Atkins remained at the door, and the doctor seated himself by Hale's head with a glass of brandy. It might be needed for the revival of Hale, who, having lost much blood, was terribly weak. But the poor wretch was bent upon confession, and even told his story with pride.

"You had a job to take us, Jennings," he said with a weak chuckle. "I don't know how you found us out though."

"It's too long a story to tell. But, first of all, tell me did Maraquito come here to-night?"

"No. Are you after her?"

"Yes, I know she isn't an invalid."

"Ah, she diddled you there," said Hale with another chuckle, "a very clever woman is Maraquito. I wished to marry her, but now I'm done for. After all, I'm not sorry, since my pals are taken. But I did think I'd have been able to go to South America and marry Maraquito. I've made plenty of money by this game. Sometimes we sweated four hundred sovereigns a day. The factory has been here for five years, Jennings—"

"I know. The man Maxwell, who was Susan Grant's father, made the secret entrance, and you had him killed."

"No, I didn't. Miss Loach did that. I thought she was a fool at the time. I told her so. We could have taken Maxwell as a pal. He was willing to come. But she thought death was best."

"And Maraquito killed Tyke?"

"No. I did that. I sent Gibber to fix him up. Tyke was a drunkard and made a fool of himself in being arrested. He would have given the show away, so I sent Gibber with a poisoned bottle of whisky. I knew Tyke couldn't resist a drink. He died, and—"

"Did you kill Miss Loach also?" interrupted Jennings, casting a glance over his shoulder to make sure that the clerk was noting all this.

Hale laughed weakly.

"No!" he said. "I fancied you would ask that. I tell you honestly that none of us know who killed her."

"That's rubbish. You do know."

"I swear I don't. Neither does Maraquito. You haven't caught her yet and you never will. I'm not going to split on the pals I have left, Jennings.

You have nabbed some, but there are others, and other factories also. I won't tell you about those."

"Clancy is captured—he will."

"Don't you make any mistake. Clancy is not the fool he looks. He has the cleverest head of the lot of us. But I'd better get on with my confession, though it won't do you much good."

"So long as you say who killed Miss Loach—"

"Miss Loach," sneered Hale, "why not Emilia Saul?"

Jennings was almost too surprised to speak. "Do you mean to say—"

"Yes, I do. All the time you and Miss Saxon and that idiot of a brother thought she was Selina Loach. She wasn't, but she was very like her. Emilia met Selina in the house that is now burnt and pushed her off the plank. The face was disfigured and Selina was buried as Emilia."

"Then Mrs. Octagon must know—"

"She knows a good deal. You'd better ask her for details. Give me a sup of brandy, doctor. Yes," went on Hale, when he felt better, "I laughed in my sleeve when I thought how Emilia tricked you all. She was Maraquito's aunt. Her name—"

"Maraquito's name is Bathsheba Saul."

"Yes. I expect Caranby told you that. He was too clever, that old man. I was always afraid that he would find out about the factory. A long while ago I wished Maraquito to give up the business and marry me. Then we would have gone to South America and have lived in peace on no end of money. Emilia left six thousand a year, so you may guess that Maraquito and I made money also. But she was in love with Mallow, and would not come away. I feared Caranby should take it into his head to search the house—"

"Was that why you had it burnt?"

"No. Tyke did that out of revenge, because Maraquito marked him with a knife. Do you think I would have been such a fool as to burn the house. Why, Caranby would have probably let out the land, and foundations would have been dug for new villas, when our plant would have been discovered."

"Who are you, Hale?"

"Who do you think?" asked the dying man, chuckling.

"One of the Saul family. You have the same eyebrows as Maraquito."

"And as Mrs. Herne, who really was Maraquito."

"Yes, I know that. But who are you?"

"My real name is Daniel Saul."

"Ah! I thought you were a member of the family. There is a likeness to Maraquito—"

"Nose and eyebrows and Hebrew looks. But I am only a distant cousin. My father married a Christian, but I retain a certain look of his people. He died when I was young. Emilia's mother brought me up. I knew a lot about the coining in those days, and I was always in love with Bathsheba, who is my cousin—"

"Bathsheba?"

"You know her best as Maraquito, so by that name I shall speak of her. Jennings," said Hale, his voice growing weaker, "I have little time left, so you had better not interrupt me." He took another sup of brandy and the doctor felt his pulse. Then he began to talk so fast that the clerk could hardly keep pace with his speech. Evidently he was afraid lest he should die before his recital ended.

"When old Mrs. Saul lost Emilia—" he began.

"But she didn't lose Emilia," interrupted Jennings.

"She thought she had. She never knew that Emilia took the name of Selina Loach. You had better ask Mrs. Octagon for details on that subject. Don't interrupt. Well, when Mrs. Saul lost Emilia, she took more and more to coining. So did her son, Bathsheba's father. They were caught and put in prison. I was taken in hand by a benevolent gentleman who brought me up and gave me the profession of a lawyer. I chose that because I thought it might be handy. Then Mrs. Saul came out of prison and her son also. Both died. Maraquito tried various professions and finally went in for dancing. She hurt her foot, and that attempt to gain a living failed. I was in practice then and we started the gambling-house together. But by this time I had found Emilia living here as Selina Loach. Mrs. Octagon can tell you how we met. Emilia persuaded me and Maraquito to go in for the coining. She already had Clancy interested. He was a good man at getting the proper ring of the coins. Well, we managed to make a tunnel to the cellars of the unfinished house, and then Emilia built the extra wing to the villa. The secret entrances were made by—"

"By Maxwell. I know that. Go on."

"Well, we started the concern. I haven't time to tell you in detail how lucky we were. We counterfeited foreign coins also. We all made plenty of money. Emilia suggested Maraquito feigning to be an invalid, so as to make things safe. False coins were passed at the gambling-house. Maraquito came here as Mrs. Herne and had a house—or rather lodgings—at Hampstead. We came here three times a week, and while supposed to be playing whist, we were at the factory. Emilia kept guard. Sometimes we went out by the door of this house and at times by another way—"

"I know. Up the tree-trunk."

"Ah, you have found that out," said Hale in a weak voice; "what a place it is," he murmured regretfully, "no one will ever get such another. I can't understand how you came to find us out."

"Tell me what happened on that night?" asked Jennings, seeing that the man was growing weaker, and fearful lest he should die without telling the secret of the death.

"On that night," said the dying scamp, rousing himself; "well, Maraquito quarrelled with Clancy, and went with me to the factory."

"Then you were not out of the house?"

"No. We went by the underground passage to work. Clancy went away, as he had business elsewhere. The moment he had gone I came up from the passage. Emilia was seated with the cards on her lap. She came with me to the factory, and thinking Clancy might come back, she went out by the tree-trunk way."

"What, that old lady?"

"She wasn't so very old, and as active as a cat. Besides, she did not want Clancy to come down, as she was afraid there might be a fight between him and Maraquito. They had quarrelled about the division of some money, and Maraquito can use a knife on occasions."

"She did on that night."

"No. Miss Loach—I mean Emilia—never came back. We became alarmed, as we knew people had been round the house of late—"

"Mr. Mallow—"

"Yes, the fool. We knew he had come prowling after ghosts. But he found nothing. Well, I—" here Hale's voice died away. The doctor gave him some more brandy and looked significantly at Jennings.

"Get him to tell all at once," he whispered, "he's going."

"Yes, I'm going," murmured Hale. "I don't mind, though I am sorry to leave Maraquito. Well," he added, in a stronger voice. "I went out to see what was up. We found Emilia lying dead near the tree. She had been stabbed to the heart. A bowie knife was near. In great alarm I got Maraquito to come out, as the body could not be left there. We dropped it down the tree-trunk and got it into the factory. Then we wondered what was to be done. Maraquito suggested we should take it back to the sitting-room, and then, people being ignorant of the passage, no one would know how Emilia had met with her death. I thought there was nothing else to be done. We carried the body through the passage and placed it in the chair. I arranged the cards on the lap, knowing the servant had seen Emilia in that position, and that it would still further throw prying people"—here Hale glanced at Jennings—"off the scent. Hardly had we arranged this and closed the floor, over us when we heard that someone was in the room. It was a woman, and we heard her speaking to the corpse, ignorant that the woman was dead. Then we heard a suppressed shriek. We guessed it was a woman, at least I did, but Maraquito was quicker and knew more. She said it was Miss Saxon, and at once became anxious to fix the blame on her. But I was afraid lest things should be discovered, so I dragged Maraquito back to the factory. I believe Miss Saxon found the knife and then ran out, being afraid lest she should be discovered and accused. This was what Maraquito wanted. She suddenly escaped from me and ran back to the secret entrance. By shifting the floor a little she saw into the room. It was then eleven. She saw also that the knife was gone, and it struck her that Miss Saxon could not be far off."

"She was not," said Jennings, "she was hidden in the field of corn."

"Ah. I thought so. Well, Maraquito fancied that if she was arrested with the knife before she could leave the neighborhood she would be charged with the murder."

"But would Maraquito have let her suffer?" asked Jennings, horrified.

"Of course she would," said Hale weakly, "she hated Miss Saxon because she was engaged to Mallow, the fool. To get her caught, Maraquito jumped up into the sitting-room and rang the bell."

"At eleven o'clock?"

"Yes, I believe—I believe—" Hale's voice was getting weaker and weaker. "She did ring—bell—then closed floor. Servant came—I—I—" he stopped and his head fell back. Suddenly he half rose and looked wildly into blank space. "Maraquito," he cried strongly, "the game's at an end. Fly, my love, fly. We have fought and—and—lost. Maraquito, oh my—" his voice died away. He stretched out his hand, fell back and died with a look of tender love on his pallid face.

"Poor wretch!" said Slane pityingly, "at least he loved truly."

XXIV

Revenge

The capture of the coiners caused an immense sensation, and the papers were filled with descriptions of the raid. Jennings came in for much congratulation, and his feat considerably improved his position with the authorities. He was confined to his bed for some days by his wound and, meanwhile, events transpired in which he would have been considerably interested had he heard of them. They had to do with Maraquito.

Since her flight from the Soho house nothing had been heard of her, although every inquiry had been made. Guessing that Jennings knew much more than was suspected, she was wise enough not to go to the Rexton factory, and congratulated herself on her foresight when she read the accounts of the raid in the papers. But she was furiously angry at losing all, when on the point of realizing her desires. She had sent her money to be banked abroad; she hoped, by means of threats to induce Mallow to give up Juliet, and she had trusted to win his love by assiduous attentions. But the trick played by Jennings which revealed her deception, and the raid on the factory and the consequent death of Hale, upset her plans, and caused her to take refuge in hiding. She did not fear being arrested, especially as her arch-enemy, the detective, was confined to bed, so she had time to make her plans. Maraquito particularly wished to revenge herself on Mallow and Juliet. She still loved the young man as much as ever, despite his contemptuous rejection of her suit. But she blamed Juliet Saxon for the hardening of his heart, and it was on the girl that she determined to revenge herself. At first she intended to call at the "Shrine of the Muses," but thinking she would meet with opposition from Mrs. Octagon, likely to prevent the realization of her malignant wishes, she changed her mind. It was no use visiting Mallow, as with him she could do nothing. Therefore she resolved to write to Lord Caranby and arrange a meeting with Juliet at his rooms in the Avon Hotel. Then, when in the presence of the girl, she hoped to revenge herself in a way likely to cause Mallow exquisite pain.

Thus it happened that Lord Caranby, who was very ill and confined to his rooms, received a letter from Maraquito, asking him to invite

Miss Saxon to a meeting with the writer. "I see that the game is up," wrote the artful Maraquito, "and I am willing to put things straight. I know much which will be of service in clearing up matters, as I was a partner with Hale and Clancy in the coining. I do not mind admitting this, as I am not afraid of the police arresting me. I can look after myself, and I am quite sure that you will not betray me when I call at your rooms. I also have something to tell you about my dead Aunt Emilia whom you so deeply loved. Therefore, if you will arrange for me to meet Miss Saxon, and allow me to make a clean breast of it, all will be well."

When Caranby received this letter his first idea was to send for Mallow. But he reflected that Cuthbert was bitterly angered against Maraquito, and would probably hand her over to the police. Caranby, from a remembrance of his love for Emilia, did not wish this to happen; therefore, he refrained from letting Mallow learn of Maraquito's determination. He hoped to get the complete truth from her and arrange matters once and for all. Also, there was another reason, and a very strong one, which prevented the old gentleman from having his nephew present at the projected interview.

Maraquito soon received an answer to her letter. It stated that Lord Caranby would be pleased to receive her on Sunday afternoon at three o'clock, and that Miss Saxon would be present. When Maraquito read this she smiled an evil smile and went out to make a certain purchase which had to do with her visit. Had Lord Caranby known of her wicked intention he would rather have cut off his right arm than have subjected Juliet to the danger she was about to undergo. But he never credited Maraquito with such calculated wickedness.

On Sunday afternoon the old gentleman was seated near the fire, carefully dressed as usual, but looking very ill. He suffered, as he had told Jennings, from an incurable complaint, and there was no chance of his recovering. But he refused to take to his bed, and insisted on keeping his feet. Cuthbert often came to see him, but on this particular afternoon Caranby had manoeuvred him out of the way by sending him to see an old friend with a message about his illness. Cuthbert never suspected what was in the wind or he certainly would not have gone. Afterwards, he bitterly regretted that he had not told Caranby of Maraquito's threat against Juliet. Had he done so, Caranby would never have received her. As it was, the old lord waited patiently for the woman who was about to bring disaster in her train. Precisely at three o'clock his servant showed up a lady. "Madame Durand," he announced, and then retired, leaving his master alone with a bent, crooked old woman who walked with the aid of a cane, and seemed very ill.

"I should never have known you," said Caranby, admiring Maraquito's talent for disguise.

"Necessity has made me clever," she replied in a croaking voice, and glanced at the door.

Caranby interpreted the look and voice. "You can speak freely," he said ironically, "I have no police concealed hereabouts."

"And Miss Saxon?" asked Maraquito, speaking in her natural voice.

"She will be here at half-past three. I wish to have a talk with you first, Miss Saul."

The woman darted a terrible look at her host. In spite of the mask of age which she had assumed, her eyes filled with youthful vigor and fire betrayed her. They shone brilliantly from her wrinkled face. Her hair was concealed under a close cap, above which she wore a broad-brimmed hat. This head-dress would have been remarkable a few years back, but now that ladies are reverting to the fashions of their grandmothers, it passed unnoticed. With a plain black dress, a black cloak trimmed profusely with beads, mittened hands and an ebony cane, she looked quite funereal. To complete the oddity of her dress a black satin bag dangled by ribbons from her left arm. In this she carried her handkerchief and—something else. As usual, she was perfumed with the Hikui scent. Caranby noticed this, and when she did not reply to his remark, pointed out its danger to her.

"If you wish to escape the police, you must stop using so unusual a perfume, Miss Saul—"

"Call me Maraquito; I am used to that name," she said harshly, and seated herself near the fire, shivering to keep up a character of old age, with slowly circulating blood.

"Let us say Maraquita," answered Caranby, smiling, "we may as well be grammatical. But this perfume betrays you. Jennings knows that your friends use it as a sign."

"Quite so," she answered, "it was clever of Jennings to have guessed its meaning. I invented the idea. But he is ill, and I don't think he has told anyone else about it. He is fond of keeping his discoveries to himself. He wants all the glory."

"Surely he has had enough by this time, Maraquita. But the scent—"

"You are quite right, I shall not use it for the future. But what do you think of my disguise? Would anyone know me?"

"Certainly not. But I wonder you have the courage to show yourself so disfigured to the woman who is your rival."

"Oh, as to that, she is my rival no longer," said Maraquito, with a gesture of disdain, "your nephew is not worthy of me. I surrender him from this moment."

"That is very wise of you. I expect you will go abroad and marry a millionaire."

"I might. But I have plenty of money of my own."

"The way in which you made it is not creditable," said Caranby.

"Bah!" she sneered. "I did not come here to hear you talk morality, Lord Caranby. You were no saint in your young days. I have heard all about you."

"From whom?"

"From my Aunt Emilia."

"I scarcely think that. You were but a child when she died."

"She did not die," said Maraquito coldly. "I have come to tell you that she lived as Miss Loach at Rose Cottage."

Caranby started to his feet. "What is this you tell me?"

"The truth. Emilia is dead now, but she lived alone for many a long day. I knew that Selina Loach was my aunt, and," Maraquito looked at him with piercing eyes, "Mrs. Octagon knew also."

By this time Caranby had recovered from his emotion. "There is nothing bad I don't expect to hear of Isabella Octagon," he said, "so this then was why she visited you?"

"Yes. I ordered her to come by threatening to reveal what she knew to the police. I could have done so by an anonymous letter. She came and then I forced her to promise to stop the marriage. I may as well add that I wrote insisting on the marriage being stopped as soon as Emilia died."

"Ah! And I thought along with Cuthbert that it was hatred of me that made Mrs. Octagon—"

"Oh, she hates you sure enough. But are you not astonished by my news?"

"Very much astonished," responded Caranby thoughtfully, "how came it that Selina died and Isabella lived?"

"The three met in the unfinished house," explained Maraquito. "I had the story from Emilia myself. There was a quarrel. All three were in love with you. Selina was standing on a plank at a considerable height from the ground. In a rage Emilia pushed her off. Isabella held her tongue as she hated Selina."

"But the substitution?"

"Well. In the fall Selina's face was much mutilated. I believe," added Maraquito, in a coldblooded manner, "that Emilia made it worse"— here Caranby shuddered and Maraquito laughed—"oh, my aunt was not a woman to stick at trifles. She insisted on changing dresses with the dead. It was the workmen's dinner-hour and no one was about. She forced Isabella to assist her by threatening to tell the police that Isabella had murdered her sister. As the sisters were on bad terms, Isabella knew that she might be accused, and so she held her tongue."

"But she could have accused Emilia."

"Emilia would have denied the accusation. Moreover, Isabella was intimidated by the fierce nature of my aunt."

"A fierce nature, indeed, that would mutilate the dead. But I do not see how Emilia hoped that the substitution would pass undiscovered by Selina's friends, to say nothing of her father."

"The idea was that Emilia, as Selina, should go abroad and return to England in a few years. Owing to the unexpected death of Mr. Loach, the father, the substitution was easy. You know how Isabella alone appeared at the inquest, and how Selina—really my aunt—pretended to be sick. Then the two went abroad and came back; Emilia as Miss Loach went to Rose Cottage, and Isabella married Mr. Saxon."

"But why did Emilia take Selina's name and—"

"Because Emilia was in danger of being arrested along with her mother and brother for coining. You could not have saved her. The accident of Selina's death—"

"The murder of Selina, you mean."

Maraquito made a gesture of indifference. "Call it what you like. It happened opportunely however. It gave Emilia safety, and by threatening to denounce Isabella, she stopped her from marrying you."

Caranby looked up. "Ah! Now I see why Isabella left me alone. She made one attempt, however."

"And did not succeed in inducing you to marry her. But had she succeeded, Emilia would have stopped the marriage. Emilia loved you."

"No," said Caranby coldly, "she loved my title and my name and wealth. I never loved her nor she me. She exercised a kind of hypnotic influence over me, and I dare say I would have married her. But her heart I am sure was always in the coining business."

"You are quite right," said Maraquito, looking keenly at him, "though I can't guess how you came to think so, seeing you thought my aunt dead. Yes, she loved coining. When I grew up she sent for me and for Daniel Saul—"

"Who is he? Another of your precious family."

"A distant cousin. You know him best as Hale the lawyer."

"Oh, indeed," said Caranby, considerably surprised, "and what did Emilia do with you two?"

"She got us to help her to coin. We made use of your house. I need not tell you how we dug the tunnel and arranged the factory. Emilia knew that you would not disturb the house—"

"I was a sentimental fool. If I had been wiser you would not have carried on your wickedness for so long."

"Oh, we have other factories," said Maraquito coolly, "Jennings has not discovered everything. But your house was certainly an ideal place. I can't understand how Jennings learned about the secret—"

"The entrance. He learned that from plans left by Maxwell who designed the same. Emilia poisoned him."

"She did—to preserve her secret. Hale and I thought it was unwise; he would have joined us. But it was all for the best."

"Apparently you think so," returned Caranby, looking at her with abhorrence, "seeing you poisoned Tyke in the same way."

"Hale did that and I agreed. It was necessary," said the woman coldly, "but you appear to know all about the matter."

"Jennings has told me everything. Even to the fact, which he learned from Hale that you rang that bell."

"I did. I knew Juliet Saxon was in the room, and I wished to get her arrested. She left the house and I rang the bell as soon as I could get away from Hale, who did not wish me to draw attention to the murder. But Juliet was too far away by that time to be caught."

"Why did you wish to hang the poor girl?"

"Because I loved Cuthbert. I would have hanged her with pleasure," said Maraquito vindictively. "I hate her!"

"Then why do you wish to see her to-day?"

"To tell her that I give up your nephew."

"That is not in accordance with the sentiments you expressed now."

Maraquito made a gesture of indifference and made no reply. Caranby now began to suspect that she intended harm to Juliet, and wondered if she had any weapon about her. That dangling bag could easily carry a stout knife or a neat little revolver. And Maraquito, as was evident from the deaths of Maxwell and Tyke, had no idea of the sacredness of life. Caranby wished he had kept Cuthbert at hand to avert any catastrophe. He was about to ring and order his servant not to bring Miss Saxon into the room when Maraquito roused herself from her reverie.

"Do you wish to know anything further?" she asked.

"No. I think you have told me everything."

She smiled scornfully. "I have told you very little. But for the rest of the information you must apply to Mrs. Octagon."

"Ah! Supposing I wish to learn who killed Emilia?"

"Mrs. Octagon can tell you!" said the woman significantly.

"Do you mean to say—"

"I say nothing. Emilia came to the factory and went out into the open air by another exit to see if anyone was about. She never returned and Hale and I went in search of her. We found her dead, and—"

"I know all this. Hale confessed it. But he does not know who killed her. Do you?"

"I can't say for certain. But I suspect Mrs. Octagon stabbed her."

"But how could Mrs. Octagon get the knife?"

"Basil got that from Mallow's room. He gave it to his mother, and—"

"This is all theory," said Caranby angrily, "you have no grounds."

"None at all," replied Maraquito calmly, "but if anyone had a wish to kill my aunt, Mrs. Octagon had. Emilia kept a tight hold over that woman, and made her do what she wished."

"About the marriage?"

"Yes, and other things. I have never been able to understand why Aunt Emilia took such a fancy to Cuthbert and that girl. But she certainly wished to see them married. She asked Juliet for a photograph of your nephew, and Juliet gave her one. I took it, and that girl Susan Grant stole it from me. It was strange that the photograph should have gone back to the cottage. Aunt and I quarrelled over the marriage. She knew I loved Cuthbert, but she would never help me to marry him. It was all Juliet with her—pah! I detest the girl. I could do nothing while Emilia lived. She knew too much. But after her death I made Mrs. Octagon stop the marriage."

"I think Mrs. Octagon will consent now," said Caranby, calmly.

"I doubt it. She hates you too much. However, she can, for all I care, Lord Caranby. I have done with Cuthbert."

The old man hoped she had done with Juliet also, for he was still uneasy. The expression of her face was most malignant. More than ever persuaded that she intended harm, Caranby again was about to summon his servant and forbid the entrance of the expected girl, when suddenly the door opened and Juliet; looking bright and happy, entered. She started back when she saw the supposed old woman, who rose. Caranby jumped off the sofa with an activity he had not shown for years, and got between Juliet and her enemy. Maraquito burst into tears. "Ah, you will be happy with Cuthbert," she wailed, "while I-" a fresh burst of tears stopped her speech and she groped in the satin bag for her handkerchief.

Juliet looked amazed. "Who is this, Lord Caranby?"

"Senora Gredos."

"Maraquito!" cried Juliet, starting back with an indignant look. "I never expected to meet that woman—"

"You call me that?" cried Maraquito, flashing, up into a passion. "I am the woman Cuthbert loves."

"He does not. He loves me. You, so old and—"

"Old!" shrieked Maraquito, snatching off her hat and cap. "I am young and much more beautiful than you. Look at my hair." It came streaming down in a glorious mass on her shoulders. "My face is as beautiful as yours. I disguised myself to see you. I hate you!—I loathe you! I forbid you to marry Cuthbert."

"How dare you—how dare—"

"I dare all things—even this." Maraquito raised her arm, and in her hand Caranby saw a small bottle she had taken out of the bag. "What will Cuthbert say to your beauty now?"

She flung the bottle straight at Juliet. It would have struck her in the face, but Caranby, throwing himself between the two, received it fair on his cheek. It smashed, and he uttered a cry. "Vitriol! Vitriol!" he shrieked, his hands to his face, and fell prone on the hearth-rug. His head struck against the bars of the grate, and a spurt of flame caught his hair. Juliet seized him and dragged him away, calling loudly for help.

"You devil—you devil!" cried Maraquito, striking the girl on the face. "I dare not stay now. But I'll spoil your beauty yet. Wait—wait!"

She hastily put on her hat and ran out of the room. The servant of Lord Caranby burst into the room, followed by some waiters. "Send for the doctor," cried Juliet, trying to raise Caranby—"and that woman-"

"She has left the hotel," said a waiter, but at this moment there was a loud shout in the street, followed by a shriek and a crash.

XXV

Nemesis

In the midst of the confusion caused by Maraquito's wickedness Cuthbert arrived. Juliet flew to him at once and flung herself sobbing into his arms.

"Oh, Cuthbert—Cuthbert!" she cried, her head on his shoulder, "that woman has been here. She tried to throw vitriol at me, and the bottle broke on Lord Caranby's face. He has burnt his head also; he is dying."

"Good heavens!" cried Mallow, pressing her to his heart, "thank God you are safe! How did Maraquito come here?"

"I don't know—I don't know," sobbed Juliet, completely unstrung; "he asked me to see him, and she arrived disguised as an old woman. Oh, where is the doctor!"

"He has just arrived, miss. Here he comes," said an excited waiter.

While the doctor examined Caranby's injuries, Cuthbert, very pale, led Juliet out of the room, and taking her into an adjoining apartment, made her drink a glass of port wine. "An old woman," he repeated, "it must have been the disguised Maraquito then who was killed."

"Killed! She is not killed. She came here and—"

Juliet began to tell the story over again, for she was badly frightened. Mallow interrupted her gently.

"Maraquito is dead," he said, "she was run over by a motor-car a quarter of an hour ago."

"Was that her cry we heard?"

"I don't know," replied Cuthbert gloomily. "I was coming round the corner of the street and saw a woman flying along the pavement. A car was tearing towards me. I had just time to see the woman as she passed and note that she was old. She caught a glimpse of my face, and with a cry ran into the centre of the street. I never thought she was Maraquito, and could not understand why she acted as she did. I cried out in alarm, and ran forward to drag her back from before the approaching motor. But it was too late, the car went over her and she shrieked when crushed under the wheels. The impediment made the car swerve and it ran into a lamp-post. The occupants were thrown out. I fancy someone else is hurt also. Maraquito is dead. I heard a policeman say so. I then saw a waiter gesticulating at the door of the hotel, and fancied something was wrong; I ran along and up the stairs. But I never expected to find you here, Juliet, much less to witness the death of that wretched woman."

"I am sorry," faltered Juliet, as she sat with his arms round her, "I don't know why she wanted to throw vitriol at me. She failed to hurt me, and I think she has killed Lord Caranby, and—"

"I must see to my uncle," said Mallow, rising, "stay here, Juliet."

"No! no," she said, clinging to him, "let me go home. Get a cab. I dare not stop. That terrible woman—"

"She will never hurt you again. She is dead."

"I wish to go home—I wish to go home."

Mallow saw that the poor girl was quite ill with fright; and small wonder, considering the catastrophe of the last half hour. To have vitriol thrown is bad enough, but when the act leads to two deaths—for Maraquito was already dead, and it seemed probable that Lord Caranby would follow—it is enough to shake the nerves of the strongest. Mallow took Juliet down and placed her in a cab. Then he promised to see her that same evening, and to tell her of Lord Caranby's progress. When the cab drove away he went again upstairs. As he went he could not help shuddering at the thought of the danger from which Juliet had escaped. He remembered how Maraquito had threatened to spoil the beauty of the girl, but he never thought she would have held to her devilish purpose. Moreover, he could not understand how Maraquito in disguise came to see Caranby. The disguise itself was an obvious necessity to escape the police. But why should she have been with his uncle and why should Juliet have come also? It was to gain an answer to these questions that Cuthbert hurried to the sitting-room.

Lord Caranby was no longer there. The doctor had ordered him to be taken to his bedroom, and when Mallow went thither he met him at the door, "He is still unconscious," said the doctor, "I must send for his regular medical attendant, as I was only called in as an emergency physician."

"Is he very ill?"

"I think the shock will kill him. He is extremely weak, and besides the shock of the vitriol being thrown, he has sustained severe injuries about the head from fire. I don't think he will live. To whom am I speaking?" asked the young man.

"My name is Mallow. I am Lord Caranby's nephew."

"And the next heir to the title. I fancy you will be called 'my lord' before midnight."

Mallow did not display any pleasure on hearing this. He valued a title very little and, so far as money was concerned, had ample for his needs. Besides, he was really fond of his uncle who, although consistently eccentric, had always been a kind, good friend. "Will he recover consciousness?"

"I think so," said the doctor doubtfully, "I am not quite sure. His own medical attendant, knowing his constitution and its resisting power, will be able to speak more assuredly. How did this happen?"

Cuthbert, for obvious reasons, explained as little as he could. "Some old woman came to see my uncle and threw vitriol at Miss Saxon, the young lady who was with him. He intercepted the stuff and fell into the fire."

"What a demon! I hope she will be caught."

"She is dead," and Cuthbert related the accident in the street. The doctor had strong nerves, but he shuddered when he heard the dreadful story. Nemesis had been less leaden-footed than usual.

In due time Dr. Yeo, who usually attended Caranby, made his appearance and stated that his patient would not live many hours. "He was always weak," said Yeo, "and of late his weakness increased. The two severe shocks he has sustained would almost kill a stronger man, let alone an old man of so delicate an organization. He will die."

"I hope not," said Cuthbert, impulsively.

The physician looked at him benignly. "I differ from you," he declared, "death will come as a happy release to Lord Caranby. For years he has been suffering from an incurable complaint which gave him great pain. But that he had so much courage, he would have killed himself."

"He never complained."

"A brave man like that never does complain. Besides, he took great care of himself. When he came back to London he was fairly well. I think he must have done something rash to bring on a recurrence of his illness. Within a few days of his arrival he grew sick again. In some way he over-exerted himself."

"I don't think he ever did," said Mallow, doubtfully.

"But I am certain of it. Within a week of his arrival here he had a relapse. I taxed him with going out too much and with over-exertion, but he declined to answer me."

"Will he become conscious again?"

"I think so, in a few hours, but I cannot be sure. However, you need not be alarmed, Mr. Mallow. His affairs are all right. In view of his illness I advised him to make his will. He said that he had done so, and that everything was in apple-pie order."

"It is not that, doctor. I wish to ask him some questions. Will you remain here?"

"Till the end," replied Yeo, significantly; "but it will not take place for a few hours, so far as I can see."

"I wish to go out for an hour. Can I, with safety?"

"Certainly. Lord Caranby will live for some time yet."

Mallow nodded and left the bedroom, while Yeo returned to the bed upon which lay the unconscious form of the old man. Cuthbert took a walk to the end of the street where the wreckage of the motor car had now been removed, and asked the policeman what had become of the victims. He was informed that the chauffeur, in a dying condition, had been removed to the Charing Cross Hospital, and that the body of the old woman—so the constable spoke—had been taken to the police station near at hand. "She's quite dead and very much smashed up," was the man's report.

Mallow thanked him with half-a-crown and, having learned the whereabouts of the police station, he went there. He introduced himself to the inspector and, as the nephew of Lord Caranby, received every attention, particularly when he described how the vitriol had been thrown. Cuthbert thought it as well to say this, as the waiters at the Avon Hotel would certainly inform the police if he did not. He looked at the body of the miserable woman in its strange mask of age. "She went to see Lord Caranby in disguise," said the inspector, "you can see her face is made up. Does his lordship know who she is?"

"Yes. And Mr. Jennings, the detective, knows also."

"Perhaps you do yourself, Mr. Mallow?"

Cuthbert nodded. "She is Maraquito, the—"

"What! the gambling-house coiner we have been looking for?"

"The same. Jennings can tell you more about the matter than I can."

"I'll get Mr. Jennings to come here as soon as he is on his feet, and that will be to-morrow most probably. But why did Maraquito throw vitriol at Lord Caranby?"

"Jennings can tell you that," said Mallow, suppressing the fact that the vitriol had been meant for Juliet. "Perhaps it had something to do with the raid made on the unfinished house which, you know, belonged to my uncle."

"Bless me, so it did. I expect, enraged by the factory being discovered, Maraquito wished to revenge herself on your uncle. She may have thought that he gave information to Jennings about the place."

"She might have thought so," said Mallow. "I am returning to the Avon Hotel. If you want to see me you can send for me there. But Jennings knows everything."

"What about his lordship?"

"He will die," said Cuthbert abruptly, and departed, leaving the inspector full of regrets that Maraquito had not lived to figure in the police court. He looked at the matter purely from a professional standpoint, and would have liked the sensation such an affair would have caused.

When Mallow came back to the hotel he found that his uncle had recovered consciousness and was asking for him. Yeo would not allow his patient to talk much, so Cuthbert sat by the bedside holding the hand of the dying man. Caranby had been badly burnt about the temples, and the sight of one eye was completely gone. Occasionally Yeo gave him a reviving cordial which made him feel better. Towards evening Caranby expressed a wish to talk. The doctor would have prevented him, but the dying man disregarded these orders.

"I must talk," he whispered faintly. "Cuthbert, get a sheet of paper."

"But you have made your will," said Yeo, rebukingly.

"This is not a will. It is a confession. Cuthbert will write it out and you will witness my signature along with him, Yeo."

"A confession!" murmured Cuthbert, going out of the room to get pen, ink and paper. "What about?"

He soon knew, for when he was established by the side of the bed with his writing materials on a small table, Caranby laughed to himself quietly. "Do you know what I am about to say?" he gasped.

"No. If it is nothing important you had better not exhaust yourself."

"It is most important, as you will hear. I know who murdered the supposed Miss Loach."

Cuthbert nearly dropped the pen. "Who was it?" he asked, expecting to hear the name of Mrs. Octagon.

"I did!" said Caranby, quietly.

"You!—that's impossible."

"Unfortunately it is true. It was an accident, though. Yeo, give me more drink; I must tell everything."

Yeo was quite calm. He had known Caranby for many years, and was not at all disposed to shrink from him because he confessed to having committed a murder. He knew that the Earl was a kind-hearted man and had been shamefully treated by three women. In fact, he was secretly glad to hear that Emilia Saul had met her death at the hand of a man she had injured. But he kept these sentiments to himself, and after giving his patient a strong tonic to revive his energies, he sat by the bedside with his fingers on the pulse of the dying man. Caranby rallied considerably, and when he began his recital spoke in stronger tones.

Cuthbert dipped his pen in the ink, but did not dare even to think. He was wondering how the death of Emilia had come about, and also how his uncle had gone to the unfinished house on the same night as he had done. Remembering how Basil stated he had been chased by someone unknown, Cuthbert began to fancy he saw light. However, at this moment Caranby began to speak, and as every moment was precious, both men forbore to interrupt him unless desirous to have a clearer understanding on certain points.

"When I came back to England," said Caranby, "I never thought that Emilia was alive. Owing to the clever way in which the substitution was effected by Isabella, I always thought Selina lived at Rose Cottage. Several times I tried to see her, hoping she would marry me. But she always refused. I was puzzled at the time, but now I know the reason. I never thought of looking at the unfinished house. It was a piece of sentimental folly my shutting it up, but afterwards, as time slipped by, I never troubled about looking into the matter. As Cuthbert will tell you, Yeo, laziness is a vice with me."

"Go on with the story and save your strength," said Yeo softly.

"Yes." Caranby heaved a sigh. "I haven't much left. Well, Cuthbert, you told me about the ghosts supposed to be haunting the house. I asked you to go down and see. You came here one night and left at eight o'clock to go down to Rexton."

"I never expected you to follow. Why did you not come with me?"

"Because I was keeping something back from you. On the previous day I received a letter. There was no name to it, and the writing was disguised. It advised me to see Selina Loach, and said I would be surprised when she spoke to me."

"Because then you would recognize the woman you believed to be dead."

"Exactly," said Caranby faintly, "but at the time I knew nothing, and was much puzzled with the letter. On that night I intended to tell you, but I did not. Then I thought I would go down to Rose Cottage and prove the truth of the letter. I went almost immediately after you, Cuthbert."

"What, in your state of health?"

"Yes. I was stronger then."

"And have been less strong since," murmured Yeo. "I understand now why you refused to tell me how you had over-exerted yourself."

"I had my secret to keep," said Caranby coldly, "some more drink, please." Then, when he felt better, he continued "Yes! I was wonderfully well and strong on that night. I climbed the wall—"

"Impossible!" said Mallow, "I can't believe that."

"Nevertheless it is the truth. I expect the excitement made me unnaturally strong. I suffered greatly when it was over."

"You were a wreck," said the physician bluntly.

"When what was over?" asked Mallow, anxiously.

"The event of the night to which I am coming. It took me some time to get to Rexton, and a long time to walk to the unfinished house. I did not go down Crooked Lane, but round by the wall."

"Did you come by the railway station path?"

"I did not. I took a wide detour and arrived at the unfinished house on the side opposite to where Rose Cottage stood."

"Ah!" murmured the young man. "No wonder I missed you. But I thought you were calling on Miss Loach."

"I intended to, but first I thought I would assure myself about the ghosts. Certainly I had set you to perform that task, but, as I was on the spot, I determined to see for myself. I climbed the wall, not without difficulty, and found myself in the park—"

"About what time was this?"

"After ten. I can't say how long. But I really cannot be precise as to the time. I wandered aimlessly about the park, threading my way amongst the trees and shrubs and undergrowth. I was astonished to find paths, and it struck me that someone used the park."

"I believe Miss Loach did—that is, Emilia," said Cuthbert. "Jennings learned that in some way. She always was on the watch for anyone coming into the park and learning the secret of the factory."

"I did not know that at the time," said Caranby, his voice growing weaker. "Well, I walked about. Sometimes it was moonlight and at other times the moon would be obscured by clouds. I struggled to get near the house and succeeded. Then I saw a man standing in the shadow. At once I went up to him—he fled. I don't know who it was?"

"I can tell you," said Mallow, quietly, "young Saxon."

"Then why did he fly?"

"He was there with no very good purpose and his conscience smote the miserable creature," said Cuthbert, "go on—or will you wait?"

"No! no! no!" said Caranby, vehemently; "if I stop now you will never know the truth. I don't want anyone else to be accused of the crime. I know Maraquito hinted that Isabella Octagon was guilty, but she is not. I don't want even Isabella to suffer, though she has been a fatal woman to me and wrecked my life's happiness."

His voice was growing so weak that Yeo gave him more cordial. After a pause Caranby resumed with a last effort, and very swiftly, as though he thought his strength would fail him before he reached the end of his dismal story.

"I followed the man, though I did not know who he was, and wondered why he should be trespassing. He fled rapidly and I soon lost him. But when the moonlight was bright I saw that he had dropped a knife from his pocket. In stooping to pick it up I lost sight of the man."

"Basil crossed the park and ran away. But he came back for the knife afterwards," explained Mallow. "Juliet saw him. He had on my coat. I wonder you didn't think Basil was me, as Juliet did."

"I am not acquainted with your clothes," said Caranby, dryly, "as I have been absent from England for so long. But no wonder Saxon did not find the knife. I picked it up. It was a bowie—"

"Belonging to me, which Basil had stolen."

"I didn't know that either. Well, I went again towards the wall surrounding the park. I thought I might meet you."

"I wonder you didn't. I was about at that time."

"The park was so thickly filled with trees and shrubs that we missed one another I suppose. Don't interrupt—I am going. Write quickly, Cuthbert." Then with a gasp Caranby resumed: "I halted to get breath near the large oak which the fire spared. I heard a rustling, and a woman came out of the shadow of the tree. I wondered who she was and where she had come from. The moon then came out brightly, and I recognized her face with a sensation almost of terror. It was Emilia."

"How did you recognize her after all these years?"

"By her Jewish look, and especially by the eyebrows. Moreover, she revealed herself to me when dying."

"What happened?" asked Yeo, sharply.

"I was standing with the knife in my hand. Emilia, seeing that I was an intruder, came swiftly towards me. She had a revolver in her hand but did not fire. She cried out something and rushed at me. In doing this she came straight against the knife. I was holding it instinctively in an attitude of defence, with the point outward. She rushed at me to bear me down by the weight and force of her charge, and the next moment she dropped to the ground dying."

"She was not dead then?"

"No! not for the moment. I knelt beside her and whispered 'Emilia!' She opened her eyes and smiled. Then she replied, 'Emilia—yes!' and died. I did not know what to do. Then it struck me that I might be arrested for the crime, though it really was no crime. Had she not rushed at me, had I not been holding the knife, she would not have met with her death. I wonder she did not fire, seeing she had a pistol."

"Perhaps she recognized you," said Yeo, glancing at Cuthbert, who was writing rapidly.

"No. Had she done so, she would never have attempted to hurt me. She thought I was some spy searching for the factory, and without giving herself time to think dashed forward, believing I would give way and fly. It was all over in a second. I made up my mind to go at once. I did not even wait to pick up the knife, but climbed the wall and came home here. What happened then I don't know."

"I can tell you," said Mallow. "Maraquito and Hale came to look for Miss Loach and took her body into the villa sitting-room. They placed the knife at her feet and the cards in her lap, thinking it would be thought she had been stabbed in the room, and—"

"Sign, sign!" said Caranby, unexpectedly, and Mallow hastily brought him the written document and the ink. He signed feebly, and the two men signed as witnesses. Yeo then turned to his patient, but he drew back. Death was stamped on the face.

Cuthbert called in the servant. "Lord Caranby is dead," he said quietly.

"Yes, my lord," replied the servant, and Mallow started on hearing the title. But he was now Lord Caranby and his uncle was dead.

XXVI

Cuthbert's Enemy

Before leaving the death-chamber, Mallow—now Lord Caranby—sealed the confession in the presence of Yeo, and went with him into the sitting-room. "What will you do with that?" asked the doctor, indicating the envelope with a nod.

"I shall place it in the hand of my lawyers to be put with family papers," replied Cuthbert. "I am sure you agree with me, Yeo, that it is unnecessary to make the contents public. My uncle is dead."

"Even were he still alive, I should advise you to say nothing," replied Yeo, grimly; "the woman deserved her fate, even though it was an accident. She destroyed Caranby's life. He would have married Selina Loach and have been a happy man but for her."

"There I think you wrong her. It is Isabella Octagon who is to blame. She has indeed been a fatal woman to my poor uncle. But for her, he would not have been prevented from marrying Selina and thus have fallen into the toils of Emilia. Emilia would not have murdered Selina, and the result would not have come out after all these years in the death of my uncle at the hands of Bathsheba Saul."

"Who is she?"

"Maraquito. But you don't know the whole story, nor do I think there is any need to repeat the sordid tragedy. I will put this paper away and say nothing about it to anyone save to Jennings."

"The detective!" said Yeo, surprised and startled. "Do you think that is wise? He may make the matter public."

"No, he won't. He has traced the coiners to their lair, and that is enough glory for him. When he knows the truth he will stop searching further into the case. If I hold my tongue, he may go on, and make awkward discoveries."

"Yes, I see it is best you should tell him. But Miss Saxon?"

"She shall never know. Let her think Maraquito killed Emilia. Only you, I and Jennings will know the truth."

"You can depend upon my silence," said Yeo, shaking Cuthbert by the hand; "well, and what will you do now?"

"With your permission, I shall ask you to stop here and arrange about necessary matters in connection with the laying-out of the body.

I wish to interview Mrs. Octagon this evening. To-morrow I shall see about Caranby's remains being taken down to our family seat in Essex."

"There will be an inquest first."

"I don't mind. Maraquito is dead and nothing detrimental to the honor of the Mallows can transpire. You need say nothing at the inquest as to the bottle being thrown at Juliet."

"I'll do my best. But she will be questioned."

"I intend to see her this evening myself."

"What about Mrs. Octagon?"

"Oh," said the new Lord Caranby with a grim smile, "I intend to settle Mrs. Octagon once and for all."

"Surely you don't intend to tell her of the murder."

"Certainly not. She would make the matter public at once. But her knowledge of the real name of Emilia, and her hushing up of the murder of her sister, will be quite enough to bring her to her knees. I don't intend that Juliet shall have anything more to do with her mother. But I'll say very little."

After this Cuthbert departed and took a hansom to the "Shrine of the Muses." He arrived there at ten o'clock, and was informed by the butler that Miss Saxon was in bed with a headache, and that Mrs. Octagon had given orders that Mr. Mallow was not to be admitted. Basil was out, and Mr. Octagon likewise. Cuthbert listened quietly, and then gave the man, whom he knew well, half a sovereign. "Tell Mrs. Octagon that Lord Caranby wishes to see her."

"Yes, sir, but I don't—"

"I am Lord Caranby. My uncle died this evening."

The butler opened his eyes. "Yes, m'lord," he said promptly, and admitted Cuthbert into the hall. "I suppose I needn't say it is really you, m'lord," he remarked, when the visitor was seated in the drawing-room, "I am afraid the mistress will be angry."

"Don't trouble about that, Somes. Tell her Lord Caranby is here," and the butler, bursting to tell the news in the servants' hall, went away in a great hurry.

Cuthbert remained seated near the table on which stood an electric lamp. He had the confession in his pocket, and smiled to think how glad Mrs. Octagon would be to read it. However, he had quite enough evidence to force her into decent behavior. He did not intend to leave that room till he had Mrs. Octagon's free consent to the marriage and a promise that she would go abroad for an indefinite period with her hopeful son, Basil. In this way Cuthbert hoped to get rid of these undesirable relatives and to start his married life in peace. "Nothing less than exile will settle matters," he muttered.

Mrs. Octagon, in a gorgeous tea-gown, swept into the room with a frown on her strongly-marked face. She looked rather like Maraquito, and apparently was in a bad temper. Mallow could see that she was surprised when she entered, as, thinking Lord Caranby was incapacitated by the accident described by Juliet, she did not know how he came to call at so late an hour. Moreover, Lord Caranby had never visited her before. However, she apparently was bent on receiving him in a tragic manner, and swept forward with the mien of a Siddons. When she came into the room she caught sight of Cuthbert's face in the blaze of the lamp and stopped short. "How—" she said in her deepest tone, and then became prosaic and very angry. "What is the meaning of this, Mr. Mallow? I hoped to see—"

"My uncle. I know you did. But he is dead."

Mrs. Octagon caught at a chair to stop herself from falling, and wiped away a tear. "Dead!" she muttered, and dropped on to the sofa.

"He died two hours ago. I am now Lord Caranby."

"You won't grace the position," said Mrs. Octagon viciously, and then her face became gloomy. "Dead!—Walter Mallow. Ah! I loved him so."

"You had a strange way of showing it then," said Cuthbert, calmly, and he also took a seat.

Mrs. Octagon immediately rose. "I forbid you to sit down in my house, Lord Caranby. We are strangers."

"Oh, no, we aren't, Mrs. Octagon. I came here to arrange matters."

"What matters?" she asked disdainfully, and apparently certain he had nothing against her.

"Matters connected with my marriage with Juliet."

"Miss Saxon, if you please. She shall never marry you."

"Oh, yes, she will. What is your objection to the marriage?"

"I refuse to tell you," said Mrs. Octagon violently, and then somewhat inconsistently went on:

"If you must know, I hated your uncle."

"You said you loved him just now."

"And so I did," cried the woman, spreading out her arms, "I loved him intensely. I would have placed the hair of my head under his feet. But he was never worthy of me. He loved Selina, a poor, weak, silly fool. But I stopped that marriage," she ended triumphantly, "as I will stop yours."

"I don't think you will stop mine," replied Cuthbert tranquilly, "I am not to be coerced, Mrs. Octagon."

"I don't seek to coerce you," she retorted, "but my daughter will obey me, and she will refuse your hand. I don't care if you are fifty times Lord Caranby. Juliet should not marry you if you had all the money in the world. I hated Walter Mallow, your uncle. He treated me shamefully, and I swore that never would any child of mine be connected with him. Selina wished it, and forced me to agree while she was alive. But she is dead and Lord Caranby is dead, and you can do nothing. I defy you—I defy you!"

"We may as well conduct this interview reasonably."

"I shall not let you remain here any longer. Go."

She pointed to the door with a dramatic gesture. Cuthbert took up his hat.

"I shall go if you insist," he said, moving towards the door, "and I shall return with a policeman."

Mrs. Octagon gave a gasp and went gray. "What do you mean?"

"You know well what I mean. Am I to go?"

"You have nothing against me," she said violently, "stop, if you will, and tell me the reason of that speech."

"I think you understand what I mean perfectly well," said Mallow again, and returning to his seat. "I know that your sister died years ago," Mrs. Octagon gasped, "and that Emilia feigned to be Selina Loach. And perhaps, Mrs. Octagon, you will remember how your sister died."

"I didn't touch her," gasped Mrs. Octagon, trembling.

"No, but Emilia Saul did, and you condoned the crime."

"I deny everything! Go and get a policeman if you like."

Cuthbert walked to the door and there turned. "The statement of Emilia will make pleasant reading in court," he said.

Mrs. Octagon bounded after him and pulled him back by the coat-tails into the centre of the room. Then she locked the door and sat down. "We won't be disturbed," she said, wiping her face upon which the perspiration stood, "what do you know?"

"Everything, even to that letter you wrote to my uncle, stating he should see the pretended Selina Loach."

This was a chance shot on Mallow's part, but it told, for he saw her face change. In fact, Mrs. Octagon was the only woman who could have sent the letter. She did not attempt to deny it. "I sent that letter, as I was weary of that woman's tyranny. I thought it would get her into trouble."

"She would have got you into trouble also. Suppose she had lived and had told the story of Selina's death."

"She would have put the rope round her own neck," said Mrs. Octagon in a hollow tone, all her theatrical airs gone. "I was a fool to wait so long. For twenty years that woman has held me under her thumb. It was Emilia that made me consent to your engagement to Juliet. Otherwise," she added malevolently, "I should have died rather than have consented. Oh," she shook her hands in the air, "how I hate you and your uncle and the whole of the Mallows."

"A woman scorned, I see," said Cuthbert, rather cruelly, "well, you must be aware that I know everything."

"You don't know who killed Emilia?"

"Maraquito said it was you."

"I" shrieked Mrs. Octagon, "how dare she? But that she is dead, as Juliet told me, I would have her up for libel. Maraquito herself killed the woman. I am sure of it. That coining factory—"

"Did you know of its existence?"

"No, I didn't," snapped Mrs. Octagon. "I knew nothing of Emilia's criminal doings. I let her bear the name of my sister—"

"Why?" asked Mallow, quickly, and not knowing what Maraquito had said to Caranby.

"I don't know," replied Mrs. Octagon, sullenly, "Emilia was in some trouble with the law. Her brother and mother were afterwards arrested for coining. She might have been arrested also, but that I agreed to hold my tongue. Emilia pushed Selina off the plank. Then she turned and accused me. As it was known that I was on bad terms with Selina, I might have been accused of the crime, and Emilia would have sworn the rope round my neck. Emilia made me help her to change the dress, and said that as the face of the dead was disfigured, and she was rather like Selina—which she certainly was, she could arrange. I did not know how she intended to blind my father. But my father died unexpectedly. Had he not done so, the deception could not have been kept up. As it was, I went to the inquest, and Emilia as Selina pretended to be ill. I saw after her and we had a strange doctor. Then we went abroad, and she came back to shut herself up in Rose Cottage. I tried to marry Caranby, but Emilia stopped that."

"Why did she?"

"Because she loved Caranby in her tiger way. That was why she insisted you should marry Juliet. She always threatened to tell that I had killed Selina, though I was innocent."

"If you were, why need you have been afraid?"

"Circumstances were too strong for me," said Mrs. Octagon, wiping her dry lips and glaring like a demon. "I had to give in. Had I known of that factory I would have spoken out. As it was, I wrote to Caranby when in a fit of rage; but afterwards I was afraid of what I had done, as I thought Emilia would tell."

"She certainly would have done so had she not died so opportunely."

"Do you mean to say that I killed her? I tell you, Maraquito did so."

"What makes you think that?" asked Mallow, delighted at the mistake.

"Because she was always fighting with Emilia about you. Maraquito wished to marry you, and Emilia would not let her. After Emilia died, Maraquito saw me, and we arranged to stop the marriage, and—"

"I know all about that. I saw you—or rather my uncle saw you—enter Maraquito's Soho house."

"I went on Basil's account also," said Mrs. Octagon, sullenly, "however, I have told you all. What do you wish to do?"

"I wish to marry Juliet."

"Then I refuse," said Mrs. Octagon, savagely.

"In that case I'll tell."

"You will disgrace Juliet. Besides, the law can't touch me."

"I am not so sure of that. You were an accessory after the fact. And if the public knew that you had acquiesced in the death of your sister and had held your tongue for years, you would not be popular. I fear your books would not sell then."

Mrs. Octagon saw all this, and glared savagely at Cuthbert. She would have liked to kill him, but he was the stronger of the two, and knew much which she wished kept silent. Mallow saw the impression he was making and went on persuasively. "And think, Mrs. Octagon, Juliet can give you up the six thousand a year—"

"Not she," laughed Mrs. Octagon, sneering.

"She will, at my request. I don't want my wife to possess money made out of coining. The income will be made over to you by deed of gift."

"Six thousand a year," mused the lady, "and you will hold your tongue?"

"Of course, for Juliet's sake as well as for yours. But I think it will be advisable for you to travel for a few years."

"I'll take up my abode in America forever," said Mrs. Octagon, rising, "do you think I'll stop here and see you my daughter's husband? Not for all the money in the world. Besides, Mr. Octagon has been insolent over money, and I sha'n't stay with him. Basil and myself will go to America and there we will become famous."

"It is certainly better than becoming famous in another way," said Mallow, dryly, "you will, of course be quite amiable to Juliet. Also to me, in public."

"Oh," she replied, with a short laugh, "I'll kiss you if you like."

"There is no need to go so far. I am sorry for you."

"And I hate you—hate you! Leave me now at least. You can come to-morrow, and I'll consent publicly to the marriage. But I hope you will both be miserable. Juliet does not love me or she would despise you. I wish you had died along with your uncle."

She was becoming so wild in her looks that Cuthbert thought it best to leave the room. The key was in the door, so he departed, quite sure that Mrs. Octagon, to avoid scandal about her shady doings, would be most agreeable towards him in public, however much of a demon she might be in private. Thus ended the interview.

Next morning Mallow drove to Jennings and related everything, including the confession of Caranby regarding the accident, and added details of the interview with Mrs. Octagon. Jennings listened, astonished.

"I am glad you told me," he said, "of course I don't want you to make all this public. The general impression is the same as that of Mrs. Octagon, that Maraquito murdered Miss Loach. It need not be known that Emilia was masquerading under a false name. She need not be brought into the case at all. What a wonderful case, Mallow."

Cuthbert assented. "It's more like fiction than fact."

"Fact is always like fiction," said Jennings epigrammatically, "however, we've got a confession from Clancy about the other factories. The whole gang will be caught sooner or later. And, by the way, Mallow, on second thoughts, I think it will be best to state the real name of Emilia."

"I think so too. If she is pilloried as Miss Loach, everyone will know that she is the aunt of Juliet. Tell the truth, Jennings."

"We'll tell everything, save that Lord Caranby inadvertently murdered that woman. She was the fatal woman—"

"No," said the new Lord Caranby, "Mrs. Octagon is the fatal woman. She was at the bottom of everything."

"And has been rewarded with six thousand a year. I don't suppose the State can seize that money. However, I'll see. I should like to punish Isabella Octagon in some way. And Susan Grant?"

"You can give her a thousand pounds on my behalf, and she can marry her baker. Then there's Mrs. Barnes—Mrs. Pill that was. She is quite innocent. Thomas her husband will be punished, so you had better tell her, I'll provide for her. As to yourself—"

"That's all right, Mallow, this coining case means a rise of salary."

"All the same, I intend to give you a few thousands on behalf of myself and Juliet. Without you I would probably have been accused of the crime. And, in any case, things would have been awkward. There might have been a scandal."

"There won't be one now," said Jennings. "I'll settle everything. Mrs. Octagon will go to the States with that young cub, and you can make Miss Saxon Lady Caranby. It is good of you giving me a reward. I can now marry Peggy."

"We all seem to be bent on marriage," said Mallow, rising to take his leave. "How's the shoulder?"

"All right," said the detective, "and it's worth the wound to have Peggy nursing me. She is the dearest—"

"No, pardon me," said Cuthbert, "by no means. Juliet is the dearest girl in the wide world," and he departed laughing.

Needless to say, under the careful supervision of Jennings, all scandal was averted. The gang with Clancy at its head were sentenced to years of imprisonment, likely to put a stop to all pranks. Maraquito was buried quietly and Mallow erected a gravestone to her, in spite of her wicked designs against Juliet. In six months Jennings married Peggy and took a house at Gunnersbury, where Peggy and he live in the congenial company of Le Beau, who has become quite reconciled to Jennings' profession. The old professor teaches dancing to the children of the neighborhood. Susan Grant also married her baker, and the two now possess one of the finest shops in Stepney. Mrs. Octagon went to America almost immediately. She managed to keep the six thousand a year, in spite of Jennings. No one knows how she managed to do this, but envious people hinted at Government influence. However, with Basil she departed to the States, as she confessed to being weary of constant triumphs in England. Mrs. Octagon now has a literary salon in Boston, and is regarded as one of the leading spirits of the age. Basil married an heiress. Peter, weary of playing the part of husband to a celebrity, remained in England but not in London. He sold the "Shrine of the Muses" and took a cottage on an estate in Kent belonging to Lord Caranby. Here he cultivates flowers and calls frequently on his step-daughter and her husband, when they are in the neighborhood. Peter never knew the true history of his wife. He always refers to Mrs. Octagon with respect, but shows no disposition to join her in America. Peter has had quite enough of sham art and sham enthusiasm.

And Cuthbert was married to Juliet within the year. The wedding was quiet on account of his uncle's death, and then Lord Caranby took his bride for a tour round the world. To this day Lady Caranby believes that Maraquito murdered Miss Loach, and knows also from newspaper reports that the pretended aunt was really Emilia Saul. Mrs. Octagon also expressed surprise at the infamous imposture, and quite deceived Juliet, who never learned what part her mother had taken in the business. In fact Juliet thought her mother was quite glad she had married Cuthbert.

"Mother really liked you all the time," she said to her husband when they set off on their honeymoon.

"I doubt that," replied Lord Caranby, dryly.

"She told me that it was always the dream of her life to see me your wife, but that Maraquito had threatened to ruin Basil if—"

"Oh, that is the story, is it? Well, Juliet, I am much obliged to Mrs. Octagon for loving me so much, but, with your permission, we will not see more of her than we can help."

"As she is in America we will see very little of her," sighed Lady Caranby, "besides, she loves Basil more than me. Poor boy, I hope he will get on in America."

"Of course he will. He will marry an heiress—" And Cuthbert's prophecy proved to be correct—"Don't let us talk of these things any more, Juliet. This dreadful murder nearly wrecked our life. My poor uncle talked of a fatal woman. Maraquito was that to us."

"And I?" asked Juliet, nestling to her husband.

"You are the dearest and sweetest angel in the world."

"And you are the greatest goose," said she, kissing her husband fondly, "we have had enough of fatal women. Let us never mention the subject again."

And they never did.

The End

A Note About the Author

Fergus Hume (1859–1932) was an English novelist. Born in Worcestershire, Hume was the son of a civil servant of Scottish descent. At the age of three, he moved with his family to Dunedin, New Zealand, where he attended Otago Boy's High School. In 1885, after graduating from the University of Otago with a degree in law, Hume was admitted to the New Zealand bar. He moved to Melbourne, Australia, where he worked as a clerk and embarked on his career as a writer with a series of plays. After struggling in vain to find success as a playwright, Hume turned to novels with *The Mystery of a Hansom Cab* (1886), a story of mystery and urban poverty that eventually became one of the most successful works of fiction of the Victorian era. Hume, who returned to England in 1888, would go on to publish over 100 novels and stories, earning a reputation as a leading writer of popular fiction and inspiring such figures as Arthur Conan Doyle, whose early detective novels were modeled after Hume's. Despite the resounding success of his debut work of fiction, Hume died in relative obscurity at a modest cottage in Thundersley.

A Note from the Publisher

bookfinity & MINT EDITIONS

Enjoy more of your favorite classics with Bookfinity,
a new search and discovery experience for readers.
With Bookfinity, you can discover more vintage
literature for your collection, find your Reader Type,
track books you've read or want to read,
and add reviews to your favorite books.
Visit www.bookfinity.com, and click on
Take the Quiz to get started.

Don't forget to follow us
@bookfinityofficial and @mint_editions

CPSIA information can be obtained
at www.ICGtesting.com
Printed in the USA
JSHW011340150223
37787JS00013B/1066